Books by Tammy Kaehler

The Kate Reilly Mysteries
Dead Man's Switch
Braking Points
Avoidable Contact
Red Flags

Red Flags

Red Flags

A Kate Reilly Mystery

Tammy Kaehler

Poisoned Pen Press

Poisoned Pen Press
6962 E. First Ave., Ste. 103
Scottsdale, AZ 85251
www.poisonedpenpress.com
info@poisonedpenpress.com

Printed in the United States of America

To my father, Roger, for a lifetime of patience, support, goofiness, sports, and love.

Acknowledgments

It's always a challenge to write about a real racing series, real cars, and real tracks, especially when the names, landscape, and cars change. I do my best to make all of the details—especially the technical and racing information—as accurate as possible, but sometimes I generalize, exaggerate, and outright make stuff up. I hope readers and race fans will forgive my liberties as the line between reality and make-believe blurs.

I owe great thanks to my technical experts in a variety of fields who provided me information, insight, and encouragement: Allison Altzman, Connie Anderson, Mario Andretti, Beaux Barfield, Meesh Beer, Andrew Davis, Doug Fehan, Carolyn Meier, Martin Plowman, Kimberly van Groos, and Steve Wittich. Three people went above and beyond the call of duty to help Kate fly in an IndyCar, namely Barbara Kreisel, Mary Lascuola, and IndyCar racing driver Pippa Mann, who inspires me every day with her single-minded pursuit of her dreams (at 223+ miles per hour!).

Thank you to real-life cancer warriors and their friends for letting me use your names: Debbie Mariol and Scott James, Erin Charlton and Janel Jernigan, Tara Raffield and Tina Whittle, and Riley Warren and Deb Arora. Thanks also to Nikki and Jimmy Gray, Jenny Carless and Tristan Rhys, Tommy Kendall, and Christine Syfert for your charitable donations and/or loan of your names.

Thanks to my beta readers Christine Harvey and Bill Zahren, as well as to my alpha reader, brainstorming partner, lunch buddy, and tiara table co-host, Rochelle Staab. You all provided much-needed feedback, sanity, and perspective. To my agent, Lucienne Diver of the Knight Agency, thank you for early reads, support, and remaining Kate's champion. To the whole team at Poisoned Pen Press—Diane, Beth, Suzan, Pete, Tiffany, and Rob—and in particular my editors extraordinaire, Barbara Peters and Annette Rogers, thank you for answers, guidance, and the wonderful feeling that I'm part of a family.

Last but not least, thanks to my many families for unqualified support and encouragement. Gail, An, Roger, Aggie, Desiree, Vicente, Patsy, Randy, Linda, Jerry, Jill, and Jason, your pride and enthusiasm help keep me going. But no one keeps me going more than Chet, who gives me kudos, sympathy, space, and kicks in the behind precisely as needed. I'm grateful to you every day for our life together.

Grand Prix of Long Beach

Long Beach, California

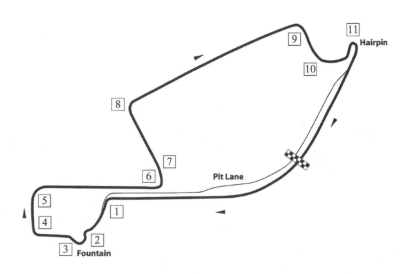

Chapter One

I stared down at the man's face and tried to care that he was dead. I tried to ignore the bloody dent in his head and focused instead on his relaxed features, which lacked the cunning and malice they'd worn in life.

"Do you recognize this man, Ms. Reilly?" I blinked as the Long Beach police detective prompted me for the second time.

"Billy Reilly-Stinson. William." I paused. "He's my cousin."

"My condolences for your loss."

"I didn't know him at all." I looked at the cop. "I only met him two years ago, and he made it clear he didn't want me in the family." I glanced at Billy again, seeing the clumpy, oatmeal-like substance in the blood on his shoulder. My stomach lurched. *Brain matter.* I turned away and breathed deeply.

The detective gestured across the parking garage toward the stairs I'd descended with him five minutes prior. I'd been a few hundred yards away in the temporary paddock for the Grand Prix of Long Beach Media Day, when he'd called asking for my help with something. His request seemed benign at the time.

He walked me around the corner of a half-wall so I couldn't see Billy's body, which settled my stomach, but not my emotions. This was my third body in as many years, and I didn't like seeing anyone dead. I felt sorry for Billy and his family—my father's family—even if I had a hard time convincing myself I'd miss Billy. Then I felt ashamed I hadn't liked him and worried about my proximity to death. Again.

The detective pulled a notepad and pen out of his sport coat pocket. "What can you tell me about the deceased?"

"You said you're Detective Barnes…you're with homicide?"

He raised an eyebrow. "That's correct. Mr. Reilly-Stinson didn't do that to himself. We're looking for another party."

I really didn't expect my ten-day trip to California to start with murder. I studied Barnes: stocky, bowlegged, of mixed Asian and Caucasian heritage. His face was comfortably lined, and his eyes shone with intelligence. I hoped he was smart and fair. I'd gone down the suspect road before, and I wasn't in the mood.

"Ms. Reilly? What do you know about him?"

"It's Kate." I stuck my hands in the back pockets of my jeans. "We were acquainted. We had no reason to communicate or be friends. Neither of us wanted to. We rarely saw each other." I considered. "I haven't run into him in more than a year. And I've never seen him alone. He's usually with his cousin, Holden Sherain."

"Is Mr. Sherain here?"

"Not that I've noticed." I bit my tongue on the fact I'd caught sight of Billy that morning and deliberately avoided him.

"Can you tell me your whereabouts today?"

I felt a flash of alarm at his question, even though I'd been through the drill before and knew I had an alibi. "I got to the track at eight to meet the race staff. From nine to twelve, I was in a pace car doing laps for media or I was with the woman I'm coaching for the celebrity race. I had lunch around noon with the other drivers. After that, more hot laps or coaching, from one until you called me. I've been with people all day."

"Who can verify that?" he asked, then wrote down the five names I gave him.

When a crime scene technician beckoned, Barnes crossed to the landing of the stairs where the tech stood next to a garbage can. A dozen other official types crawled around the half-full parking structure, moving from car to car, shining a flashlight under, around, and between, looking for evidence. Still others stood talking and looking down at Billy's body.

I shivered, not cold, but remembering Billy's bloody head. I wrapped my arms around myself. I supposed I should be mourning Billy's loss of life. I did, in theory. But I hadn't liked the guy, and I wouldn't pretend I'd miss him. I did wonder how the rest of my family would take the news. I wanted to stay out of that.

Barnes shifted, the movement drawing my attention, and I saw what he and the other man were looking at: some kind of pipe or stick and a wallet.

The detective returned to me, looking down at his notebook, and I spoke before he could. "Was that the murder weapon? In the trash can?"

He hesitated. "It could be. We'll have to test it to make sure."

"And Billy's wallet?"

"Yes, with his identification."

"How long ago was he killed?"

"Not long. Anything else?"

My big question: "Why did you ask me to identify the body?"

"The only item in the victim's pockets was a marketing card with your name and photo—a 'hero card,' someone said—with your cell phone number handwritten on it. Any idea why he'd have that?"

To cause me trouble? "Those cards get handed out by the hundreds at a race weekend. I'm sure there are bunches here for the media today. I have no idea why he'd have one, especially not with my number on it, except we're both associated with Frame Savings."

"How?"

"My father's family founded the bank more than a hundred years ago. I think Billy works there. They've just come on as one of my major sponsors for racing."

Barnes took notes. "Can you tell me Mr. Reilly-Stinson's next of kin? Who he was close to? A spouse, significant other? Best friends?"

"All I know is Billy and his cousin, Holden Sherain, were as tight as brothers. Billy's father is Edward Reilly-Stinson. And my father, James Hightower Reilly, is Billy's uncle. I only have contact information for my father, but he'll know more." With the detective's approval, I called my father, identifying myself and handing my phone to Barnes.

After that, Barnes asked one last question before letting me leave the parking structure. "You and the deceased didn't like each other. What was the problem?"

"Family issues."

"I'm going to need more."

I sighed. "I was raised by my mother's family and never met my father or his family until a couple years ago. There's still… friction with some of his family, including Billy." *Which wasn't helped by me uncovering his unethical and illegal activities a year ago.* "We were antagonistic when we saw each other occasionally, but I didn't spend time thinking about him. That's why I don't know the family very well. I'm an outsider, and I plan to stay that way."

He made a note in his book. "If you're both an insider and an outsider, your perspective could be useful. I'll be in touch."

Fine, just don't make me solve this one.

Chapter Two

I left Detective Barnes with my cell number and the mystery of who killed Billy. The other crimes I'd felt obligated to help solve had involved victims or suspects I cared about, including myself. This one did not.

My spirits lifted as I headed back to the day's activities. On my right was the Long Beach Arena, a big, round building with a huge mural of an underwater scene painted all the way around it. Yes, the building that hosted concerts, sports, and special events for the City of Long Beach was circular and blue, with life-size whales on it. Only in Southern California.

Ahead of me was a parking lot transformed into a paddock by the addition of chain link, racecars, and transport trailers. At the far side of the enclosure, I could see the brightly logoed Toyota Scions of the celebrity race competitors pulling off the track. I quickened my steps.

The conclusion of the second celebrity practice meant Media Day for the Grand Prix of Long Beach, or GPLB, was a wrap. We were ten days out from the race itself, plenty of time for local media to write stories about the coming event that would fire up the local population and increase attendance. To that end, the day was a dog-and-pony show.

In addition to getting to know the types of cars that would race during the GPLB weekend—including an IndyCar, a Porsche 911 GT3 R, and the celebrity cars—members of the press could interview the stars taking part in the ten-lap celebrity race to benefit charities. To get a real taste for the track, journalists strapped into pace cars for a hot lap at the hands of one of four pro drivers: the current Indy 500 champion, a drifting champion, a Pirelli World Challenge race winner, and me. I'd driven a couple dozen laps that day, and every passenger had exited the car with an ear-to-ear grin.

My driving duties were over for the day, but my work wasn't, since I was coaching the most famous of the celebrity competitors. I smiled at the security guard monitoring entry to the media area and hurried over to the Toyotas.

The celebrity race was made up of two groups: professional drivers from different forms of motorsport—motorcycle racing, drag racing, or even someone long-retired from sportscar racing—and a variety of celebrities from the music industry, movies, television, news, or other sports. The celebrities were always hit and miss, some years famous and attention-drawing, some years not so much. This year they'd hit the jackpot with a member of the current number-one boy-band and an Oscar-winner with critical success *and* starring roles in the two biggest box-office films of the last year. That was my client, Madelyn, or Maddie, Theabo.

I aimed for the scrum of media in the center of the celebrity cars, certain what I'd find: Maddie and the boy-band member back-to-back, fielding questions from reporters. I caught Maddie's eye and pointed to the temporary trailer where the race staff had set up for the day. She nodded, but kept talking.

Two months prior, I'd received a phone call out of the blue from a woman named Penny Warner, who was looking for a driving coach. We were most of the way through negotiations before she revealed she was calling for her employer, Maddie, one of the biggest names in movies. It took two hours for me to get over my fangirl freakout.

Maddie had gone through the standard celebrity training, four days at a track in the high desert north of L.A. But she wanted more instruction, feedback, and support. Since then, we'd met at different go-kart facilities to work on braking points and lines, and I'd prepped her as well as I could for driving the Long Beach track. But nothing compared to being out on the pavement, and part of my job was to help her make sense of her impressions.

I watched her handle the crush of fans and media, marveling that she didn't ignore anyone. I understood firsthand how a crowd of media and fans could press in on a person, and I'd only endured it briefly at a racetrack. Away from the track, I was virtually invisible. But everyone recognized Maddie, and she still handled the attention graciously, replying to greetings, smiling at photo-takers, and accommodating everyone who asked for a signature. She'd told me when we met that she knew her success was due to her fans, so she always gave them and the media time.

When she finally broke free from the reporters, we ducked into the office trailer, nodding to three staff members huddled over laptops at the far end of the room. Maddie leaned against a desk inside the door, draining the contents of a water bottle. She was thirty-three, with a slender build, an expressive face, and bouncy, wavy, auburn hair half the world coveted.

I eyed the flush in her cheeks. "How was it?"

"Nearly as much fun as sex."

I laughed. "Did anything trip you up? Was the track what you expected?"

Since the Long Beach Grand Prix track was comprised of city streets, which had to be closed to traffic, it was only available during Media Day and the race weekend. The stands, barricades, and fencing lining the course would remain, but the walls shutting down public roads would be moved aside any minute now, to be set in place again a week from Thursday, when the race weekend began. Today's two sessions, both follow-alongs, single file behind an instructor, were the first time the celebrity competitors had seen the racing surface.

"You'd warned me," she said, "but the walls were still closer after Turns 5 and 8 than I expected."

The concrete walls brought in to define the temporary circuit were big and unforgiving, and to wring the most speed out of a car, we ran right next to them. More than one reporter during the day's laps had flinched at their proximity.

We talked corners for a few minutes until I saw Maddie shiver. "You need to get changed before you catch a chill. Keep thinking about the track, and draw your racing line on the track map I gave you."

"You're still coming to the party this evening?" Maddie asked. "And the studio tomorrow? Penny has a car arranged for tonight."

"She does, but I don't need the car and driver. I drive for a living."

"It's easier. You can drink what you like, enjoy yourself, and not be unsafe driving home. Plus parking in the hills is a bitch." She put a hand on my arm. "For all you're helping me, it's the least I can do. Besides, this way, I won't worry about you."

I gave in. "What do I wear tonight? I've never been to a party in Hollywood."

"Anything you want, Kate. You'll see ripped jeans and sequins, sometimes on the same person." She smiled. "I'll see you later."

I followed her out of the trailer and watched her purposeful stride through the fenced area, her ever-present personal assistant, Penny, next to her. The fenced-off parking lot was rapidly draining of vehicles as the celebrity race staff took the Toyotas back to their staging area. My work was done. I collected my belongings from the lone IndyCar trailer, waving at one of the IndyCar Series executives as he passed. I also nodded at a member of the grand prix organization, then stopped when she spoke to me.

"Thanks again for giving the press a thrill, Kate."

"You bet." I shook her hand. "You're Erica?"

"Erica Aarons. Your team media guy, Tom, said you'd let me set up some interviews while you're in L.A. for the next week. If that's all right, I'll make a plan."

After swapping contact information, I continued on my way to the GPLB media center in the basement of the Performing Arts Center building, which—combined with the whale-muraled arena, a hotel, and the convention center—formed the heart of the Long Beach circuit. I ducked inside, downstairs, and into the women's bathroom. One thing I loved about this race facility was the abundance of real bathrooms. I'd been in lots of porta-potties in my career, and I preferred running water.

I swung the door open and came face-to-face with Elizabeth Rogers, part of the operations team for the SportsCar Championship, or SCC, the series I competed in.

Elizabeth saw me and dissolved into tears. "Kate, did you hear what happened? Holden is devastated."

My spirits fell to the ground with a thump. Billy. Dead.

Chapter Three

I blinked away the image of Billy on the ground, dented and bloody. "I heard, yes." I used the excuse of going into a stall to assemble my thoughts.

As I washed my hands a minute later, I studied Elizabeth. Aside from her red eyes and blotchy skin, her long, straight, blond hair—an Alice in Wonderland look—was her most distinguishing feature. Though we'd become acquainted through her role in operations for the SCC, I'd never gotten past the surface with her. Never seen emotion. Until now.

I dried my hands and turned to her, leaning against the counter. "Were you close to Billy?"

"Since I've been seeing Holden, Billy and I have gotten to be good friends. You know how close the two of them are. Were." That set off another round of slow tears rolling down her cheeks. "I feel so badly for what Holden's going through."

"You spoke with him?"

Another nod and a hiccupped sob. "Once I found out from the GPLB staff, I had to tell him. Holden deserved to know right away, from someone who cares."

Holden Sherain deserves a swift kick in the rear. No, be charitable. Even if you don't like him, feel sorry for him. He must be devastated. I thought about Billy, beaten to death and abandoned in the parking structure. I came up with more sympathy for both cousins.

I was fumbling for what to say to Elizabeth—I didn't know how to console her and didn't want to ask after Holden—when there was a commotion outside the door. It swung open to reveal a woman who looked like she'd taken a wrong turn somewhere on her way to a mall. I caught a flash of diamonds and a glimpse of a red-soled shoe. *Forget a mall, she's AWOL from Rodeo Drive.*

She pointed at someone outside. "Not this time. Stay there." She closed the door and slumped against it, only then noticing us watching her, our mouths agape.

I'd never seen her before, but Elizabeth had. Within seconds of the door closing, Elizabeth flung herself at the newcomer. "Nikki! I'm so sorry! How are you coping?"

Judging by her lack of tears or distress, Nikki was coping fine, except, perhaps, with Elizabeth. She patted Elizabeth on the back and extricated herself from the embrace.

She turned to me with a pageant smile, featuring loads of straight, blue-white teeth. "I'm Nikki Gray. Pardon the intrusion."

Everything about Nikki was overdone and big, unless it was supposed to be small: tiny waist, impressive cleavage, full golden-brown hair, skyscraper heels, and sparkly diamonds and other gemstones. At first glance, she was the young, slim, tan L.A. stereotype. With a second look, I revised my estimation of her age and number of surgical procedures upward, seeing the unnaturally taut skin under her eyes and the way the corners of her plump mouth tilted up even at rest.

I noted my own flat hair, how the little bit of mascara I'd put on that morning had run under my eyes, and that I'd somehow collected a stain on the front of my white team polo. I dragged a finger under each eye to scrape away mascara. "Kate Reilly. Public place. All yours."

She tee-heed. "I simply had to have a break from those cameras."

Elizabeth sniffed, though her eyes were dry. "You've got the crew here? But what are you doing about Billy? You know what happened? You can't be using that on your show!"

"They've been here all day." Nikki turned to me and smiled brightly. "I'm shooting a reality show pilot about my life since my husband's death in a tragic badminton accident."

I kept my mouth shut, not sure how badminton could be tragic or how tragedy translated to her chipper tone. Not sure how she and Elizabeth knew each other or how Billy fit in. Especially a dead Billy.

"But," Elizabeth put in, "you were dating."

I wasn't sure I'd heard correctly.

Nikki moved to the counter and peered at her reflection in the mirror. "I heard what happened. Poor Billy." She turned to me again. "We were spending time together. 'Dating' sounds so high school, doesn't it?" She tittered.

What soap opera had I been dropped into? She'd been sleeping with Billy? What did she see in him other than a pretty face and a twenty-four-year-old body? *Oh, right. Hello, rich, bimbo, Southern California cougar.*

"Won't it look bad if you're not upset?" Elizabeth asked.

Nikki pouted again, watching herself in the mirror, as if verifying a pout was a good look for her—it was—and patted Elizabeth's cheek. "The first thing you learn about reality television is not to deal with real emotion on-camera. Tamara made that mistake a couple seasons ago on her show about running her spa in Santa Monica." The last was addressed to me, before she looked back at Elizabeth. "I feel terrible about Billy, but I'll handle that at home, alone. Not in front of the cameras." Nikki might have frowned, the barest wrinkling of her brow. "But honestly, it's not as if we were deeply in love. We'd only known each other a couple months."

I couldn't tell if she was unaffected by Billy's death or if she had the self-control to hold off grieving until later.

She fluttered her fingers. "Excuse me a minute while I tinkle." She tiptoed off to the stalls in her stripper heels.

I also wondered if the clueless persona was an act or a way of life. I'd never heard anyone over the age of five use the word "tinkle." My whole experience in that bathroom had felt like a visit to a foreign country. One I was ready to leave.

I looked at a visibly calmer Elizabeth. "Will you be all right?"

"I'll be fine. Holden is on his way here from San Diego, so I'll pull myself together to be strong for him." Her eyes got watery again, and she took a deep breath. "It's kind of you to ask."

I left, thinking it was the most intimate conversation I'd ever had with Elizabeth. Then again, murder brought all kinds of people and behavior out of the woodwork.

I exited the bathroom into the glare of lights and the stares of cameras, which were quickly lowered when they saw I wasn't Nikki.

"Sorry," called a man with a clipboard.

I exited the media center building, still blinking away spots in my eyes, and almost ran into someone.

"Easy there, Kate." I heard a hint of laughter in a voice I recognized.

"Ryan Johnston. It's been a while."

To be precise, it had been fifteen months since the grim and emotional 24 Hours of Daytona where I'd met Ryan, an FBI agent undercover with a team run by a money-laundering, murderous, thug-harboring crook. Of course, no one had known Ryan was FBI until I'd unmasked the killer who tried to abduct my half-sister, Lara. I still thought Ryan could have done more to keep Lara safe, but I'd long since accepted he'd had different priorities.

"Good to see you, Kate." He smiled, offering a hand. His grip was like the rest of him: mild-mannered on the surface, hints of iron underneath. "How's Stuart Telarday doing?"

Stuart had been the killer's first victim at Daytona, though Stuart had been critically injured in an engineered hit-and-run accident, not killed. It had been a long road to recovery, and Stuart's physical healing was happening faster than the emotional. "Pretty well. He may never regain all of his memory, at least around the accident. But he's mobile now and getting back to full health."

"Are you still seeing him?"

I looked at Ryan in surprise. "What does that have to do with Billy?"

"Who's Billy?"

"The dead guy over in the garage." I pointed to the structure. "Billy Reilly-Stinson."

"More dead bodies?"

"Isn't that why you're here? I can't imagine why Billy would interest the FBI."

"He hadn't caught our attention yet, though, having met him, it was only a matter of time. I'm here to see the Series in action again. And to see you."

"Me?"

"I realize you're probably leaving after today, but you'll be back in a week?"

"I'm staying until the race."

His grin animated his entire face. "Are you still seeing Stuart? Or anyone else?"

I did the math and smiled. "Are you asking me out?"

Chapter Four

Ryan's eyes lit with amusement. "First, I'm asking if you're currently in a relationship."

FBI-man, asking me out? I looked around, expecting cameras to be capturing the moment. Instead, they followed Nikki exiting the building.

"Kate?"

I turned back to Ryan. "No current relationship. Stuart... isn't in a good place now."

"I'm sorry to hear that. I've worked with victims of similar accidents, and I know they can be tough to recover from emotionally."

I nodded, unwilling to go into the details of Stuart kicking me out of his life, telling me he wouldn't watch me waste my time on him. Not when he might be in a wheelchair the rest of his life and doubted I truly loved him. No argument I'd made had gotten through, and in the end, I'd left him alone. I kept tabs on his progress, but it still hurt.

"How about dinner?" Ryan's voice broke my thoughts. "Sometime in the next week, away from the racetrack."

Was I interested? He was smart, friendly, attractive, and a little dangerous. Of course I was. "I'd like that."

We exchanged cell phone numbers and made a tentative plan for Friday night. We'd gotten to the awkward goodbye stage when Tom Albright, the media guy and general assistant for my team, Sandham Swift Racing, trotted up the stairs from the basement media room.

"All wrapped up, Kate?" Tom turned to Ryan with a puzzled expression. "I know we've met, but I don't remember your name."

"Ryan Johnston. I was with Arena Motorsports at Daytona last year."

Tom's eyebrows shot up to his hairline. "That's right." He leaned forward, lowering his voice. "Are you still with the FBI? Are you undercover again?" Tom looked back and forth in the hallway. He wasn't subtle.

Ryan smiled. "I'm still with the Bureau, but I'm not undercover anymore. That was a special circumstance." He glanced at me. "I need to be off, but I'll see you soon."

Tom looked between me and Ryan's retreating back, but I ignored the question in his eyes. "Back to the hotel?"

At his nod, I led the way up outdoor stairs to the top-level plaza of the Long Beach Performing Arts Center. I tried to shake off the weirdness of the last couple hours: seeing Billy dead, experiencing Elizabeth's emotion, meeting Nikki, and being asked out on a date by an FBI agent. I felt a looming sadness about the glimpse I'd had of violent death—though I was angry about feeling anything at all for Billy, given the way he'd treated me. It was easier to focus on Ryan asking me out. Or on Tom at my side.

"How was the media response today?" I'd done the driving, and he'd done the talking, filling my passengers in on the specs of the racing series, the track, and the upcoming race weekend.

"Fantastic. Lots of excitement. You gave them all a great ride, and we should get some good press."

"It was a fun change of pace taking easy laps in a street car and giving the journalists a treat."

"The GPLB press person, Erica, mentioned she had an idea to pitch you to a couple reporters doing longer pieces. And I had a photographer wanting a quote to go with a photo essay. I gave him your info."

Near the fountain in the plaza we passed a woman with reddish-brown hair sitting on the lip of a planter. I'd noticed her earlier around the racing activity because of the pink-patterned scarf tied loosely around her neck.

"Hey, great scarf. I have the same one," I called to her as we passed. It was sold by one of the major breast cancer research organizations to raise funds, and I often wore mine to complement the pink shirts for my sponsor Beauté and the Breast Cancer Research Foundation.

The woman started and mumbled something I couldn't hear.

Tom slipped his phone into a pocket. "Sent you the reporter's info. Let me know if you need help with anything."

"Not that you'll be here."

"Nope, going home to Indiana. You're the one staying in La-La Land. I expect to return and find all the New Mexico drummed out of you. You'll be carrying a tiny dog around in a designer purse and doing lunch with people. Also having your people make calls for you."

"Do people really carry dogs in handbags?"

"You've got a week, Kate, and you're staying at the Beverly Hills Hotel. That's enough time for a dog *and* a movie deal. To make a splash in the 'scene.'" He made air quotes.

"I have sponsor obligations and the IndyCar test in Fontana. Beyond that, I'm hoping for downtime." I frowned, considering my schedule. "I wonder if Billy's death will impact any of the Frame Savings activities."

"Billy's—what? Your cousin Billy? Was that the dead body? I knew it!" He stopped me in the middle of the plaza. "I knew there couldn't be a body at a race without you being involved. Did you talk to the cops? Did you talk to the reporters? You saw the local TV vans doing standups, right? Are you going to find his killer?"

"No. No business of mine. No big deal."

"Dead body. Cousin of yours. Hello?"

"Yes, my cousin Billy is dead, and no, I didn't find him. They called me over to identify him. So I…" I had to stop and swallow the lump in my throat. "I saw him."

"Are you going to try to figure out who killed him? You don't even like him."

"Absolutely not. No reason for me to get involved. In fact, if it wasn't cold and heartless, I'd say good riddance." I looked around to be sure no one, especially the press, was listening. "Of course, I'm too nice to say that. Out loud."

"But your record *is* still intact for getting involved with every dead body that shows up around a racetrack." Tom started walking again.

"Unfair." I caught up with him and pushed the button to cross Ocean Boulevard. Come race weekend, that thoroughfare, as well as every restaurant and hotel on it, would be buzzing with celebrities and race activity. I didn't expect much excitement that evening.

We entered the Renaissance Hotel's long, shallow lobby from the side and stepped directly into chaos—the reality-show chaos that was already a familiar sight. I'd seen the two cameras and clipboard-man down at the track. The stylist, hairdresser, makeup artist, yapping Yorkshire terrier, and harried-looking man in the black GPLB polo shirt were new. But even with all the voices, activity, and dog-barking, Nikki Gray was in her element. Or she was too clueless to notice.

I leaned close to Tom. "You met her yet?"

He shook his head, wide-eyed as Nikki put her dog down on the ground among all the legs and feet. Predictably, the dog ran around, causing the hairdresser, stylist, and the other man—he'd dropped his clipboard—to chase after it.

"Nikki Gray. Filming a reality show. Not sure why she's here, except she was apparently seeing Billy."

"So she's got bad taste. And a dog."

I smiled at him. "It's not in a purse."

"I saw her earlier with Billy, looking angry with him. Or maybe disgusted. I also saw her with Don Kessberg—that's the GPLB guy there, the head of the Grand Prix Association. She didn't have as much of her entourage at the time. But she and Don were arguing. That's when I saw Billy. He was the same as always."

"Supercilious, arrogant." I stopped, feeling guilty for maligning the dead.

"Exactly. Nikki was annoyed with Billy, and Don was mad at them both." Tom considered. "Don seemed frustrated with Nikki, but furious with Billy. Like he wanted to wring Billy's neck. It was quite the drama."

"I get the feeling it's usually a drama around her. But is it real or for the cameras? And Billy's neck wasn't wrung. His head was caved in."

Tom and I looked at each other.

"Oops." I made a zipped lips motion.

The hairdresser scooped the dog up, cooing to it.

Nikki raised her voice. "You're not going to tell me to stay away." She stood in front of Don Kessberg, hands on her hips. "I have every right to be here. It's not my fault what happened."

That's when Detective Barnes walked in.

Chapter Five

Tom and I settled back against a low planter to watch the action, and I identified Detective Barnes and one of the uniformed officers from the scene of the crime.

"Ms. Gray?" The detective required only his presence and those words to quell the noise and activity buzzing around Nikki. Even the dog stopped yapping.

Nikki turned away from Don Kessberg. "Yes? Officer?"

"Detective," Barnes corrected. "We'd like a few words with you. Alone."

"You all, take a couple minutes." She fluttered her hands at the entourage.

When the cameramen zoomed in, Barnes fixed an unamused eye on them. "Go away."

Clipboard man tried to protest. "We're filming—"

"No." Barnes saw me and raised an eyebrow before focusing on Nikki.

She turned to Kessberg. "Donnie, can you wait, so we can work this out?"

Barnes looked at the GPLB boss also. "Don Kessberg? You'll need to wait. I'd like to speak with you."

Barnes led Nikki and the uniformed officer past a cordon into the closed restaurant area next to the lobby. I was ready to leave when Don crossed to us.

"Kate Reilly?" He extended a hand. "Don Kessberg, president of the race organization. I didn't get to meet you earlier, but I greatly appreciate your efforts today. I heard the journalists had a great time."

I introduced Tom. "We were glad to help. The members of the press all seemed happy. I hope they generate some good stories and race attendance."

Don gestured to the police. "You heard what happened? Why they're here?"

"It's a shame."

"Right, of course it is." His inflection teetered between sadness, regret, and sarcasm.

I shrugged. "Time for me to be off. Don, nice to meet you. Tom, see you in a week."

Half an hour later I was headed north on one of the many Los Angeles freeways, but not at any real pace. I eyed the sheer mass of humanity around me. As many as six lanes each way, half of them unmoving. I wondered where everyone was going.

The scene was perfect. The sun was setting to my left, painting the sky in shades of blue, pink, and gold, and the air temperature hovered around seventy degrees. In the lanes around me were more Porsches, Ferraris, BMWs, and Mercedes than I'd ever seen outside of a racetrack. Not to mention Bentleys, Aston Martins, Teslas, and a couple Maseratis and Lamborghinis. Plus a few Corvette C7s, the new Stingray model my racecar was built from. I enjoyed the view all the way to Beverly Hills.

I checked in to the iconic Beverly Hills Hotel, trying not to gawk like a tourist at the pale pink stucco exterior, green and white striped ceilings, and quiet marble elegance. Every furnishing was plush and tuned for visitor comfort. After sampling the complimentary toiletries in my bathroom, I had time to eat dinner, see, and be seen in the Polo Lounge before standing in front of the hotel at the appointed time for my ride to the movie-star party. I felt almost famous.

A black Lincoln Town Car pulled up, and I prepared myself. Instead of picking me up, it disgorged a man in a tuxedo and a woman in a short, fringed and sequined dress. A second Town

Car arrived, empty, and I got ready for action, but a man in a meticulously tailored suit strode past me and greeted the driver.

Five Town Cars later, I'd stopped reacting, and I began Tweeting about not being in Albuquerque anymore. A throat cleared in front of me. "Ms. Kate Reilly?"

I looked up to see a slim Asian man in his early twenties. He installed me in the rear seat of a Mercedes S-class sedan—black, of course—and drove me up into the hills. We passed house after perfectly landscaped and illuminated house marching up the canyons, Mediterranean architecture next to colonial next to modern. Some homes extended over air, propped up by giant stilts.

The views were tremendous, I discovered when I arrived at the party. That house occupied a big, flat spot on one of the Hollywood hills, saving all outdoor space for the pool and the panorama in the back yard. Standing out there at the edge of the drop-off, I could see Santa Monica and a dark blot I presumed was the Pacific Ocean on the right, all the way across the city basin to downtown L.A. on the left. All glittering with lights. It left me breathless.

"Kate, you made it!" I turned away from the pool and the view as Maddie approached, barefoot in the grass. She gave me a quick hug. "And you look great."

I'd hoped plain, black fitted trousers and a silver sequined tank, with a worn leather jacket for warmth, would blend in. I gestured at the city lights. "This is amazing."

"I know. I've got a similar view, and my favorite thing to do is sit with coffee or a glass of wine and enjoy." We were quiet a moment, and then she hooked an arm through mine. "Come on inside, I want to introduce you to some people. Lucas is eager to meet you."

"Lucas" meant Lucas Tolani, Maddie's co-star in the film she was currently shooting. He was also the current "hottest," "most beautiful," or "most desirable bachelor," depending on which entertainment magazine you read. I swallowed. "Why would he want to meet me?"

"I've raved about you." She smiled. "Lucas is great. Don't let the press scare you. Plus, I think he's in talks to play a racecar driver. He probably wants to pick your brain."

I relaxed. I understood being a source.

I followed Maddie's lead through the crowd, realizing as I met people that politics and power-plays were the same the world over, whether your industry was racing or film. It was easy to tell when someone Maddie greeted wanted something from her and when they were friends. Suddenly, Lucas was next to me.

Maddie patted him on the shoulder. "Lucas, introduce yourself and look after Kate for a minute. I need to chat with someone." She winked at me and crossed the room to a small cluster of people in ragged but expensive clothing.

Having been around racing for eighteen years, I was used to famous people. I was also used to well-honed, fit bodies and good looks. Lucas Tolani was all that and more. Charisma radiated off of him, an easy, friendly charm that warmed his audience and made them smile. Plus he had green eyes, an engaging grin, and thick, wavy dark brown hair. He was flat out, drop-dead gorgeous. I tried to remember to breathe.

Lucas held my hand in both of his. "I'm thrilled to meet the woman who led her class at the 24 Hours of Daytona this year."

"You're a racing fan?" I blurted out. I never expected anyone I met outside of the racing world to know about anything but NASCAR or, occasionally, Formula 1. The idea that someone not only knew sportscar racing but was aware of me? Surprising. The fact that Lucas freaking Tolani did—or knew enough to pretend he did? Unbelievable.

He laughed, displaying perfect, white teeth, the kind Hollywood cornered the market on. "I learned about racing when I did a movie with Neil." He nodded to a group of people in a far corner of the large, stark-white living room, and I recognized Neil Welch, a successful TV actor–turned–sportscar racer.

The owner of the world's sexiest smile still hadn't released my hand. "Your story is fascinating, Kate. I always like seeing how the underdog will perform. If they'll rise to the occasion and prove the world wrong. I love watching people do that, you among them."

I glanced around the room at the polish and fame and tried to smile. "Keep an eye on me here. I'm out of my element."

Lucas leaned closer. "The secret is none of us fits in. You learn to ignore it. How do you deal with it in the racing world?"

I thought of feeling both at home and isolated. "I don't let anyone tell me what I can't do."

"What a great approach."

I felt my cheeks burn. "I keep meaning to ask Maddie about the movie you're making together. What's it about?"

"Big picture, it's about how people react to pressure, to warning signs, or to obstacles in their path. How people are rarely what they seem. And how, all too often, we don't even know ourselves and what we're capable of." He paused. "Specifically, I'm a man who steals someone else's identity and becomes that person, convincing others the real person is the identity thief. Maddie is an investigator trying to uncover the truth." A suited man got Lucas' attention from across the room, and Lucas gave him a "one minute" sign, apologizing to me for needing to go conduct some business.

I jumped in. "I'm sorry for monopolizing you."

He quirked the side of his mouth up in a half smile. "I'm the one guilty of that. The question is, can I do it again? Are you free for dinner soon?"

I managed to give him a smooth acceptance and my cell number. When he left me and crossed the room, I found the nearest bathroom, locked the door, and freaked out for five minutes. The most sought-after, lusted-after, dreamed-about man in the world asked me out on a date. Maybe it was research for an upcoming role. Maybe the date wouldn't actually happen. I savored the moment, regardless.

Chapter Six

My first thoughts Wednesday, the morning after the party, were of three different men: Lucas Tolani, Ryan Johnston, and Billy Reilly-Stinson. Lying in my fluffy bed, I felt smug about dates with two of them. And, despite the fact we hated each other, I felt sympathy for Billy and the people who'd loved him. He'd never again know the anticipation of a first date or the comfort of a bed like this. I remembered the scene and grimaced. It hadn't been a gentle way to die.

I shook off my mood and got ready to meet my father, James Hightower Reilly III, for breakfast at the famous Canter's Deli on Fairfax. I didn't spot the celebrities that apparently flocked there, but I did see a woman in a wedding dress sitting at a table. No one else paid any attention to her. As we settled into an orange-red vinyl booth, my father saw me looking around.

"It's an L.A. institution," he told me. "Been here more than eighty years, open twenty-four hours. I love diners."

Yet another thing we share. "Holly hates it when I want to stop at every hometown spot."

After we'd ordered corned beef hash and eggs for him and an avocado, mushroom, and Swiss omelet for me, conversation lagged. We'd gotten the pleasantries out of the way on the drive over. Now it was time for the heavy topics.

After a lifetime of no connection, I was slowly coming to terms with my father. And possibly with his wife and two children. The other members of the family I'd met were "uncle" Edward, "cousin" Billy, and "cousin" Holden. They'd greeted me with open hostility and disdain, which stemmed from the events surrounding my birth, when my mother died and my father walked away, leaving me to be raised by my maternal grandparents.

My father claimed not to have known his family gave money to my grandmother when she took me home with her, and whether that was a kind gesture to help with my rearing or a payoff to stay away from the Reilly family forever was under dispute. My father believed the former. My uncle and cousins believed the worst. The bigger question that had nagged at me for the last year, if not my whole life, was why my father had walked away from his newborn child all those years ago.

My father took a deep breath. "Did you talk with your grandparents?"

"Yes. Did you get information from your family?"

"I did. But first, I want us to agree we won't blindly adhere to either story. That we'll work together and agree on the truth."

"You think one side is lying?"

"I'm suggesting one person's truth isn't the same as another's. I'm also suggesting we commit to staying civil, since the families couldn't manage that." He paused. "My relationship with you is more important to me than my family being right twenty-six years ago. I don't want to lose you again."

I tried to decide how I'd feel rejecting what my grandparents had told me. My father and I had made progress in our relationship over the past year, and I was starting to trust him with my thoughts and emotions. But I didn't feel connected to him, not the way I was connected to my grandparents.

"Can you do that, Kate? Can you commit to working with me on this relationship and promise not to walk away when it gets difficult?"

I sucked in a breath. *Direct hit.* Different responses leapt to my lips, including "The way you walked away from me all those years ago?" and "Maybe I don't want this relationship if it means betraying my grandparents." But I held onto them. Finally responded. "I'll do my best."

The facts weren't disputed. My parents fell in love, married, and had me while they were students at Boston University. But three days after my birth, my mother died in the hospital. I'd gone home with my mother's parents, and I'd had no contact with my father or his family until three years ago. That's where stories diverged.

One year ago, Billy and Holden informed me my father's family had paid my grandparents to take me away. Since that information was news to my father also, we agreed to ask our respective families what had happened. I'd been dreading today's discussion.

My father wasn't a popular subject in my grandparents' house—his name was anathema, in fact. But I was an adult now, and I needed information. It took me nine months to wear my grandmother down. Three months after I'd finally cornered her, she still barely spoke to me. I didn't have the full story, but I had the idea.

My father cleared his throat. "Would you like to start with what you learned?"

"It wasn't much." I paused. "You have to understand, my grandmother doesn't talk about you or your family. It was all I could do to get her to confirm she'd talked with members of the Reilly family back then. She wouldn't say who. She said all parties agreed I should be raised by her and Gramps, and that was that."

"And the question of money?"

"She said your family provided some funds for my upbringing."

"That's it?"

"That's all she'd tell me, but Gramps helped me piece together more of the story. He has no more love for the Reillys than Grandmother does, but he understands I need to know." I sighed. "That's what Grandmother can't see. I'm going to make my own decisions, and it's better for me to have all the facts."

"I'm sorry they're still so angry." He pressed his lips together and looked away.

"Me, too. I don't like hurting them."

We stayed quiet while the waitress delivered our meals.

"Gramps nosed around and figured out my savings account was started with a deposit of fifty thousand dollars, so that must have been from your family." I dug into my omelet. "I didn't get any further details about who Grandmother spoke with or what was discussed. All she'd ever say was you and the Reillys didn't care about me, didn't want me, and wouldn't see me in the hospital, which we know is untrue, based on the photo you gave me of your father holding me. Gramps said Grandmother came back from Boston with me and all she said was, 'We will raise the child, and we will never communicate with them.'"

I looked up from my plate to see my father staring out the window with tears in his eyes. I hadn't ever seen him emotional about the past, and it startled me. "I shouldn't have dumped all that on you at once."

He shook his head. "I didn't know how much it was, but I knew they'd handed over money. They say your grandmother demanded it for taking you."

A mouthful of eggs prevented me from an outraged response.

"I don't believe it," he said. "Any more than you believe every word your grandmother said about me and my family."

"Fair enough. Lots of bias on both sides. Who's 'they'?"

"My mother and my brother."

I set down my coffee cup with a clunk. "Your brother Edward. Maybe that explains why he hates me so much. But how old was he?"

"Only twenty."

"And he was involved in your business?"

"He wouldn't have seen it as my business, but as family business."

"That's bullshit."

"It's how the Reilly family has always operated."

"And you put up with that?" I paused, feeling a tightness in my chest. "I should ask this instead, why did you put up with that? Why did you let them get in your business?"

He took a long, deep breath and released it. "That's the explanation I owe you. I've been trying to prepare for it, and I'm not sure I have an acceptable response."

I waited.

"I have reasons, but no excuse. I failed you. I know that, and I can't tell you the pain I feel knowing how much of your life I missed. How sorry I am I wasn't there."

"That's *now*. I need to understand then." Regrets didn't help me make sense of the past.

"I was devastated. I'd never lost anyone close to me before, and I was out of my mind grieving for your mother. My family swooped in, patting my hand and telling me not to worry about anything. By the time I understood what was happening, I was back at home." He stared out the window again, his eyes—his whole face—bleak. "I woke up one morning and asked about the funeral." He turned back to me. "Your grandparents had taken your mother back to New Mexico to bury. They'd taken you with them."

"You could have come after me."

"I should have. The truth is, I wasn't strong enough to go against my family." He paused. "They told me your grandmother called me a killer and told me to stay away. They said she'd threatened to come after me and my family if I attempted to see you."

"That doesn't sound like my grandmother at all."

"I only half-believed it, but I understood she didn't want me around. My family didn't want us in contact either. That was too much pressure to fight."

My chest was tight. "Even though you'd have been fighting for me?"

He froze, eyes on his plate. He opened and closed his mouth twice. "I was young and foolish. A coward."

Has that changed? "You went against your family when you found me three years ago."

"Over the years, I'd wanted to find you, but I told myself my appearance would disrupt your life. Then, when we were both in the racing world, it seemed like fate."

I wasn't sure I was happy with fate, but when it came to my relationship with my father, I'd learned not to make knee-jerk responses. Especially not to voice them. I needed time to sort through my feelings about his story.

Chapter Seven

While I drove back to the Beverly Hills Hotel, emotions still reeling from my father's revelations, I received a voicemail from Nikki Gray—with no trace of a giggle—asking me to talk with her and Don Kessberg, because only I could help them.

I debated ignoring the message, but professional responsibility got the better of me, and I called her back, then detoured to her Bel Air mansion. She'd offered no specifics, only begged me to meet with her and Don, telling me they needed my help to save the Long Beach Grand Prix from "certain disaster." I didn't believe her dire predictions, but I'd been unable to resist her repeated entreaties. I pulled into her driveway ready for anything. Or so I thought.

To start with, her house wasn't what I expected. Given Nikki's overblown appearance, I'd braced myself for artificial Tuscan opulence. Instead, the space I entered was all clean lines and walls of glass. Nikki pranced ahead on another pair of platform heels to an enormous living room with one open wall looking south, from the ocean to downtown L.A.

"It's an amazing sight, isn't it?" Don claimed my attention and shook my hand. "Thanks for meeting with us, Kate."

"Nikki said you're desperate. I have no idea how you think I can help you." I sat down in a low, dark-gray leather armchair and watched him as he settled in the matching chair opposite me. He had the lean build of an athlete and a full head of thick, white hair.

Nikki sank down on the couch to my right, kicking off her shoes and tucking her bare feet under her—no small achievement in a short, skin-tight, stretchy dress.

I jumped as the small accent pillow next to Nikki stood up and stretched.

Nikki noticed and giggled, the same high-pitched fake sound as the day before. "Pookie-bear surprised Kate, didn't she?" She picked up the white fluff, which resolved itself into a tiny dog, and made kissing sounds. A little pink tongue darted out to lick Nikki's face, and I thought I saw jewels glinting on the dog's collar.

"You had a different dog yesterday." I couldn't tell what breed this one was, but the other had been a silvery-gray and black Yorkie.

"That was Teenie. She went better with my outfit."

As I worked to keep the surprise and amusement off my face, I saw three more dogs run across the backyard. A large, brown Lab with a big tongue hanging out of a graying face and a Terrier-mix nipping at the Lab's heels. Bringing up the rear was a short, golden fuzzball, wearing a blue vest with an insignia I couldn't read, that stumbled and rolled butt-over-head before righting itself and dashing out of sight.

Don cleared his throat. "Dogs aside."

"What exactly do you think I can do?" I glanced from Nikki to Don.

"I think you know I'm the president of the Long Beach Grand Prix organization. What you may not know is Nikki owns the race event itself."

I glanced at her, now rubbing noses with Pookie. Pookie-bear? I'd soon be ready for a movie role myself, with all the practice I had in hiding my thoughts.

Nikki settled the dog on her lap. "My late husband, Quentin, owned the naming and promotion rights for the race, which I inherited a few months ago. I leave most everything to Don to handle."

"I've been running the day-to-day of the event for the last

seven years," he explained. "While we've missed Quentin, we've been able to carry on smoothly."

"I still don't understand why I'm here." I looked between the two again.

Don sat forward. "We're uneasy about negative publicity for the race and the race organization concerning Billy's death."

"His murder," Nikki corrected.

"I know they say all publicity is good publicity, but I'm not sure that will be the case. At Nikki's request, Billy had recently gotten involved, helping us put on the event." Don spoke the last few words through a clenched jaw.

"Billy had experience in the racing world, you know," Nikki explained, as she adjusted her trio of pink sparkly— diamond?—bracelets.

I made a non-committal sound. I'd seen Billy's "racing experience" at Daytona when he ran roughshod over ethical behavior and series rules to advance his father's position.

"We're concerned the race organization will come out the worse for the police investigation into his death. Or that a killer on the loose at the racetrack will affect attendance." Don paused, jaw tense. "Billy managed to ruffle a few feathers within the organization, so we're looking for some damage control."

"I'm still not clear—"

"Isn't it obvious?" Nikki leaned forward, her breasts defying gravity by staying in her dress. "Donnie here is afraid he'll be arrested for Billy's murder, and we want you to figure out who really did it."

Don sighed, but didn't speak.

Oh, no. No, no, no. Not a chance. When I had air in my lungs, I asked the obvious. "Why do you think I can do anything? You should be talking to the police."

"They're already looking at me," Don returned. "I don't— can't—trust them to look deeper. You've caught three murderers. You know racing. People will talk to you."

"People will also talk to a private investigator when you hire one. I'm a racecar driver, not a detective!" I took a couple deep breaths to calm down.

"The cops won't care about preserving the reputation of the longest-running street race in North America," Don pointed out. "And a PI can't talk to people in the racing world like you can. The racing world will trust you to investigate, because you've done it before."

"Please?" Nikki pleaded.

I tried to marshal my arguments. All I came up with was, *No, no, no, no, no.*

Nikki narrowed her eyes at me. "You don't want to be responsible for the destruction of the Long Beach Grand Prix, do you?"

"That's not on me."

Don's face hardened. "But you could help save its reputation. Could you live with knowing Billy ended the long tradition of the race, when you could have prevented it?"

Nikki lifted Pookie and rubbed the fluffy dog against her cheek. "I don't know, Donnie. I'm not so sure she's right for the job. Maybe she should stick to driving."

"Right," I replied. "That makes sense."

"She has so much to do already. So much to prove. This would clearly be too much."

"Right, thank you. I…" I stared at her. "What?"

Her eyes widened. "As a woman, I understand the uphill climb it is to be taken seriously. I see how hard it is for you to prove yourself every weekend, I wouldn't want to give men more reason to think you can't cut it."

I stared at her. *How did this go from "help us" to "you're a sub-par driver"? I'm not falling for that trick.*

"Don't say no right now," Don jumped in. "Please consider it."

Nikki smiled, slyly. "I'll make sure it's worth your while."

"This isn't about money."

"But you always need sponsorship," she continued. "I know a lot of people. I could make things easier for you."

I imagined the corollary: she could also make things more difficult for me. I saw a flicker of something in her eyes, before she nuzzled Pookie and gave me another smile. A more calculating one this time. My feelings warred with each other. *Oh, hell, no,* doing battle with, *I'll show them.*

I turned to Don. "Do the police think you killed Billy?"

He gazed out at the magnificent view of Los Angeles. "If they don't, they will, after they stop thinking Nikki did."

"Did you?"

Nikki giggled. "Donnie couldn't do that."

"Donnie" grimaced, and I thought he probably could have. I turned to Nikki. "Did *you?*"

Her eyes went wide. "Why would I?"

"You were tired of him?" I speculated.

"Tired? Oh, my, no. He could be sweet, and he was talented." She purred the last word.

Don shifted in his seat, uncomfortably. I felt nauseated.

Nikki pouted. "But he was going to leave me soon."

"The cops were asking if that's why she killed him," Don added.

Her brow creased that tiny amount. "Why would I? He'd be gone either way."

She had a point.

"So you'll consider looking into it for us," Don said. A statement, not a question.

I opened my mouth to decline, but he cut me off. "Consider it, please, that's all we're asking."

"It's not *all* we're asking," Nikki put in.

Don nodded. "For now, it is."

They wouldn't hear "no," I wasn't going to say "yes," and I had another meeting to get to, so I took the contact information they handed me and got out of there.

As I looked back at them from my car, Don held a hand up in farewell and Nikki waved Pookie's paw at me. I understood their level of concern about the race organization, but didn't get how they thought I could help. I also couldn't comprehend their alliance. How two such different people worked together. How he could put up with her.

I didn't understand a lot.

Chapter Eight

I worked through shock over Don and Nikki's request for help as I drove down the hill from Bel Air. I instinctively wanted to rise to any challenge, and, I admit, I was curious why Billy was killed.

But you didn't like him, you don't care.

I tapped my fingers on the steering wheel, waiting at a red light on Melrose Avenue. It was true, I hadn't liked Billy. I didn't care that he wasn't around anymore, but I did care that he, or anyone, was murdered. That wasn't right. Anything I could do to make the world fairer or more just, I should do. Right?

Now you're a crusader for justice, Batgirl?

I spotted an open red curb and pulled over to call my best friend, manager, and PR person, Holly Wilson. Voicemail.

"Checking in, Holly. You won't believe what's going on. Or maybe you would. I feel like I've been dropped into the middle of a television show. It's Real-Housewives-meets-CSI. Or maybe it's Murder-She-Wrote-meets-the-Kardashians. You'd love it." I paused. "I'd say I wish you were here, but I think I'm hearing you in my head. Tell Miles to win this weekend, and I'll see you Monday."

I pulled back into traffic, thinking about Holly's upcoming public debut as the girlfriend of Miles Hanson, the most beloved NASCAR driver of the current era. She and Miles had been dating for a year and a half, but they'd been cautious about publicity. This would be her first weekend by his side on national television. My own experiences with Miles' super-fans made me doubtful they'd welcome her, but I'd kept my concerns to myself. After all, wrecking the man in a race—which I'd done—was different than dating him. I hoped. For her sake.

Holly returned my call when I was back in my hotel room. I filled her in on the last twenty-four hours and heard only silence for ten seconds. "I left you alone for two days, sugar."

I laughed. "I'm not sure how this happens."

"Are you all right about what your father told you?"

I squeezed my eyes shut. "I'm trying not to think about it right now. What I want to know is, would I benefit by looking into Billy's death for Don and Nikki?"

"It couldn't hurt to have the Long Beach race promoter—a man with influence—owe you."

"And ditzy as she may be, Nikki's got access to serious funds."

"Not a bad person to have on your side. But…"

"I know. My gut is screaming for me to stay away from my father's family. I don't need them in my life."

"Do you *want* to find out why Billy was killed?"

"No. I mean, I'm curious, but happy to leave it to the police."

"Do you feel like you need to?"

"Not sure."

We were both quiet a minute, then she spoke. "Your decision. I'll do my job and remind you to focus on business. You're headed to the bank for the board meeting soon?"

"I am." Even I heard my lack of enthusiasm.

"Be excited about the people planning to fund your racing for the next five years, Kate."

"I'm grateful. I'm excited, you know that." I sighed. "It's hard to separate my father and his family from the bank."

"I know." Her voice was stern. "But you need to go in there and charm the entire Frame Savings board of directors. This is business, not personal, even if some of the people in the room are your long-lost, and irritating, family. Suck it up, and give them what they want for their sponsorship dollars. Those don't grow on trees."

I pictured Holly, one hand fisted on her hip, tossing her red, corkscrew curls. I took a deep breath, let it out, and took another. I sat up straight. "Okay, I'm good. Pleasant and professional. Appreciative and enthusiastic." I paused. "I still don't know what to say to Nikki and Don."

"Don't think about it until after tomorrow. Right now you need to focus on the sponsor meeting. After that you need to think about the IndyCar test. Do not distract yourself with anything else."

Holly was right, the next twenty-four hours would be crucial to my racing career. Most of all, I needed to perform well in the boardroom and on the track. "I'll update you after the meeting."

I tried to calm the butterflies in my stomach as I rode the elevator to the twentieth floor of the Frame Savings building in the Wilshire District. I arrived in the middle of a spacious lobby filled with brown leather furniture and oil paintings featuring Los Angeles. The sixtyish female behind a big, curving cherrywood desk took my name and asked me to wait for the break the board members were about to take. It was only five minutes before my father came out to greet me.

"Thanks for coming. Are you all right after our discussion this morning?"

"I'm fine, and I'm very happy to be here. To meet the team that's willing to support my career." I eyed him. "Thank you again for making this happen for me."

"You're welcome, though it didn't take much convincing. I wasn't even the first to propose you. Frame Savings has a long tradition in motorsports, we'd simply…gotten away from sponsoring anyone in the professional ranks."

I knew he meant while the bank had sponsored his brother, Edward, and his nephews, Billy and Holden. The bank had withdrawn sponsorship from that trio fifteen months ago, after they tried to cheat their way to better results. I'd been instrumental in revealing those misdeeds, which apparently hadn't prejudiced the bank's board of directors against me.

"You're the perfect answer," my father continued. "A professional with a long career ahead of her, and part of the family."

"I'm glad that works for all of us."

"Since we have a few minutes, I thought I'd give you a quick tour of our headquarters." James led the way to the elevator.

As we descended, he studied me. "That's one of the new shirts?"

Though the board would be in suits, I'd stuck with my uniform: team shirt and khakis. But this was a new white polo, sporting a prominent Frame Savings logo. "I thought I'd demonstrate that everyone seeing me sees Frame Savings."

"It makes the point effectively." He led the way through a glass door from the elevator lobby to a Frame Savings branch office on the building's ground floor.

"This is your flagship branch here in Los Angeles?" I asked. Until I started negotiating with them about a sponsorship deal, I hadn't known the East Coast-based bank was national or that it had a significant presence in Southern California.

"This was the first branch out west." He related the bank's history as he led me back to the elevator and through the executive floors of the tower, introducing me to key personnel along the way.

I tensed as we rounded a corner on the nineteenth floor and discovered Edward Reilly-Stinson and Holden Sherain talking with an assistant outside Edward's large corner office. My father stayed cordial and professional. "Of course, you know Holden and my brother, Edward. Also Edward's assistant, Trina. Edward's jointly in charge of West Coast operations with Coleman Sherain. Holden's been running San Diego regional operations for the last year."

I was surprised to see Edward at the office the day after his son was killed, especially given his red eyes and haggard demeanor. Holden was always grim and angry, in my experience, and today was no different.

"I'm very sorry for your loss," I offered.

Silence.

After a few fraught seconds, my father spoke. "Kate, perhaps you'd wait by the elevators for a moment?"

"Sure." I walked fifty feet away, turned the corner, and stopped before I reached the elevators. I could still hear most of what was said.

Edward spoke first. "I can't believe she's here. I can't believe you're going to pay her."

My father remained calm. "Trina, will you take a break, please?" A pause, I presumed, while the assistant left. "Edward, you should be at home. I'm sure there are arrangements..."

"Holden's helping me make them. You stay out of it."

"Please let me know if there's anything I can do to help."

Edward barked out a ragged laugh. "If you cared, you wouldn't bring that—"

"Careful," my father warned.

"*Fine*. You wouldn't bring her here. Not after what happened to Billy."

"Kate had nothing to do with Billy's death. You're not thinking straight."

He thinks I killed Billy?

Holden broke his silence. "You don't know her. You can't be sure."

Chapter Nine

I had to stop myself from darting around the corner and yelling. *You don't know me either! How dare you insinuate I'd do anything that awful? I wasn't the one caught cheating at a race!*

"Holden, Edward, I'm not going to hear it. Ever. Give up or get out." My father's tone softened. "Ed. Both of you. Take time to grieve. Don't be here today."

There was no response. I heard footsteps coming my way, so I tiptoed to the elevators.

My father reached past me to push the up button. "Sorry about that. It's a tough day for them. I know it can't have been easy for you yesterday, either. Identifying Billy. Thank you for doing that and for putting the police in touch."

"Of course."

"Everyone in the offices here is still a bit shocked." He glanced at me. "Billy was working here at headquarters, you know."

I hadn't known, and I bordered on "I didn't care." Fortunately, the elevator arrived. Time to focus on the board meeting instead.

This time we passed through the big lobby on the twentieth floor and entered a small, plush anteroom of the executive boardroom. Half a dozen men and two women stood chatting next to a buffet of snacks and beverages. My father started the introductions.

The men were a blur of basic names—Bob, John, Tim, Mark—and executive titles from the financial ranks of big corporations. They were all friendly and welcoming. The only female board member was Sharon, CFO for a movie studio in town, and she was also pleasant, happy to hear I'd be on her studio lot later that day to visit Maddie.

The remaining woman in the room was an executive assistant. The brief words we exchanged, the glances she shot me, and her general demeanor told me she was territorial. She didn't like interlopers, particularly female ones. She also thought I was too young and too female to be so bold and confident—I got that from her derisive sniffs as I explained my racing career to two of the men. I hated it when another woman tried to keep me down, but I kept my frustration and sadness in check. Since I knew I couldn't change her mind, and since I'd only intrude on her turf briefly, I tried to ignore her attitude. I watched her soften and smile as someone new entered the room.

Coleman Sherain, Holden's father and president of the bank, was tall, with a jock's muscled physique on the verge of going soft and dark hair starting to gray at the temples. He wore a confident smile and radiated power, and I shook his hand with as steely a grip as I could muster. I'd spoken with him a few times, working out the details of the sponsorship, and met him briefly at the 12 Hours of Sebring race a month before. I'd been on guard at first, given his son's attitude toward me, but Coleman had been straightforward, professional, and emotionless. All business.

His smile stretched wider, but didn't touch his eyes. "Good to see you again, Kate. Glad to have you on the team." I wondered if the coolness and insincerity I felt came from him or from my own mistrust of his son. He adjusted his tie and glanced around. "Let's resume."

Once we were all settled around the large conference table in the next room, Coleman took charge, the executive assistant typing on a laptop as he spoke. He started by introducing me to the room, waving a hand at nameplates in front of each member. Then he requested a summary of the contract and planned expenditures be read out by the assistant and asked me to explain my plans in more detail, without the contractual language.

I stood and remembered to smile before launching into my story. I outlined my early days and success in go-karts and Star Mazda, then my leap to sportscars. "I love racing the Corvette, and the people at Sandham Swift Racing have been wonderful. But I have dreams of racing other, faster cars on bigger stages and tracks. That's where Frame Savings comes in. I'm excited to represent the Frame Savings name and brand to a larger and broader audience."

One of the board members—Robert Roberts, he went by "Bob"—asked exactly what I meant by "bigger stages."

"I have a big career wish list: the Daytona 500, 24 Hours of Le Mans, Indy 500, and more. Each race is in a different series and requires a different kind of car, but that means I have a lot of options, depending on where you'd like to see Frame Savings represented."

"It also means money," another man mumbled, halfway down the table.

I turned to him. "You're right. I said those were on my wish list. I didn't say I expected to race them all. I make choices about where I race. It's my career, after all." I smiled and saw answering grins on a couple faces. "But I'm aware where I end up is also dependent on my partners. Where the money is coming from, and what goals that organization has."

I glanced around the table. "Which brings me to a question for this group. I've had conversations with the executive team, but I'd like to be sure I understand *your* goals for your sponsor-ship dollars. Where do you want to see Frame Savings in the racing world? And how can I get you there?"

The man who'd mumbled about money snorted. "We'd like to get attention for winning, instead of for trailing the pack or being reprimanded by the people in charge."

Coleman looked down his nose. "We're all in agreement. That's why we've got a professional. How many podiums were you on last year, Kate?"

"Six podiums from ten races, with one win, three seconds, and two third places. In what's widely regarded as the most competitive class in current racing."

I saw signs of satisfaction, and I hated to burst their bubbles. "I want to set your expectations correctly. Those results come from a team that works together extremely well—has done so for almost a dozen years now, including before I came along three years ago. It didn't happen overnight."

Coleman took the floor and adjusted his tie again. "We've discussed a measured approach to building Kate's skills, the team around her, and her exposure, as well as ours."

The grouchy man spoke again. "What about our spend? What do we get during this slow build? And how long will this take? Why aren't we at the 500 this year?"

"We'll go next year." I cut through the murmurs running around the room. "And for at least two years after that. That's thirteen months to the first Frame Savings car at the Indy 500. We'll set modest goals that year, such as qualifying for and finishing the race. I'll have bigger hopes and expectations for the years that follow."

I met the eyes of each board member. "As much as I'd love to get out there next month for this year's race, it's a terrible idea on a variety of levels. We need time to find the right team and prep the car, and I need to get comfortable with both. That's why, this year, I'll run some lower-level races with a team that could take us to Indy next year, to get used to an open-wheel car again and to try out the team."

"And you're testing tomorrow." My father spoke for the first time.

"Tomorrow I'm on the oval in Fontana with that team, testing an IndyCar on the track."

"How can you do that, if you're driving for your current team?" Sharon, the lone female on the board, asked.

"My contract with Sandham Swift means I drive their Corvette in the SportsCar Championship. It doesn't prohibit me from driving other cars in other series, though I clear other rides with Sandham Swift out of courtesy. I can have more than one driving contract, like I can have multiple sponsors."

"What kind of car is it, and have you driven one before? Driven on an oval?" Bob wanted to know.

"IndyCars are what's considered open-wheel, meaning no fenders around the wheels, as well as open-cockpit, meaning no roof. I drove smaller, less-powerful open-wheel cars in my Star Mazda days. Some of those races were on ovals, and I've also driven other kinds of cars on oval dirt tracks here and there. But the answer is I haven't done much of either, so I need practice before tackling the fastest cars on the biggest oval at the Indianapolis 500."

I answered questions for another fifteen minutes about my racing plans and how those had changed, based on their sponsorship. One board member insisted I should move straight to NASCAR, to "make a splash." I explained why sending me into a high-level series with zero experience in the cars or tracks was a recipe for disaster, whereas building slowly would get us somewhere. I think I got my point across.

At least, they all seemed satisfied when they called for a break after an hour and twenty minutes. But there was one last topic on a few minds.

"We've covered the racing, Kate," noted Bob, as everyone pushed back their chairs and stood up from the table. "What about Billy's murder? I assume you'll get that figured out also."

Chapter Ten

I froze. "Excuse me?"

Board member Bob replied. "You've solved crimes before. Figuring out what happened to an executive at your new sponsor ought to be part of your duties. Don't you think?" The last was addressed to the others in the room, who mostly agreed.

Sharon raised her eyebrows. "Are you an investigator also, Kate?"

"She's a racecar driver." My father's cold, flat voice cut through the murmurs. "*Not* an investigator."

Coleman frowned. "She knows the racing world, and that's where Billy's death took place. Haven't you unmasked killers before?"

You know very well, since your son was collateral damage. I replied to the group. "I've been lucky to help the police catch a few criminals. But it's not what I do. Besides, we don't know Billy's death had anything to do with racing."

"You know the players in the Reilly family, the bank structure, and racing," Bob put in. "It couldn't hurt us to have someone involved in the investigation making sure Frame Savings is the number one priority. Someone we can count on to bring a minimum of publicity to Billy's...situation."

It could hurt me.

My father's voice got frostier. "We have no business asking her to have anything to do with Billy's death. No right. Much less to play on her feelings of obligation to us for the sponsorship. All she owes us for that is to race and represent us well."

"No one's threatening her sponsorship." Sharon looked me in the eye. "Whatever happens, Kate, you have a contract. We're delighted you're representing us."

I could hear the "but" coming.

"Right, gentlemen?" Sharon surveyed the room, eliciting nods. "Don't worry about that, Kate. But—" *There it is.* "—it's true you're in a unique position."

"I didn't know Billy. Or his friends." I tried to stay calm, to keep the desperation and panic out of my voice.

"But you are more familiar with his various activities or circles than anyone else." Sharon smiled. "Perhaps you can keep an eye or ear open, in case his death had anything to do with the racing world? So there's no negative blow-back on the Frame Savings brand."

Sharon glanced at my father and spoke to me. "While we're not asking you to whip out your magnifying glass and outdo the police to capture Billy's killer, it's fair to say the promotion of the Frame Savings brand is ultimately one of your goals as our representative. Wouldn't you agree?"

She'd backed me into a corner. I hoped my frustration and reluctance didn't show on my face, at least not as much as anger and fear showed on my father's.

I forced a smile. "I'll see what I can find out and keep the board posted."

Everyone was in a congenial mood after that, except for my father. For my part, the request to solve Billy's murder—clearly that's what they wanted me to do—only added to how conflicted I felt about having Frame Savings as a sponsor. The upside was the fulfillment of my racing dreams. The downside was dealing with my father's family. Being beholden to them. Having to interact with them.

Coleman stopped me on my way out of the conference room, shaking my hand again. "Looking forward to your results, on and off the track, Kate."

"I can only guarantee you performance in a racecar. I'm a driver, not an investigator."

"Perhaps you need to figure out how to be both, since that's what our brand needs right now. I'd hate to have to make more changes so soon." He touched a hand to the knot of his tie and walked away, leaving me reeling.

As I pulled myself together, I heard a new voice whisper, "An attractive girl, but not feminine. And quite aggressive."

I stiffened, suspecting it was the only board member who hadn't spoken a word in the meeting. I slowly turned to survey the room. As I expected, the whisperer stood with the grouchy board member and the executive assistant, all of them trying to pretend they hadn't been talking about me.

Sharon touched me on the shoulder. "Thank you for being here, Kate, and for representing us."

"Thank you for the support."

"Don't worry about them." She glanced at the critical trio. "It takes time for the old guard to accept women in new roles."

"I assume you'd know?"

"Indeed." She smiled. "Best of luck tomorrow."

I felt better after that, but I still felt the weight of the words and requests as my father escorted me into the elevator.

He waited to speak until we exited on the ground floor and stood near the elevators to the parking garage, out of the bustle of people moving in all directions. "I think the meeting went well. Thank you again for coming to speak with everyone."

"Of course. Thank you for everything you did to arrange the sponsorship."

"All I did was suggest your name. I abstained from the voting, in fact. The marketing team and board of directors made the decision. It's not a gift, you earned it."

"Having Reilly as a last name helped."

"Of course it did. But, as we know, there are other members of the family not being sponsored. It's not only about the name. You heard them, they want visibility and results."

I understood the line between a gift from family and sponsorship by Frame Savings. I was almost comfortable with it. But I knew outsiders wouldn't grasp, or care about, the subtleties, and I knew I'd hear about "daddy paying for my ride." The sponsorship was worth it.

I looked at my father, seeing the same blue eyes and almost-black hair I saw in the mirror every morning. He was also short, though taller than me, and slim. Much as I sometimes wanted to, I couldn't deny our obvious genetic connection.

"Thank you anyway, and thanks for the help today." My poise deserted me. I could talk potential sponsors out of hundreds of thousands of dollars, but I fumbled around my father, afraid of saying too much and committing myself beyond my comfort level, but also afraid of losing the connection. Family was complicated.

He cleared his throat. "You may feel obligated to look into Billy's death. I don't want you doing that."

I don't want to either, but the board certainly does.

He struggled with something, starting to speak twice and stopping, before saying simply, "I don't want you hurt. Let the police handle it. Leave it alone."

I agreed with him in theory. "It's hard for me ignore a request from a brand-new sponsor, much less when it's the same request made by the race organizer." I described the meeting I'd had with Nikki Gray and Don Kessberg. "At this point, it's hard to say no. If I *can* say no." Coleman hadn't made it seem like an option.

"Try."

"We'll see." I shrugged, feeling like a recalcitrant teenager. "I need to get moving, and I'm sure you need to get back to the meeting. Thank you again."

His lips compressed to a tight line, but he didn't make any more demands. He kissed my cheek goodbye. "Good luck tomorrow. I'll try to get out there for part of it."

"It's the first step. I guarantee it'll go well."

The elevator arrived with a chime, and my father put a hand on my forearm to stop me moving forward. "I'm sure it will. Be careful. *Please.*" He watched me as the doors closed.

I spent the first five minutes of the drive back to the Beverly Hills Hotel whining to myself, variations on the theme of "But I don't want to!"

I considered the issue rationally. I didn't have to confront Billy's killer. I didn't even have to figure out who it was. All I needed was for the race organizers and my sponsors to *think* I was helpful. Keeping them happy with me, for whatever reason, was a good idea. I'd ask some questions and, in the unlikely event I dug up useful information, I'd turn it over to the police.

I got back to the hotel with a couple hours to kill before my visit to Maddie's movie set. When I found the housekeeper cleaning my room, I wandered out to the pool and marveled at the immaculate cabanas, colorful chaise lounges, and beautiful people arrayed around the water that no one swam in. Apparently "pool" in L.A. meant "place to be seen" not "place to get wet."

Before I could do more than pull my feet onto the pink chaise, an attentive and stunningly attractive male server appeared, asking if he could get me anything to eat or drink. If my order of a simple iced tea disappointed him, he didn't let on.

I dug through my handbag for a small notebook and a pen, squared my shoulders, and called Don Kessberg. He met me at the pool half an hour later.

He perched on the center section of the next chaise over, facing me, elbows on his knees. I couldn't see his eyes behind his mirrored aviators.

We'd done no more than exchange greetings when the attractive server was back.

"Club soda, lime, no ice." Don waved him away. "Thank you for agreeing to look into this. Nikki and I are both grateful."

"She's interesting." It was the best I could come up with.

He surprised me with a grin. "She's got her idiosyncrasies, but she's not dumb. She puts on an act."

Yet she took up with Billy...

Chapter Eleven

I eyed Don Kessberg. "What was Billy doing to help the race organization?"

The server reappeared. Don took the glass, refusing the straw, and drank a third of the club soda down in one go. "Billy was supposed to be contributing marketing ideas to increase press and attendance. He was nominally in charge of logistics for the SportsCar Championship paddock. And he had stepped in to take the lead on the celebrity race."

That was a whole lot to dig into. "What does 'take the lead' mean?"

"He interpreted it as trying to be every celebrity's best friend."

"Anything else?"

Don took another long drink, silent and unreadable behind his sunglasses.

"Don, you've got to give me something. I can't do anything if you won't talk to me."

"You can't repeat this to Nikki. I don't want to ruin my relationship with her."

"Fine. I'm not here for gossip."

"All right." He took a deep breath and finally removed his glasses, revealing bloodshot eyes. "Billy supposedly had experience in the racing world and in big business. All he was really good at was talking a good game."

"You said he had three roles."

"Two of them, paddock logistics and marketing work, were small projects, easy to hand over. To be honest, I thought he couldn't do much damage."

"What happened?"

"He promised innovative ideas for pitching stories to new media, but in the end, all we got was half-illiterate posts from racing bloggers no one's ever heard of and a spread in a trade journal for the porn industry—excuse me, the adult film industry. He did zero work, though he did spend an afternoon with the adult film reporter."

I hoped my mouth wasn't hanging open. "What does a magazine about adult films have to do with the race weekend?"

"Sponsorship. There's always a car in the paddock sponsored by an adult film company, usually racing in one of the support series. Sometimes the producer or distributor is driving the car, since it's big business on the other side of these hills in the Valley. Haven't you seen the porn stars walking around the paddock at the Grand Prix?"

"Someone pointed out one woman last year. Until then, I thought everyone was kidding." I remembered the woman wearing six-inch platform heels, a bikini top that was three sizes too small, and a skirt the width of an Ace bandage. Plenty of race fans or workers wore skimpy or revealing clothing, but that outfit was extreme.

"They show up every year. Paddock regulars." He was amused. "Anyway, Billy talked big about marketing and press coverage. He left all the work to the office staff. He couldn't return follow-up calls or e-mails to the journalists who responded to his pitch, which we had to edit to correct misspellings and factual inaccuracies. We got basically nothing out of it. That was one project."

He finished his beverage and set the glass on the ground next to him. "The other was the SCC paddock setup. He completely screwed that up, too."

I knew the SportsCar Championship, a support race at Long Beach to the main event of the IndyCar race, had been in the same patch of parking lot for the last five years, almost without change in arrangement. "How hard could that be?"

"He'd had a *better* idea about paddock configuration, and he sent out a notice with a schematic to all the teams, without telling anyone else. It took three phone calls from irate owners before I caught on." He rubbed both hands over his face. "I don't know what he was like in the rest of his life, but in my experience, everything that boy touched turned to shit."

No shock there. "What was his role with the celebrity race?"

"He was on the in-house team organizing it. He liked to think he was in charge. We have a committee that picks the celebrities and hands them over to the racing school, which does their thing. Once the celebs are trained, we set up the press opportunities and manage their schedules. He was on the committee at Nikki's insistence, and he introduced himself to the celebrities as in charge of the event. Then didn't do anything."

"That must have been annoying."

He shrugged. "It was more embarrassing than anything. You're not from here, right?"

"Albuquerque."

"The thing about L.A. is we don't pay attention to celebrities. We see them, but we don't gush, we don't freak out, we don't posture in front of them. We treat them like fellow human beings and let them live their lives." He glanced around the pool area. "Like those two over there—" he gestured with his chin to the opposite corner "—hottest power couple right now, but no one's freaking out."

I craned my neck and stared at Kim and Kanye for a few seconds, before realizing what I was doing. *Play it cool, Kate.*

Don smirked. "At the Grand Prix Association, we've always prided ourselves on creating a no-ego environment with this race. We treat the stars equally, whether you're an Oscar winner, Olympic gold medalist, or the local, non-famous auction-winner. And our staff doesn't ask for autographs, doesn't ask for a selfie with them. Like members of the media, we don't take advantage of our access to them for our own purposes. But not Billy. He acted like an asshole. Photos and autographs all around, sucking up to the biggest names and ignoring everyone else."

"Billy was a jerk, caused extra work, and pretended he knew it all. How did you put up with him? *Why* did you?"

"Nikki wanted him there, and ultimately, she signs my paychecks. It was…frustrating."

"Couldn't you push back? You're the one with years of experience. Couldn't you fire him?"

"Seven damn years of running this race, and eight years before that running my own damn team. You think I didn't *try* to push back?" Don surged to his feet and loomed over me. "You think I wasn't angry that a twenty-five-year-old with more talent in his dick than between his ears was supposed to help me? That the loser screwing my boss was shoved in my face?"

Anger rolled off of him. I sat still, ready for anything, as he clenched and unclenched his fists. He bit out the next words. "But you tell me how I was supposed to boot his ass if I wanted to keep my job and put on a race."

I understood why Don and Nikki thought the cops might arrest Don for Billy's murder. "I wasn't accusing you. I was trying to understand."

Don gave one curt nod and slipped his sunglasses back on, turning and starting to pace back and forth in front of our seats.

I exhaled and glanced around the pool area. No one seemed to notice Don's tension. Or they weren't acting like they noticed, which was close enough. I decided to get the tough questions out of the way.

"At the risk of making you mad again, why might the cops start looking at you?"

His smile was laced with chagrin. "My temper, though I don't often lose it." He walked back and forth two more times, then stopped. "Plus the fact I've never had anything good to say about Billy. Plenty of people can attest to the opposite. To be blunt, I'm not sorry the asshole is dead."

I agreed, but kept it to myself. "You said he'd ruffled feathers in the race organization. Who in particular did he make angry?"

Don sat down again and propped his sunglasses on top of his head. "Mostly me. I didn't want to burden my staff. But also my marketing and PR guru Erica Aarons, because she had to pick up the extra work he created with his *genius* press ideas."

"That's it?"

"I think so. He pissed off Elizabeth Rogers over at the SCC, with how much he bungled their logistics." He thought a moment. "I think Penny, Maddie Theabo's assistant, was furious at him the other day."

"He got around."

"I'm not saying any of those gals killed Billy."

"I don't think they did either. But I want to find out what he was up to and come up with some ideas why he was killed. Maybe that'll help the police figure out who did it."

"You're the pro."

I stifled an eye-roll. "Anyone else you can think of who might have been mad at Billy?"

"Honestly, Nikki wasn't happy with him lately. She said one more stunt and she'd show him the door. I didn't take her seriously at the time, but maybe there was something to it."

"She said he was going to leave her."

"Maybe he was. Maybe she was going to dump him. I have no idea." He checked his watch. "I need to go sweet-talk a sponsor."

We both stood up, and he smiled easily this time. "I'm sorry for getting riled up a minute ago. I appreciate your help. The whole race organization does. I can't offer to pay you, but we'll do what we can to promote you."

Back in my room, I thought about what Don had told me and wondered if Billy had angered as many people in the business world or his personal life as in the racing world. Those would be harder questions to answer, since there was no one I wanted to talk to for information, except my father. He might not want to help.

Chapter Twelve

I gave up on my attempts at sleuthing and packed what I needed for my afternoon adventure and an overnight in Ontario, loading it into my car and triple-checking I had all of my racing equipment. I traversed Beverly Hills from north to south, worked my way west to Overland Avenue, and drove to Sony Studios in Culver City. I felt both important and pretentious telling the guard at the gate I was there to visit Maddie Theabo. By the time I parked in the large, multi-level structure to the right of the gate, Maddie's assistant Penny was waiting.

She worked her phone non-stop as always, but it didn't dim her attentiveness or friendly nature. "How are you, Kate? Excited to be on the set?"

I tried not to be a fangirl about meeting celebrities, whether in the racing world or out, especially considering Don Kessberg's advice about interacting with them. But I was on a studio lot, about to go behind the scenes of a major motion picture, and I felt giddy. I didn't bother hiding my grin. "I'm pretty excited."

"First rule of movie-making: it's a boring process." She waved me forward into the maze of large warehouse-sized sound stages. "But I'll admit, it's amazing to see a movie later and know how the scenes were built. To have been there for that."

"I'm excited to see how movies are put together."

"Maddie's glad to have you here to show you off. The whole set knows how much fun she had at the practice session yesterday. You'll get questions. Especially from Lucas."

I gulped. I'd done my best to ignore the fact I'd not only be seeing Maddie, but also the hottest man in America. Who claimed to have an interest in me. *You ignored it so much you changed into your best jeans and a shirt that matches your eyes.* "I can handle racing questions." I wondered if Penny would understand. "Movie stars are still intimidating."

"I get it. But they're normal people. Ones everyone thinks they know."

"Gorgeous normal people."

Penny chuckled. "True. But also goofballs. Insecure. Obsessed with stupid stuff. Like the rest of us. They're human. Focus on the personality, not the movie-star persona."

"I'll do my best." *Still, drop-dead gorgeous Lucas Tolani.*

Penny stopped at a small door in the side of a big building. "Keep your voice down most of the time, don't say anything when they're rolling, and watch where you're stepping."

I followed her inside. I expected to enter the fictional world of the movie being filmed. What I saw instead was a forest of metal stands holding lights, cameras, and backdrops clustered around a set for a three-walled coffee shop, with multiple tables full of people. No sign of Maddie or Lucas, even as we drew closer to the brightly lit action.

For the next three hours, I watched while movie magic happened, as Penny had warned, at a snail's pace. Discussions, rehearsals, makeup, lighting, and reblocking all took place before the scene was shot. And shot. And reshot. Over and over, take after take. Finally, the thirty-second-long scene was done, and the cast and crew took their lunch break. At five in the afternoon.

Penny explained. "They started at noon today, and they'll go to midnight or later. This really is lunch for most people."

She knocked on the door of Maddie's small trailer and entered without waiting for a response. Inside, Maddie had changed out of her character's costume and was handing it over to a woman I'd seen on set earlier.

Maddie turned to me. "Hallelujah! Time for food and racing talk. You ready, Kate?"

"Do you have your marked up track map?"

Maddie pulled a folded piece of paper from the back pocket of her jeans and waved it in the air. "I'm ready. And hungry. Penny?"

Penny dropped onto the couch. "I'll meet you after I deal with some e-mails."

Maddie and I settled at a dark-stained wood table in the Sony Studios Commissary with our trays of food: meatloaf, mashed potatoes, and broccoli for me, and a chicken Caesar salad for her. Light streamed in from two walls made entirely of windows.

She eyed my plate. "Damn you athletes."

"Remember to fuel up before race day."

"I've been working out more to prepare." She frowned at her salad. "And eating more. But I'll be in a tight dress for tonight's scenes."

I smiled and dug into my potatoes. "A firesuit is more forgiving. Tell me about the track, now you've had a full day to think about it."

Maddie forked up a bite of her salad. "I got better as the session went on. More confident. Not as afraid I couldn't keep up with the leader. Like you said, the capability is there in the car, and I have to find it in myself."

"But do the right things with the car," I added. "Remember the traction circle."

I referred to a simple diagram of a circle split into four quadrants, representing acceleration and braking in the top and bottom halves and left and right turning in the left and right halves. The point of the diagram was to show where the limit of traction was for any combination of turning, acceleration, or braking. At the limit of tire grip for acceleration or braking, there could be no turning; at the limit of grip for turning, there could be no throttle or braking. Or the car would break loose. Plenty of novices thought they were doing the right thing by pushing the limits of tire adhesion, only to end up outside the circle and in the wall.

"I kept that in mind the whole time, and I was *very* careful to do one thing at a time. I got smoother by the end. But I'm sure I was doing something wrong." She took another bite of salad.

"Show me your lines." I moved my plate to the side and studied the notes she'd made on the map of the Long Beach temporary street circuit. I quizzed her on them, particularly coming out of Turns 5 and 8, where drivers wanted to use every inch of the track on exit to carry speed through the corners and get on the throttle quickly. Which meant we ended up a hairsbreadth away from the solid, concrete walls that lined the track, something that could rattle even pros.

She scrunched up her nose. "I probably wasn't that close."

"I didn't expect you to be." I smiled. "But when you get back out there, remember you're supposed to be close to the walls there—don't look at them or you'll drive into them. Look down the track and see yourself running next to the wall. You want to be slow in and fast out of Turns 5, 8, and 11, to lead onto your straights."

"Even though the front straight is one big curve with an apex."

"Right. You're flat out down Shoreline Boulevard, so that makes it straight enough. There and the back straight are where you can build speed and sneak up on slower cars."

She stared at her half-eaten salad. I suspected she was seeing herself driving the track in her mind.

I folded the map and handed it to her. "You looked comfortable yesterday in practice, and I know you can add speed. Keep thinking about hitting your apexes, placing your car closer to the wall, and that traction circle. You'll be great."

"You'll be there for practice and qualifying?"

"You bet. I really want to see you kick some celebrity ass."

"That sounds like something I want in on." Lucas pulled out a chair with one hand, holding a tray of food in the other. "May I?"

"Sit down," Maddie told him. "I'm going to kick some ass on the track next week."

Lucas unloaded his own meatloaf and leaned over to set his tray on a nearby empty table. "I'm not interrupting, right? I don't mind if you need to finish talking racing."

She shook her head. "We're done. I was getting my wrap-up pep talk."

"Am I that predictable?" I asked, struggling to gather my wits. I wasn't sure if it was the fame or his drool-worthy looks, but Lucas scrambled my brain. *Pull yourself together.*

Maddie smiled at me. "You leave me knowing I can improve, but you also make sure I feel good about what I've done and what I'm capable of. You're a good coach."

"I'm glad to hear it. That's what you're paying me for." I noticed Lucas gulping down his food at record-setting pace.

Maddie waved a hand. "I pay a lot of people for services and consultation. You're good because you take the trouble to get inside my head and understand what I need. Plus I like you. I've found a friend, not only a coach."

I couldn't help grinning at her. "Agreed. And it'll be even better when you show people how it's done next weekend on the track."

A speculative look replaced the teasing glint in Lucas' eyes. "Maddie, there's that racing movie I've been talking with people about. Maybe you want to look at it. Do it with me."

"What's the story?" I asked.

"The early days of racing Corvettes: back in the nineteen-sixties, racing the cars in Florida and over at Le Mans. I'd need you to consult, of course." He winked at me, and my insides fluttered.

Maddie collected her silverware on her empty plate. "It's possible. Could be fun. Who's producing?"

"Right now, me," Lucas replied. "I'm not sure if it'll get off the ground, but I'm looking into it. I'll keep both of you in mind."

"Sure." Maddie stood and stopped me from gathering my utensils. "I need to head back and run some lines. Kate, since you're not done, stay and keep Lucas company. We start again in forty minutes, so come to my trailer before that." She left before I could reply.

I looked at Lucas. "You don't need time to rehearse?"

"I'm not in the next scene, but I'll be here later than Maddie tonight. Tell me what you did today."

I explained the various meetings I'd had, skipping the part about being asked to investigate a murder and focusing on the business aspects. I folded my napkin. "How serious are you about doing a movie about racing? Have you raced at all?"

"I went to a Skip Barber school, and I've been to a few races. I think it's an appealing and interesting world most people don't know about. With lots of cinematic possibilities and challenges. I'm serious about a movie, but it's also the first project I've taken on myself." He turned his brilliant smile on me. "Meeting you has to count as a good omen, right?"

"You could see it that way." I felt out of my element...on a movie studio lot, eating dinner with one of the most famous and eligible men in the world. I checked the time on my cell phone and noticed I had new messages.

Lucas covered my hand with his, blocking my view of my phone. "What's wrong?"

"I don't know how to do this."

He frowned. "Get to know someone? Flirt? Date?"

"It's not that simple. I'm just Kate from Albuquerque."

"You race cars around the world, and you're featured in the media wherever you go. And you're scared of me? I'm just Lucas from Boise."

"Boise?" I laughed and the rest of what he said clicked. "I'm not scared of you. I'm...all this." I stopped and thought about my surroundings. Sure, the commissary was more glamorous and permanent than Linda's catering tent at a race. But the rest was much the same: an elaborate, temporary show staffed by teams of people with special talents and a couple stars at the center of the action. Racecar driver and movie star, who'd have thought our worlds were similar?

I eyed Lucas. "I get the similarities. But one of us shows up in the tabloids a whole lot more." I paused. "One of us dates supermodels."

"No, one of us wants to date a sexy racecar driver."

He thinks I'm sexy? He wants to date me? Both were tough to believe.

Chapter Thirteen

Lucas leaned back in his chair and crossed his arms over his chest, a move that highlighted his substantial muscles. "I saw you in the tabloids over that wreck with Miles Hanson."

"Once, because they hated me. Not because I was sleeping with—"

He held up a hand. "If one of us here has dated or slept with supermodels, it must be you. It isn't me."

He met my blank look, and as I opened my mouth to challenge his statement, he spoke again. "Be careful, Kate. This is where you choose to listen to me or to the bloggers, paparazzi, and anyone courting fame by making things up about people they don't know."

He had a point. I'd had my own run-ins with the great, uninformed public. I knew better than to trust the anonymous hordes online that lived for gossip, innuendo, and criticism. I also heard what Lucas didn't say. This was where I chose if we'd be friends—or more—or not. I studied him: stunningly attractive, intently focused on me, and interested. And one of the top twenty most famous people in the world in that moment.

All at once, I got mad. My problem? I didn't think I was good enough for the perfect, famous man who could have anyone. *What the hell? Screw that.*

I straightened my spine. Smiled at him, trying to convey warmth through the anger and self-disgust I felt. I held out my hand. "Lucas from Boise? I'm Kate from Albuquerque. Would you like to have dinner sometime?"

Lucas laughed and drew me up from my seat. "I would love that." He held onto my hand as we walked out of the building and back to the sound stage. "Next Monday night? Unless you're free tomorrow?"

"Tomorrow I'll be out in Fontana at the speedway. Monday works."

"It's a date." He laced his fingers with mine. "Now, tell me about your test tomorrow."

I felt uncharacteristically giggly about holding hands, and I tried to focus. "Fontana, big oval track. I've only driven smaller ovals and smaller cars. And not often." I took a deep breath, held it, exhaled. "Tomorrow I'll be in an IndyCar on an oval to start preparations for racing the Indy 500 next year."

Lucas gave me a crooked, sideways smile. "That's pretty freaking cool. You're kind of a rock star. It sounds like big pressure."

The butterflies in my gut started circling again. "Some pressure. Some excitement. Nerves. But it'll be good. I can do this."

He squeezed my hand. "I have no doubt."

We'd reached Maddie's small trailer outside the soundstage where they were filming, when I remembered Ryan Johnston. I pulled Lucas to a stop and extricated my hand. "You should know something."

He put his hands on his hips, but didn't speak.

I had to stop myself from blurting out apologies. "I have another date this week."

"Is that all?" His shoulders relaxed. "I'll be out with someone for a thing on Friday. That's not a real date, but a favor for my agent and another client of his trying to break in. But it'll look like a date for the photos, since that's the point." He stepped closer to me and looked into my eyes. "Be honest with me, and I'll do the same. Deal?"

I nodded, dazed, and he lowered his head to kiss me. I closed my eyes and tried not to freak out, though the kiss lasted only

a moment before he stepped back. I belatedly popped my eyes
open to find him grinning at me.

"Looking forward to next Monday."

I felt my face flush and decided I didn't care. I smiled back.
"Me, too."

He escorted me into Maddie's trailer, where we found her
sitting on the small couch, script pages on her lap. She waved
us to the small armchairs across from her.

"While I'm thinking about it, Lucas—sorry, Kate, this'll only
take a second." Maddie pointed to the script.

I waved them on, and while they discussed the phrasing and
timing of a specific line in the script, I pulled out my phone,
remembering the message notices I'd seen.

I had a text message and a voicemail, along with a dozen
e-mails that didn't need immediate response. The text from
Holly sent my spirits and nerves soaring with her query about
how the set visit had gone and her instruction to knock 'em
dead at the test session.

The voicemail made my emotions flatline. It was from Nikki
Gray. About Billy. *My murdered cousin, cut off in the prime of life
while I gallivant around with movie stars.* I'd almost forgotten.

"Kate, it's Nikki." I heard a yip in the background, and
Nikki giggled. "And Pookie. Say hello to the nice lady, Pookie!"
A pause, during which, to my great relief, I did *not* hear a dog
say "hello." "Good girl. Anyway, Kate, I wanted to see if you'd
discovered any *leads* in poor Billy's murder. I just know you're
going to figure this all out for me and dear Don, and I can't
thank you enough. Let me know if you need anything from
either one of us—oh! I meant to offer you a free salon treatment.
Haircut, massage, mani-pedi, whatever you want. My treat at
Dino's in Beverly Hills. Call them anytime, they've got your
name. Thanks, doll, ciao!"

I stared at my phone, confused, and saved the message.
Murder investigation to free salon services seemed like a strange
leap, even for Nikki.

"Problem, Kate?" Maddie asked. She and Lucas looked at me with curiosity.

"I agreed to look into something for someone, and she's... high strung?"

"Was this the woman you met with today?" Lucas asked. "The people involved in organizing the race?"

I nodded. "Maddie, did you ever meet anyone with the race organization? Specifically Don Kessberg and Nikki Gray? She'd be memorable."

Maddie thought a moment. "I know who you mean. Diamonds and a dog?"

Lucas laughed.

"I met her and Don," Maddie confirmed. "To be fair, the outfit isn't unusual around here, only at the racetrack."

"Did you ever meet...if they call them cougars, what do they call the younger men?"

Lucas raised both eyebrows. "Prey?"

I was embarrassed. "Did you ever meet Nikki's? Billy?"

"Fair hair? Young and stupidly attractive?"

I shifted in my seat. "I suppose so."

"I met him." She eyed me. "Most people would think he was hot. You didn't?"

I grimaced. "He was my cousin, and he was a jerk."

Lucas asked, "Was?"

"He was killed yesterday, at the track in Long Beach. Nikki and Don are afraid they'll be charged with his murder."

"How are you involved?" Maddie leaned forward, her eyes wide, script pages forgotten.

"They asked for my help. I know how this works. I've been through it before."

"Murder investigations?" To his credit, Lucas didn't sound incredulous or disbelieving.

"Three of them. But I'm not doing that here." I sighed. "It's that I know the racing world, and I know Billy's world, which is partly the bank that's my new, big sponsor and partly my distant family. And of course, I saw the scene when I identified Billy for the police."

Maddie and Lucas stared at me, mouths open. *Why did you blurt all that out?* "I shouldn't have—don't tell anyone, please."

"We tell the media nothing," she assured me. "Your secrets are safe with us."

Lucas furrowed his brow, and I braced myself for the standard protective-male response. "That's amazing. You'll have to tell me more."

Surprising. "I guess." I turned to Maddie. "You met Billy?"

"He was buzzing around at one point. Trying to make connections, you know? You learn to spot them pretty quickly. I'm sure it's the same for you."

"The players and the operators. You must see more of them than I do."

Lucas spoke up. "At least we have people to run interference."

"Penny dealt with him, so I didn't have to. Talk to her." Maddie checked her watch and excused herself to change into her next costume.

Lucas pulled me to my feet, then framed my face with both hands and looked into my eyes. "I have so many questions to ask you. You fascinate me, Kate Reilly."

He kissed me longer and with more emotion this time, making me lose touch with my extremities for a moment. With a smile, he let his hands fall and stepped back. "I'll see you Monday. Take care of yourself and kick ass tomorrow."

I sank back down into the armchair.

Maddie exited the back room in costume and eyed me. "I take it things are going well?"

I managed another nod.

She laughed. "I guess so. Lucky for you, he's a good kisser."

Okay, *that* was strange.

Chapter Fourteen

Maddie saw the surprise on my face and got serious. "Kate, we make movies, and we pretend to be in love. We kiss for the cameras, not for each other. But I've kissed enough people for the cameras to know when they're good at it. And Lucas is good at it."

My mind whirled.

She spoke again. "Now you're wondering if you can trust him, since he acts for a living."

"I'm that transparent?"

"It's everyone's first question. It's our job. We don't use our job to play tricks on normal, nice people, unless we're psychopaths getting off on others' misery. Which most actors are not—certainly Lucas and I aren't. My advice is treat Lucas like any ordinary guy, and trust him enough to get to know him and decide for yourself."

"It's odd, hearing you say you've kissed him, right after he kissed me."

"Better to get it out there now, rather than later. I have to roll around mostly naked with him in a couple weeks, but I can promise I won't enjoy it nearly as much as you would, should you ever reach that point." Her smile was wicked this time.

My cheeks burned. "Let's not get ahead of ourselves." Of course, I couldn't stop myself from remembering magazine photos of Lucas shirtless.

Penny entered the trailer. "You ready, Maddie?"

"Yep. And while I go do my job," she smiled at me, "Kate needs to ask you about Billy with the Long Beach race organization."

Penny grimaced. "All right."

"You don't have to, Penny," I rushed to say. "I've taken enough of your time."

Penny slipped her black-framed glasses off and squeezed the bridge of her nose. "You're never a problem. He, however, was an asshole."

"Stay here as long as you need to, Kate." Maddie hugged me. "Good luck tomorrow. And thanks again for the help."

"We're still karting on Sunday? One last lesson before race week?"

"I'll be there."

Maddie left the trailer, and Penny and I sat down. She apologized and typed furiously into her phone, while I studied her.

Everything about Penny screamed no-nonsense, from her simple tee-shirt and cargo pants, in which she carried various notebooks, electronic devices, and items to help repair Maddie's makeup or clothing. On her own, she was pretty. Next to Maddie, we were all ordinary. But Penny didn't care. She preferred to be support staff, out of the limelight. My best friend and manager, Holly, was the same way.

"There! Go away." Penny tossed her phone on the chair across from her and stood up, moving to the small fridge. "Want some water?"

"Thanks. Lots of interview requests?"

She sat back down, taking big gulps. "And appearance requests, inquiries about the celebrity race, and so forth. Enough of that. What did you want to ask me about that…person?"

I didn't bother hiding my smile. "You know he was killed yesterday?"

"Saw it in the news. Sorry for his family. Not sorry I won't have to deal with him again." She eyed me. "Are you with the police or something? Investigating his death?"

"Not with the police. Not investigating. Asking questions for his employer and the race organization so they know what happened and can be prepared if anything embarrassing comes up." I decided to tell Penny the truth. "I'm doing it against my better judgment, as a favor. I wasn't a fan of his either."

"Sounds like you have stories also."

I nodded. "What did he do that made you so angry?"

"He wouldn't stop pushing. He wouldn't listen to me or to Maddie. More than once, even after we both said we weren't interested."

"In what?"

"In an interview, in his help with promotion of Maddie's part in the racing weekend, in his connecting her with big money men who could help her fund any project she wanted." She paused. "In having sex with him."

I almost spit out my water. "He propositioned her for sex?"

"Both of us. He couched it as dinner or 'treating us right.'" She looked revolted. "He talked about helping us with any *needs* we might have, and he spoke to her while trying to grind himself against me."

I felt queasy. "What did you do?"

"I shoved him away. I thought Maddie was going to slap him, but I stopped her in time—it's worse if the celebrity makes contact. Maddie told him we'd report him for sexual harassment, and he laughed in our faces. He knew we wouldn't want the publicity for something the cops couldn't act on anyway. But he threatened us with taking his story to the media."

"What good would that do?" The answer started to dawn on me as she spoke.

"He'd get a lot of coverage on a story of how we'd propositioned him for a three-way and became violent and abusive when he turned us down."

I sipped my water again, hoping it would calm the roiling of my gut. I'd known Billy and his cousin Holden were vile, but this was a new low. "What happened?"

"Maddie called his bluff. Told him to stay the hell away from us, or we'd have him arrested."

"When was this?"

Penny blinked at me, her hazel eyes still angry behind her glasses. "He slithered around Maddie from day one, back in March, at those dinners during the training sessions. The physical approach—"

"Assault?"

She shrugged. "Aggression. That was yesterday morning, first thing." She grimaced. "Just what I needed, a little molestation before my second cup of coffee."

"I wish I could say I'm surprised. He was a disgusting asshole."

She glanced at her phone, which was buzzing in the other chair, but didn't pick it up. "I didn't talk with him after that. I saw him from a distance, but I made sure to avoid him and keep Maddie away. Then he was killed."

"Did you see him with other people?"

"I saw him at least four times throughout the day. I swear he paraded around so we'd be sure to see him with different women." She rolled her eyes. "He was always with women."

"As if he was God's gift."

She laughed. "Right. He was with the Beverly Hills cougar a few times. And her cameras."

"That's Nikki Gray. She owns the race—or the organizing company."

"That explains his air of entitlement. I also saw him with Erica Aarons, the PR person from the race staff. He was talking to her, looming over her, you know?"

"Been there."

"I got the sense she was barely being civil, but she'd probably have to if she wanted to keep her job."

I made a mental note to talk to Erica. "Anyone else?"

"A blond woman, also short. He wasn't trying to intimidate her as much as the others."

"Can you describe her more?"

Penny closed her eyes a moment, thinking. "That's tough. She was so forcefully bland. Long, straight hair."

It was the perfect description of Elizabeth Rogers. "I know who you mean."

"I did see him with one man. Don someone? The guy running the race?"

"Don Kessberg."

"Right. I saw Don yelling at someone around the side of a trailer, waving his hands and looking pissed off. I couldn't see who he was talking to at the time, but a couple minutes later, Billy walked around the corner." She paused. "Funny, I'd forgotten that until now."

I frowned. *Don didn't mention arguing with Billy yesterday. He's still got plenty of motive and opportunity. Speaking of opportunity...* "Penny? Don't take this wrong, but you weren't alone at any point yesterday, were you?"

"I need an alibi?" She smiled at my discomfort. "As it happens, I wasn't ever alone, except when I went into one of the God-awful porta-potties while someone else held my phone and bag. And Maddie was with me unless she was in the car."

"Sorry to ask."

"I've got nothing to hide. I didn't kill him. Didn't want to kill him." She shook her head. "If he'd been found strung up by the balls, you might be looking for me. I'd have gone for humiliation and revenge."

Chapter Fifteen

Wednesday evening, I drove east on highway 10 toward Ontario and the Fontana Speedway, with the sun setting behind me and darker skies ahead. I thought about what Penny had told me. I'd known Billy was a creep, but I hadn't realized he was also a sexual predator. I was shocked by his arrogance, dumbfounded he'd think his crude attempts at seduction would appeal to women. Or that they'd be bullied into remaining quiet.

He obviously didn't care much about Nikki. I wondered how much she'd cared about him in return—and how to ask her that question.

I had a list of people to talk to, starting with Nikki. Also Don, to find out what he argued with Billy about, and Elizabeth Rogers and Erica Aarons to see what they knew of Billy's last hours. Some questions would go unasked. I wouldn't talk to Edward, not after he'd called me a whore like my mother. Or Holden, who'd never had a civil word for me.

I still wondered about Coleman. I'd been wary of him because he was Holden's father and part of the Reilly family by marriage. My interactions with Edward, Billy's father, had gone so wrong I wasn't sure how Coleman would act. But working with him on the terms of the bank's sponsorship had been fine. We'd both been professional and respectful. Up until he steamrolled me into investigating Billy's death.

I unclenched my jaw and relaxed my shoulders. I shook off my gloom, mentally walling off everything to do with Billy, murder, and my family. I shoved it all in a room in my head and turned the key in the lock. It was time to think only about the next day's task. The car and the track waiting for me.

My excitement about the test got me up early the next morning. I ate a hearty breakfast, drank a lot of water along with my coffee, and checked out of my hotel by eight o'clock.

I felt a familiar surge of adrenaline as I drove through the tunnel under Turn 4 and up into Fontana's Auto Club Speedway infield. My first view of the track got my heart beating even faster, and I flexed my fingers on the rental car's wheel, imagining steering around the oval. I followed the paved road past grassy parking lots to concrete lots in the center of the infield. Aside from light standards and trash barrels, the acres of flat ground were only broken up by three low garage buildings and a two-story building that paralleled the front straight, housing pits, suites, and rooftop viewing. I parked next to a small group of cars near the fueling station and garages, and I headed for pit lane, after a stop to change into my firesuit.

I was there to test with Beermeier Racing, whose drivers had ended the previous season seventh and fourteenth in the standings—respectable, but not all the team hoped for. Beermeier had yet to field a top-five driver, but team co-owner Alexa Wittmeier was a former competitor with a best season-long result of sixth. Though she'd never won a race, she'd amassed dozens of top fives and only failed to finish a race an astonishing four times in six years. She'd been the benchmark for consistency as a driver, and she'd slowly built a strong team from the other side of the pit box, making a big leap in Series standing when she joined forces with Tim Beerman five years ago.

I'd done a lot of research into the team and its results, and I thought they were poised to break out and take a driver to a championship. I wanted that driver to be me. But it all depended on how I performed and what kind of chemistry I had with the crew. Like many teams, Beermeier Racing employed two drivers, one a star and the other a rookie or near to it, along with a possible third car only at the Indy 500. In addition, Beermeier still ran a racing program in Indy Lights, the lower-level feeder series to IndyCar, which I'd tested with a couple months prior. All in all, there were a variety of options for working with the team, should the day's test go well.

I found the team set up near a break in the pit wall, equipped with the bare essentials—tires, tools, and a handful of crew members—plus a fueling rig and a timing stand for each car, where the crew monitored cars and laptops receiving data. Most importantly, there were two racecars.

"I guess that's us," said a male voice.

I turned to see a late teen with a wiry build and a worn firesuit.

"Must be." I held out a hand. "I'm Kate Reilly."

"Matt King. Good to meet you. I know you've been racing sportscars. And winning. But now IndyCar?"

"I'm thinking about it. Matt King…you've been in Indy Lights?"

"For three years."

I revised my estimate of his age up to twenty. "Time for a step up to the big leagues."

He nodded, his eyes on the cars in front of us.

"I'm all for collaboration and sharing information, if you are," I offered. I couldn't tell if he'd be willing to compare notes or would need to "beat the girl." I'd seen plenty of both attitudes.

But he smiled. "Anything to make me faster. Let's both kick some IndyCar ass today."

"Deal."

There would be ten car-and-driver combinations testing IndyCars, run by four teams splitting the facility rental cost. In general, test days were money-makers for teams: they got paid to bring out their cars and coach a new driver around the track. For the driver, test days were pay-to-play. We paid—or hopefully, our sponsors paid—for the opportunity to show this team and others what we could do. A solid performance might reaffirm a sponsor's plans to fund the driver in the future, and with sponsor dollars in hand, the driver could knock on team doors to find an available car. I needed a good performance to prove to my sponsor I was worth the money and to interest teams in providing a car for me.

The reality of racing these days was that drivers, even at top levels, had to bring money to a racing team. The story of a driver with no associated sponsors being hired and paid by a team, strictly based on talent, was as much a fairy tale as finding Prince Charming. Of course, the better and more well known a driver, the easier it was to secure sponsors. Those of us in the middle ranks struggled more. A lot more. I'd met plenty of talented racers without enough dollars to launch themselves out of the local circuits.

I was one of the lucky ones, especially on a bright, sunny, but not too warm day at a California Speedway. The buzz coursing through me bumped up a notch.

As Matt and I moved toward the pits, Alexa Wittmeier, co-owner of Beermeier Racing, saw us and gestured to the cars: low-slung, rear-engined, open-wheel, and open-cockpit. "Welcome. There's your transportation for the day."

Matt and I looked at the cars, then at each other, and broke into identical grins.

Alexa smiled also. "We should have some fun." She opened two cabinets in the pit cart where Matt and I stored our helmets, gloves, and other gear. We followed her around the end of the wall to stand in pit lane.

"Kate, you'll be in the front car, the 40. Matt, in the 41," Alexa explained. "I'll introduce you to the crew, and then Mick and I will take you around the track in street cars to orient you." Mick was Michel Poirier, a French driver and Beermeier's star.

"After that, we'll get you two strapped in and familiar with the controls and send you out individually for your rookie tests," Alexa went on. "We'll have a couple short sessions before lunch, and two or three longer ones this afternoon. Does that work for you both?"

Matt and I both nodded.

"Great, let's get to it."

Chapter Sixteen

I'd made a trip to the Beermeier Racing shop in Indianapolis a month prior to make a seat—a two-day process that involved me sitting in the car for two hours while a vacuum pump helped chemicals and foam beads cure to my shape—as well as to fit belts and make pedal adjustments. But it still took some doing at the track to get me strapped down and comfortable, get a refresher on the buttons and knobs I had in the cockpit, and be sure the radios worked. I'd have Xavier, one of the team's race engineers, talking to me from the pit box and Alexa in my ear from the spotter's stand, high atop the main grandstand with a sweeping view of the full oval. She wasn't typically a spotter, but for this situation, where I needed as much driver-coaching as help staying out of traffic, she'd pull double-duty. Mick would do the same for Matt King.

Finally, I sat there in the unfamiliar position—slightly reclined, legs horizontal out in front of me—so different from my seat in the Corvette. I was belted and nervous, waiting for my turn to do a single out-and-in lap to check the car's systems, called an install lap. Each driver was sent out separately, to ensure clear track around us.

I heard Xavier's voice in my ear. "Almost time, Kate. You doing okay? Not too hot?"

I was sweating, but it wasn't due to ambient temperature. I pressed the radio button. "Temperature is okay. I'm fine, thanks."

Like each rookie at the day's test session, my goal was to prove I could drive the car. Throughout the day, I'd demonstrate working up to acceptable speed, running appropriate lines, and maintaining smooth car control. I'd start with the single-lap install check, then run laps with no one else near me on track. Eventually, I'd work up to running in traffic.

"Nervous, Kate?" That was Alexa.

"Waiting's the hard part." I hoped no one could see my knees shake.

"Remember, this lap is only to check basic functions. Use the warmup lane through Turn 2, move onto the back straight to click up through the gears, then down to the warmup lane again through 3 and 4, and back into the pits."

"Copy that." My heartbeat kicked up another level as two other cars drove down pit lane.

Xavier leaned over the pit wall as he spoke on the radio. "You're up, Kate. Ready?"

"Copy." I gave him a thumbs-up.

"Flip the ignition switch." As I complied, he twirled a finger in the air for the crew. "Let's fire her up."

I felt a tug on the back of the car as a crew member connected a rod to the engine and turned it over. The car rumbled around me. In me. My heartbeat, my breathing, my thoughts all fired in time to the rhythm of the car.

"When you're ready, Kate," Xavier told me. "Remember, cold tires mean wheel spin."

I nodded at him. Looked at my hands on the wheel. One breath in, one breath out. *You've driven an oval before, even if it was five years ago and a less powerful car. It will be familiar. Trust the car and the team. Trust yourself. Breathe, and go.*

I squeezed the clutch paddle behind the steering wheel with my left hand and flexed my right foot for throttle. I clicked the right-side paddle for first gear. Released the clutch and kept my foot in it. The tires spun, unnerving me. The car started to move. My heart leapt into my throat. *This was it. My first step to the Indy 500.*

I had no more time for thought, only instinct and reaction. I kept the car straight while the tires found grip, then watched for the pit lane exit line, the marker where I could release the speed limiter. Mostly I tried to ignore the warning messages from my nervous system about how broken the car felt on the flat ground, when it was set up for banking.

Oval tracks had multiple lanes or lines: a low one against the inside edge of the track and a high one next to the outer track wall. Fontana was wide enough for four lanes, lane one down low and lane four high. Each would be faster for different car setups, at different times of day, over different temperatures. Inside of lane one, a flat apron served as a warmup lane so drivers could merge onto the track's banking on a straight, instead of in the middle of a turn.

As I exited Turn 2 in the warmup lane, Alexa radioed, "Clear racetrack, it's all yours."

I gave the car more throttle, clicked the paddle to shift to third gear, and moved up the track. More throttle, shift to fourth, fifth, and sixth on the straight, checking out each gear. Trying to get a feel for the car.

As a driver, I actively listened to the health of my racecar with my entire body. I was attuned to the feel of balanced suspension and a happy engine—in a Corvette C7.R set up for right and left turns. This IndyCar chassis might have a Chevrolet engine, but that was the only similarity. The car felt bent—less so on the banking than on the flat. But still broken.

My conscious mind warred with my instincts. *It's bent! Get them to fix it.*

"That's what it's supposed to feel like." I muttered inside my helmet. *Bent! Turning left. Something's wrong!* "Get used to it."

Alexa spoke again. "Good job, Kate. Now slow down. Get back to the warmup lane, then the pits."

As I rounded Turn 4, the car feeling awful again on the flat, Xavier radioed. "Hit your limiter on the mark and remember where we are, midway down. There's Bill waving."

I saw a mechanic standing out in the lane, sweeping an arm to signal me for my pit location. Xavier talked me in, and I pressed the button for neutral as I braked and parked the car.

"Did the car feel good? Any issues?" Xavier asked as two crew members hopped the wall and checked out the car.

Is he kidding? It felt awful. I took a deep breath. "Fine so far."

"Great, we'll take a minute to check you both out. Then you'll go out again for real laps." All rookies would be on the track at the same time for those, but we'd be kept apart, to give us experience with open-track running.

"Copy, thanks."

I'd been nervous in the few minutes before I got the car rolling the first time, but I took anxiety to a new level waiting for laps at speed. The install check did nothing to make me comfortable with the car, and I still hadn't tackled the worst of what Fontana Speedway had to offer: the seams.

All around the track, not matching up exactly with the four lanes, were thick, black lumps of tar and paint filling the gaps between widths of concrete. They were infamous in the IndyCar world for being difficult to handle, and they'd caused more than a few wrecks.

"Mind the seams," Mick had emphasized during our orientation laps. "Debris can be another factor, as there is much grit—" it came out "greet" in his French accent "—that simply falls from the skies here. It will be slippery, with low grip. But the seams, if you try to cross them with any load on the car, they will grab you and spit you into the wall. Also, in the lower lines, there are little bumps. Too many to point out. Be ready for the car to be unsettled when you move out of the high line." He'd looked at me as he held the throttle to the floor on the back straight. "Again I say, to stay out of trouble, mind the seams. Stay high to start, and be very careful about crossing them at speed."

When I left pit lane again, I had the track's seams firmly in mind. Limiter off, throttle on. The RPM lights illuminated in a line across the top of the steering wheel, right below the number "1" indicating I was in first gear. Upshift to second in the warmup lane through Turn 2.

"Clear to blend," Alexa said, advising me there were no cars coming behind me.

Steering up onto the track. *Seam! Won't be a problem while I'm getting up to speed.* All the same, I angled the car to get higher on the banking, into that top lane. More throttle. RPM lights max out. Upshift to third. Breathe.

I take that back. The car's not balanced, it's touchy. Reacting to every input with a lunge.

RPM lights, fourth gear. Throttle. Not into top gear yet. *The car still feels bent. Ignore it!*

"Doing fine, Kate. Remember to mind the seams," Alexa called.

I stayed in the top lane away from seams as I flew toward Turn 3 of the oval. I was only in fourth gear, still building speed, and already going what felt crazy fast. Especially with a turn approaching. I knew an experienced driver with warm tires would drive the whole track in sixth gear, almost flat out, with only a bit of lifting from the throttle here and there. But my mind screamed at me to brake. I squashed the idea and lifted my foot a fraction from the throttle, then lifted it more. Held my breath. *How the hell am I going to go flat in sixth gear here?*

I turned, trying to be smooth, but fumbling and bobbling the wheel back to the right after I turned too much to the left. I lifted from the throttle more, decelerated too much. Started to panic. Got mad at myself. *Figure this out. You're not screwing this up.*

On the front straight, I kept the car moving forward, adjusted how much input I was giving the steering wheel to make it turn like I wanted, and started improving my speed. Into Turn 1, I lifted less than I wanted to but more than I thought I should, and called that a victory.

Alexa concurred. "You're doing fine. Let the tires come up to temp. If you're going to lift, do it before the corner and carry speed through it. That'll help the car feel more balanced."

I held on through Turn 2, and put the hammer down on the back straight. *Holy God, the walls are close.* I followed Alexa's advice going into 3 and realized I could have handled more speed. Tried that in Turns 1 and 2.

"That looks smoother," Alexa told me. "Keep working on it."

Another lap, a little less lifting. Up to fifth gear on the straights. I felt the foreign sensation of air flowing over my helmet.

Alexa kept talking to me. "Keep working that high line. You're doing great, keep building up to it."

Two more laps, and I finally clicked up to sixth gear. The car still felt weirdly bent, but it was starting to fit me better, and I started to find a rhythm. First a long, long sweeping left at one end of the oval, during which I focused on keeping my hands smooth and still, as well as carrying more speed each time around. Then a full-throttle sprint down a straight, barreling toward the other long, long arc of a left turn. Over and over. The walls constantly looming.

The popular notion among those who didn't know was oval racing was boring or easy, since you only turned left. Whoever thought that was wrong. Every lap—every hundred yards—was different than the one before. Track surface, car handling, tire wear, where the sunlight came from, and hundreds of factors changed from moment to moment. I was constantly adjusting. Constantly learning.

Right as I got the slightest bit comfortable, I was called off the track. On my in-lap, at Xavier's direction, I slowed on the back straight and crossed down the track to the warmup lane. The slower speed felt terrible, partly due to the increased number of bumps in that lane, but also because the car's rear end wanted to break loose and spin me up the track.

I reached the pits, turned off the car, and sat there, body thrumming even though the engine was quiet. Thinking if I didn't move, I couldn't hear bad news about my performance.

"Alexa is on her way back over to give you feedback from IndyCar." Xavier paused. "Gotta tell you though, kid. From my perspective, you looked good for a rookie."

I nodded, smiling under my helmet, though I knew he couldn't see me. I pressed the radio button. "Thanks, Xavier. Quite a ride."

I peeled my fingers from the wheel and released the belts. Time to see if I'd cleared the first hurdle. I rolled my shoulders, feeling tension and muscle fatigue.

No, time to learn you've passed the test. This is only the beginning.

Chapter Seventeen

Alexa appeared after I'd gotten out of the car and before I'd finished gulping down a bottle of water. Matt King and I had both passed the initial test and, moreover, looked confident and smooth doing it. He and I compared notes on how the cars felt. We agreed on "horrible and bent." Also "awesome."

A short while later, we climbed back in the cars for another group session. Each of us, at least the rookies, was meant to be out on track with plenty of open space around us. That was true for me until two of the four current IndyCar drivers testing with us rookies came out onto the track well ahead of me. Or so I'd have thought.

Alexa and Mick had explained how different the cars would feel once there were other cars around us. I knew the sensation, from running in Indy Lights. Out on the track alone, we had "clean" air: nothing interfering with the optimum flow of air around, over, and under the car. But when other cars were out on track with us, the air was "dirty" from being disturbed by flowing around other cars before hitting ours. Dirty air made the cars unpredictable and harder to handle, but dealing with it was part of racing.

When the two other cars pulled onto the back straight four and five car lengths ahead of me, they affected my air, and I learned Alexa and Mick were masters of understatement. The car didn't feel different, it felt awful. Disastrous. The only reason

I couldn't think of more synonyms was because I was too busy holding on for dear life and swearing.

The other cars ran single-file and then side-by-side, and whatever they did to the airflow hitting my car felt catastrophic. I had no grip, so the car felt twitchier than ever. I could barely muscle the car into a turn. And I was afraid to let off on the throttle because I thought I might unbalance the car and snap the back end around. The car was shit, and all I could do was try to lift as little and as smoothly as possible. And hold on.

"That's right, Kate, stay in it up in that high line. Get used to dirty air," Alexa said in my ear. I didn't respond, too consumed with four-letter words and wrestling the wheel.

She talked me through the turns and the back straight, but left the time I was driving down the front straight for messages from the engineer, Xavier. "Nice smooth hands on the wheel, Kate. And remember your bars if you've got push," he suggested.

"Copy, thanks."

I nudged the anti-roll bar lever to add more stiffness to the front suspension and, hopefully, keep the car from rolling or "pushing" to the outside of the corners quite so much. If that happened, in theory, the car would turn left better. Once again, I held on in the wide, open radius of Turns 1 and 2, gritting my teeth, still behind the two side-by-side cars. I nudged the bar a little more and felt improvement in Turns 3 and 4. Either that, or driving something that handled like a piece of farm equipment was starting to feel normal.

By the time the morning session ended, I'd gotten familiar with the variations in car-feel, based on clean or dirty air. I hadn't gotten happier with other cars around me, but I'd gotten more used to the sensations. I knew the afternoon session would bring a new set of challenges, specifically driving lower lines on the track, which meant crossing the dreaded seams in the concrete. Plus, I'd keep upping my speed.

I reached a personal milestone before the lunch break when I kept my foot to the floor in sixth gear for an entire lap. No lifting. I'd had clean air and fresh "sticker" tires—meaning the manufacturer's stickers were still on the rubber—and I'd kept the throttle flat the whole way around the oval. That achieved, I wanted to work on speed.

The lap record stood at something above 225 mph, which I knew was accomplished by a top driver with a car trimmed out for qualifying. In contrast, our cars were set up for today's temperature and a balance of grip and stability, which wouldn't produce the fastest speeds. I expected the four active IndyCar drivers to be the fastest, in the 210 to 220 mph range. My stated goal was to keep getting better and to impress everyone with my ability to handle the car throughout the day. Secretly, I wanted to hit 215.

I grabbed a sandwich and more water and sat on the pit wall next to Alexa as she contemplated the front straight. "Are you considering the future or feeling wistful for the past?"

She smiled. "I miss the thrill of a race sometimes, but I still get to climb in the two-seaters to give hot laps, and we do regular team trips to the go-kart track."

"Do you win?"

"Hell, yes."

"What was the hardest aspect of this kind of racing for you, when you started?"

"The same thing that will challenge you. Learning patience." She stopped my protests. "I don't mean you're impatient. You keep your wits about you in the car, and you have a good feel for continuously pushing, but not too much at once."

"But?"

"When I was starting in IndyCar, I felt I needed to prove myself right away. I needed to be the fastest every day." She narrowed her eyes and looked sideways at me, as I wolfed down the second half of my sandwich. "Can you tell me that's not what you're thinking?"

I swallowed. "No."

"You probably have a speed goal you've set for yourself today, right?"

Busted. "If a particular speed isn't a good goal, what is? Tell me what will make everyone leave more impressed with me than with anyone else." I glanced around, grateful to see no one else was watching.

She put a hand on my shoulder. "Don't be embarrassed to ask the question. It shows maturity, and while I'd answer any driver, I'm especially happy to give another woman as much help as possible."

"Thanks."

She took a sip of her diet soda. "To impress everyone today, don't think about speed. Not about setting the top speed. We want to see you're comfortable in the car."

"That's it?"

"It's a lot. I mean comfortable all day, getting used to speeds against the wall, dealing with a tough moment—and you'll have one at some point, everyone does—playing with different lanes, crossing the seams, and generally having a good feeling for the car. Also being able to talk to the engineers about how it's handling throughout."

"That makes sense. Thanks." I paused. "But if I can do that and also be pretty quick, that'd be even better, right?"

"And that's where the patience comes in." She laughed. "You're not wrong, but I'll say it's unnecessary and, frankly, unlikely."

I grinned at her. "Gotta have goals."

A few minutes later, on my way back from the restroom, I stopped short at the sight of four unexpected visitors, all wearing aviator sunglasses and black suits, like a team of special agents. My father wasn't a surprise. Even Coleman Sherain, I understood. But why were Holden Sherain and Elizabeth Rogers there?

I tamped down my irritation and greeted my father and Coleman, who stood apart from the others. "Nice of you both to come out to support me today."

"We wanted to see how you're doing," my father said. "I was also curious how it works."

"There's not much to see at a test. Ten cars in total. We'll do another session at one, and with any luck, no one will stuff a car into the wall."

Coleman straightened his tie as he surveyed the other cars and teams. "We know you won't, at least."

"That's the plan." I gestured to the team setup in front of us. "This is the Beermeier Racing team, and I'm in the 40 car, parked on the other side of the wall there."

Alexa caught sight of me with two men in suits, and she joined us, turning on the charm. She toured them through the car, pointing out the controls in the cockpit. I downed another bottle of water and pulled up the top half of my firesuit, which I'd knotted around my waist while out of the car.

Elizabeth walked over from the next team down, where she'd left Holden. "How'd the morning session go?"

Is she asking as an SCC Series representative, as my hated cousin's girlfriend, or as a woman trying to be my friend? I didn't have time to work out an answer. "Pretty well, thanks. I'm slowly getting used to the car."

"That's fantastic, I'm glad to see an IndyCar test. I've only been around sportscars."

I zipped my firesuit closed. "Did you come to see how Indy-Car does it?"

She stepped around me, into the meager shade cast by one of Beermeier's pit carts, and slipped off her sunglasses. "I guess it's strange we're here. Holden and I were in San Diego, and this, oddly enough, made a good place to meet Coleman. There's a family thing tonight for Billy, so we'll ride in to L.A. with Coleman from here. That's why all the black." She grinned. "I know the situation is sad, but we actually took a limousine here, to the track! How crazy is that? I could get used to it, I tell you."

I masked my confusion by pulling on my balaclava, a fire-retardant head sock. I'd never had such a personal conversation with Elizabeth, and I wasn't sure what to do. I might call it an odd time and place to display personality, but I couldn't call her bland. "I doubt the SCC will spring for a limo at the next race."

She laughed again. "I'm sure not. Sorry to run on. Good luck. I'm sure you'll do well." She patted my shoulder and moved away.

"Quick question," I called, and she turned around. "How long was Nikki dating Billy? And how serious was it?"

"It was serious, as in spending time together, traveling together, sleeping together. But not serious like it was leading to marriage." She laughed. "Can you imagine?"

"I really can't."

"The first time I saw them together was at the Petit Le Mans race last year, and it'd only been a couple weeks. He was already advising her on racing matters."

"They were together about six months?"

She slipped her glasses back on and nodded. "I think it'd run its course. My sense was she was ready to kick him to the curb. Definitely more irritated and less enchanted lately."

"Interesting."

Chapter Eighteen

I'd put on my helmet, HANS—or Head And Neck Support device—and gloves, and was sitting on the pit wall taking a quiet moment to visualize the car and the track, when I heard Coleman and my father behind me.

"The team says she's on target so far," Coleman said.

"As we expected," my father replied.

"I can only stay briefly into the afternoon, but you'll be here longer?"

"Yes."

"Keep me appraised. If all goes to plan, we should look at an oval race for her before this season ends. Give her a real test run in these cars."

I felt a thrill of excitement, and I held still, sure they didn't know I was in earshot.

"Coleman, how is Holden doing? About Billy?"

"He's grieving. Upset he and Billy had been separated and punished with probation and community service the last year." Coleman sighed. "He thinks if they'd been together, Billy wouldn't have been killed."

"Don't forget the fines we paid for them." My father paused. "He blames us for Billy's death?"

"Currently, yes. He's not thinking logically."

"My impression was he'd been doing better this year, overall."

"He's taken to his new role better than Billy had. But I'd always thought he was smarter. Less indulged."

I rolled my eyes.

"I don't mean Billy wasn't talented or capable," Coleman amended. "But Billy expected things to come more easily to him than Holden did. Both boys had every advantage, but Billy acted like he deserved them. Maybe that's simply a father's bias."

This time my father sighed. "I can't disagree with you. I was pleased with Holden's work in the San Diego branch, but I can't say the same for Billy in Los Angeles."

The rest of the afternoon passed in a flash and also felt two weeks long. From one to five, the track was open to all testers, and I made the most of it. Every thirty or forty minutes I pitted for more fuel, an adjustment, a chat with the engineer, or new tires. Otherwise, I turned laps. They weren't all pretty, but I stayed out of the walls, which was more than every driver could claim.

One rookie learned it wasn't only the seams we had to watch out for. We also had to be careful of the transition from the banked track surface to the flat warmup lane or apron. A young Brazilian Indy Lights driver came out of Turn 4 too low and too fast, catching the apron with his left front tire. The change in angle, at high speed, unbalanced the car enough to send it spinning up the track and slamming into the outer track wall. He was helped out of the car and walked gingerly, but under his own power, to the ambulance. It was a sobering reminder for all of us to be aware of where we placed every wheel. We were red-flagged—all track activity stopped and drivers called into the pits—for thirty minutes.

On track, I worked on feel and speed. I got better at adjusting the anti-roll bar and weight jacker, which shifted weight from one side of the car to the other, to help the car turn more or turn less. I also got better at understanding the effect of minor changes. I counted it as success when I stopped thinking "too much push, make it stiffer," and reached for the levers automatically.

Alexa and Xavier talked me through every lap, assuring me I was up to speed well and had a good feel for the car in clean air. I could tell from their reactions they liked the feedback I gave—explaining how the car felt on corner entry, mid corner, and corner exit, along with where the bars were set for different passes—and the questions I asked about the technical details.

I did 212.2 mph at my best, on fresh rubber in the cool, clean air at the end of the day, compared to one of the current IndyCar drivers who'd done 213.5 during the morning session. He'd gone faster later, when his team adjusted the car for more speed, but I'd gotten damn close when our cars were similarly set up. I called that a speed win.

But it wasn't all sunshine, roses, and clean air. The tough, real-world part was handling my own car with other cars all around. And crossing those stinking seams.

I started slowly, on my own, changing lanes and crossing the seams on corner entry and exit, to get a feel for them under the tires. Then Matt King and I teamed up to pass each other on the straights, for a sense of them with changes in airflow. The big test was side-by-side in the turns, Matt's car getting under me, close, both of us on the ragged edge of speed and grip, knowing one wrong move by either one would mean we both ended up in the wall.

The first time another driver passed me in a turn, I gave in to the knee-jerk reaction to get out of the throttle and let them fly past. The driver immediately slid up in front of me on the high line and took away my clean air, making my car go from decently behaved to garbage. That got me mad, which meant the next time someone tried a pass, I made him work for it, keeping my foot in it, hearing Alexa in my ear. "He's inside, Kate. Inside. That's good, hold your line, make him take it. Still inside. Clear."

As I shot down the front straight, Xavier chimed in. "That's good, Kate, try to stay up there longer next time. We're telling you they're coming, so hold the throttle in the clean air while you've got it. Let's work on your confidence in dirty air."

In the late afternoon, back to green after the Brazilian driver's accident, I came upon another car from a long way back. I inched ever closer over a series of laps and caught him. I needed to pass, and it would have to be done in a corner, which meant dirty air, bumps, and seams.

Alexa radioed as I was on the back straight. "You got this, Kate."

I rolled through the long sweep of Turns 3 and 4, thinking through the advice she'd given me. *Wherever possible, cross the seams early, before you're cornering hard. Stay between them or straddle them. And hang on.*

Down the front straight, I got close behind the other car, building as much speed as possible in the tow effect created by him breaking the hole in the air for both of us. As the track started to bend left for Turn 1, I tugged the wheel left and slipped below him—and lifted almost immediately, unprepared for how unsettled the car got.

I recovered, keeping the car straight and falling back in line behind the other driver.

Alexa spoke while I was on the back straight. "Doing fine, Kate. It'll feel different going inside of someone else in lane three. Squirrely. Now you're ready for it, give it a try again."

I took a lap to regroup. Got close behind the car again on the front straight. Heading for Turn 1. Slipped below him at corner entry. My heart thudded as I saw the black line slide under my car, left to right. I held on and exhaled as I realized I'd survived. Foot on the throttle, turning the wheel into the long turn.

"And he's outside," Alexa called, marking where the other car was relative to mine. "Outside. Outside. Doing great. Outside. Outside."

I was almost past him, leaving some room. Maybe too much room, because I kept my left rear tire on a seam too long. It grabbed hold of my car and didn't want to let go.

Instead of hearing the "Clear" call in my ear from Alexa, I felt myself slipping, the back end of the car tipping up the track. *Shit! Don't wreck! Don't hit the other car. DON'T LET THIS HAPPEN!*

Alexa was in my ear. "Hold it! Outside, car coming past you."

I reacted without thought. Eyes focused forward. Hands counter-steering, pointing the wheels where I was looking, not where the car was headed. Foot off the throttle. Body braced.

Feeling the car tipping, bouncing over a bump, tipping—recovering! Quick hands the other way to counteract the swing.

"*Clear!* Use all of the track," Alexa called.

Rear of the car snapping back and forth three times. Settling. Car pointed straight, foot back on throttle. *Go, get back on it!* My heart beat as if I'd sprinted a marathon distance.

"Good job, Kate," Alexa called. "Good hands. Keep it steady. Gather yourself back up."

I didn't bother replying. I focused. Tamped down emotions and looked forward. Caught that slow driver again a lap and a half later. Then I was right behind him again, staring down the track at Turn 1.

On the front straight, Xavier spoke. "Keep doing what you're doing, Kate. Nice smooth hands on the wheel."

I dropped down into the lower lane, exactly as I'd done before. Kept my foot planted. Remembered the mistake last time and looked ahead down the track, through the turn, seeing the curve. Visualized hitting lane three between the seams.

"He's outside. Outside. Keep it steady," Alexa reminded me.

I concentrated on my car, on carrying enough throttle into the corner. Eyed the seams and stayed off of them. Kept my hands still and my shoulders loose to absorb the bumps I ran over. Stayed with him through 1 and 2, but couldn't get clear. We exited Turn 2 side-by-side, and I added "exiting a turn in lane three next to someone" to my list of uncomfortable sensations. As we blasted down the back straight, the other driver made back some of the ground he'd lost.

"Still outside," Alexa said. "Keep on it. Keep working him in 3 and 4. Stay smooth."

I was still ahead by a nose turning into 3, which gave me the advantage, especially since I had no seams to contend with there. I gritted my teeth and kept my foot down. Later I thought I got through the lap on will alone.

Alexa talked me through the rest of the move. "He's still there, in lane four. Still there. Still outside. Outside. Keep working that throttle, Kate. Outside. Still outside. Outside. At the rear corner. Keep on it. Still there—*clear!* Good job." I heard delight in her voice.

I let myself breathe down the front straight. I'd had a moment and learned from it. Used the mistake to make myself stronger. I still wasn't ready to tackle a race, but I knew I was getting better, faster, and smarter about the cars. I buckled down to make the most of the last hour.

I was low in Turn 3 on my final, cool-down lap after the final session ended, when Xavier came on the radio, sounding strange. "When you pit, Kate, we want you to stay in the car until we signal. Alexa's on her way back over, and we've called security. They'll help you."

"Copy. What's going on?"

"You'll see."

I was too occupied with braking and steering down pit lane to think much about it. Once I arrived and parked, it was all too apparent what the problem was.

The paparazzi had arrived.

Chapter Nineteen

Why half a dozen pushy photographers were in pit lane, I didn't know. But given I was being told to stay in my car, and that they were being held back from entering pit lane right behind me, I assumed I was their target.

Because I found Billy? He wouldn't be important enough. Neither is the fact I'm testing for IndyCar. Because of Maddie and the celebrity race? Must be. Alexa arrived to help me out of the car and offer me a Beermeier Racing hat. When I'd pulled off the helmet, HANS, and balaclava, I wiped down with the towel she also provided and put on the hat. I could cover my flat, sweaty helmet-head, but I'd have to live with the creases in my face from tight-fitting safety gear.

"We figured there was no avoiding them, so we might as well get the team some publicity. You game?" Alexa gestured for a crew member to collect my helmet and gloves, and she handed me water.

"Any clue what it's about?"

"No, except they're not motorsport press. They're entertainment media."

Maddie. I drank down half the bottle of water and nodded at Alexa.

We walked to the rear of the car, toward the opening in the pit wall and the increasingly agitated photographers.

As they saw us, they started shouting questions and directions.

The first clear voice to rise out of the noise stopped me in my tracks.

"Kate, is it true you're dating Lucas Tolani?"

"How'd you bag the most eligible bachelor in Hollywood?" another man shouted.

Alexa turned to me, her eyebrows raised.

"Met him," I muttered.

"Kate," yet another photographer yelled. "Do you think a girl driver can hold onto Hollywood's biggest playboy?"

Alexa and I both tensed at the "girl driver" comment, and she recovered first. She spoke quietly. "Since you can't get out of this, let's give them a little girl-driver ass-whoopin'."

"I'm so sorry."

She laughed. "You didn't call them out, did you?"

I shook my head.

"Then not your fault. Besides, I think it's funny."

I was too dismayed for humor, but I was all for her team benefitting. I stepped forward and raised my hands. "I'll answer your questions if we do this calmly. I've been driving the racecar for most of the last eight hours, so I'm a little tired." The sound of shutters tripping as I spoke unnerved me, but I tried to ignore it. "Why don't you get a photo with us and the car?"

As they gathered around, I insisted on pulling Alexa into the photo, spelling her name for them. They asked for me alone, and after five minutes of that, I answered questions.

"No, I'm not dating Lucas Tolani. I met him through Maddie Theabo, who I'm coaching in the celebrity race at the Grand Prix of Long Beach next weekend. You should all come watch, it'll be fun."

"Do you want to date him? Has he asked you?" Another photographer inserted.

"No comment."

"Do you think a girl driver can hold onto him, when super-models can't?"

I tried to keep a pleasant expression on my face, but I wasn't sure I succeeded. "That's insulting on a variety of levels. One profession is no better than another, just different. I'd never presume to comment on why he did or didn't date a supermodel, an actress, or a librarian. It's none of my business."

The men clamored again, but I held up a hand and waited. "Lastly, I'd like to ask you never to use the term 'girl driver.'"

"What the hell do we call you then?"

"A driver. A racer. A racecar driver. A female driver, if you have to. But 'girl' conjures up the idea of ruffled dresses and pigtails. I'm twenty-six years old. I'm a racecar driver, and I happen to be female." I looked at Alexa and back at the men. "And in case you didn't know, Alexa was also a racecar driver. Now she owns a successful racing team, and she's one of the few women doing so. Anything to add, Alexa?"

She smiled at the group. "What she said. And please spell my name right."

I fielded a few more questions, and then we got rid of them. I slumped onto the pit wall, exhausted. Up and down pit row, teams disassembled their setups. Most had rolled their cars back to their trailers already. All other drivers, including Matt from the second Beermeier car, were gone, and I was disappointed not to have a chance to debrief with him.

Xavier approached with another bottle of water. "Not the usual end to a test day."

My adrenaline and bravado were fading, leaving a residue of embarrassment. Here I was, auditioning for a respected team on the next step up the ladder, trying to be a focused, effective, considerate team player. I might have succeeded earlier in the day, but I'd punctuated the event by attracting the circus. "You were great today, Xavier. I'm so sorry for the intrusion."

"Highlight of the day for us. The crew had a ball." He chuckled, taking off his hat with one hand and rubbing his bald head with the other. "You didn't see it, but they were photobombing your shots. They're all hoping to find themselves in the tabloids tomorrow."

I sat up a little straighter. "Good. I mean, thank you. I'm relieved to hear it."

He patted my shoulder. "Don't worry, kid. You did good today, and the idiots at the end didn't change that."

Alexa walked over. "He's right. In fact, the crap at the end shows me you can handle yourself—and dumbass questions—straight out of the car after a long day."

I stood up. "Thank you. For the day and also the backup at the end."

"You earned it, and like Xavier said, you did well." She narrowed her eyes. "I'm not saying I'd put you in the car for a race tomorrow, but you got farther along today than most rookies here. I told James you'd be welcome at Beermeier whenever you're ready."

Relief and happiness flooded my body. I tightened my grip on the water bottle, making it crackle. "Is my father still here? I thought he had to leave mid-afternoon."

Alexa shrugged. "We had that conversation at lunch. And you didn't screw up this afternoon, so it's still true."

"I almost did."

Xavier grinned. "Kid, a racecar driver who's never had a change-your-underwear moment at Fontana is a mythical creature. A unicorn. You recovered." He tapped a finger on my hands, which were clenched together in front of me holding the water. "And you've got some quick hands there. Good hands."

Mission accomplished. I stuck out one of those hands and then changed my mind and hugged them both. "Thank you for the day. The car was great. I mean, it felt broken, but I'm now used to that being great. And you both were supportive and responsive. Your whole team was. Thanks very much."

"Our pleasure," Alexa responded. "Hope we'll work with you in the future."

"I hope so."

During the hour-long drive west back to Beverly Hills, I made two calls. First, I spoke with my grandparents, though I didn't have any more than a "how-are-you-fine-good" exchange with my grandmother. Gramps, on the other hand, was able to put aside the means by which the day's test had been paid for and focus on the results. I reported only the good, and my near spin, and he was thrilled for me.

Then I dialed Holly. But instead of her voice, I heard a man.

"Kate! How'd the test go?" asked Holly's boyfriend Miles Hanson, the tall, dark, and handsome NASCAR rock star. Talk about a woman bagging an eligible bachelor.

"It was great, Miles. Big, powerful car. Probably like yours. Tell me, do you get on an oval and think the car feels bent?"

He laughed. "Only right after a road course race, and only for a couple seconds. But I remember the first time I got in a car set up for a high-banked oval. Those are really canted sideways to handle the angle. IndyCars must be also."

"Sure are. I'm not used to that in the Corvette. But these were more powerful. And bent."

"Glad to hear it went well. You looked good."

"Thanks, I—what? How did you see…there are photos already?"

"Here's Holly. Talk to you later." I heard fumbling and scraping sounds.

"Nice move, Slick," Holly told him. "Now, Kate. The test went well?"

I filled her in on the day's racing details and outcome, explaining the surprise of finding photographers and their stupid questions in pit lane. "What are you seeing, Holly? And where?"

"Well, sugar, you want the good news first or the bad news?"

I fought the urge to thunk my head against the steering wheel. Not wise while driving west on Highway 10 back to the Los Angeles metropolis.

"Actually," Holly mused. "It's not so much bad news as… tacky."

"Give me the tacky news first, then cheer me up."

"You've made the entertainment magazine sites, the Hollywood gossip blogs, and Racing's Ringer. So far. We'll see what comes up tomorrow."

"What are they saying?"

"You're referred to as Lucas' new love, his 'walk on the wild side,' since you're not a model or an actress, and a 'merely pretty, girl driver.' Which is flat out rude."

"Can I die of embarrassment?"

"Not hardly. Here's the good news. Great photos of you, Alexa, and the car."

"Are there crew members in the back? They were trying to get in the frame."

"You can see them making faces."

"Perfect. Give me the rest."

"The photos are good, and you look seriously great. Vital and strong, you know?"

"You're not saying it to make me feel better?"

"I'm not, I swear. Yes, what they say about you is tacky and embarrassing, but you look good and you got the car and Beermeier team name out to a bunch of viewers who'd never normally see it. That's great. It's what you want—minus the tacky. How did the team deal with the press?"

"I was mortified they were there about Lucas. Alexa was amused. Had fun with it, like the crew."

"There you go." Her voice lightened. "Take the good from it and flick off the rest."

"Thanks, I needed that."

We chatted a couple more minutes about my test and Miles' race that weekend at Bristol Motor Speedway, a track I'd always wanted to experience. Then I was alone with my thoughts in my rental car. That is, I was alone with a few thousand other drivers, all heading west into the fading sunlight at a minimum of seventy miles per hour. I shook my head. What a place.

Chapter Twenty

I woke up late Friday morning and dragged myself to the hotel's super-deluxe gym, knowing I needed to work out my muscle stiffness. I felt the effects of spending most of a day in an unfamiliar car all over my body, but my neck and shoulders felt it the most, due to stabilizing the wheel and handling g-forces. I'd made a point over the last four months of working on my upper-body strength, particularly my neck, but I could tell I'd need to do even more.

Once I'd cleaned up, breakfasted, and caffeinated, I braced myself and called Nikki.

This time, there was no giggle, no dog, and no BS, though the breathy tone assured me it was the same woman. "Thank you for looking into Billy's death, Kate. I have three minutes before the camera crew arrives. What can I do for you?"

"Can you get a copy of the raw footage your crew shot on Media Day?"

"Of course. What else?"

"Who was Billy close to, besides Holden? And you?"

"He spent a lot of time with Coleman. I didn't hear about other friends. Maybe an acquaintance he'd go for drinks with after the gym, but that's all." Her doorbell rang, and she disconnected with zero fanfare.

She's not as scatterbrained as I thought. I considered what she'd told me. I wanted to know who liked Billy, if anyone had, but

I wasn't willing to talk to Billy's best friend, Holden. I took a deep breath and dialed Coleman.

To my surprise, he picked up. "How can I help you, Kate?"

"In order to look into Billy's death, I need to understand who he was. Can you tell me about him? His interests? Talents?"

"I'm glad you're taking this seriously." He paused, and I wondered if he was straightening his tie on the other end of the phone.

"Billy was young and green, but he had potential," Coleman said. "He had an abundance of charm, and that would have served him well in life, once he found his niche. He was popular with women, but also enjoyed hanging out with the boys. He was deeply committed to taking care of unwanted animals, and he'd just begun volunteering his time with underprivileged children at a local community center."

"It sounds like you knew him well."

"Better over the last year. He needed firm guidance—and course correction after some the missteps you're aware of—but he had a good heart." He sighed. "I understand your relationship with him wasn't very cordial, so that might be difficult for you to believe. He was insecure about his role in the world, and he projected attitude to compensate. If he'd had the chance to mature, he'd have grown out of it."

Would he have grown out of being a sexual predator? Maybe anything's possible. Hearing the regret in Coleman's voice, I felt another trace of sorrow at Billy's death. "You'll miss him?"

"I will."

I sat in silence after ending the call, considering Billy's character. I'd seen the two-dimensional villain, as had plenty of other people. But he'd been a real person, with friends as well as enemies. Strengths as well as flaws. I might not miss him, but someone would.

I wasn't done with challenging family conversations for the day. Shortly before noon, I pulled to the curb in front of the Frame Savings headquarters building to pick my father up. He'd requested a second discussion, and I'd reluctantly agreed.

At Du-par's Restaurant in the Farmer's Market, we both ordered sandwiches and salads. My emotions were still raw from his admission that he hadn't stood up to his family for me, and I waited for him to speak.

"I felt we didn't finish our conversation two days ago, since we never talked about the money or where we go from here," he began. "This may be uncomfortable, but I want us to be open and honest with each other."

"That's what I want also."

"Did your grandmother tell you about the money, if it was offered or asked for?"

"Nothing. Did your family say?"

He frowned. "Considering it was my brother Edward, any comments aren't repeatable."

"I'm sure it was something about payment for services rendered by my mother." I studied him. "I can't believe you're calm about that."

"I know it's a lie. There's no doubt you're my daughter." He took a breath. "I won't deny it makes me mad, but that's one of many frustrations I have with my brother these days. I'm trying to pick my battles."

I wasn't as ready to swallow the insult, but I left it alone. "Especially this week."

"Yes. I wish I were in a better position to help him. At least Coleman is able to."

"You know Coleman well?"

"We've been friends since college—he even knew your mother. After college, we stayed close, and he married my sister and joined the bank. For a long time, we were as close as brothers. More so."

"Not now?"

"He's closer to Edward these days, perhaps because their sons are friends. Were. I haven't felt the same connection or comfort level with Coleman, or Edward, in a long time."

"What changed?"

"I'm not sure. Coleman started spending more time here on the West Coast, though his family was still back east. I feel Frame Savings hasn't gotten his complete attention for some time now due to his pursuit of outside interests or hobbies."

I raised my eyebrows at him, and he frowned. "I don't feel comfortable with the choices he's making of late. For instance, he sometimes makes his networking opportunities and connections a higher priority than the bank."

"Judging by his son's behavior, I don't think much of his parenting."

"That's part of it. I'm not sure where he and Edward went wrong with Holden and Billy." He waited a beat. "But perhaps neither of us should make parenting judgments?"

Fair point, James.

"Speaking of family," my father began, "I want to ask you to consider something."

This can't be good. "All right."

"This summer there will be a Reilly family reunion, and I'd like you to attend. It appears there's no conflict with a race."

"We just had a conversation dancing around the fact your brother thinks my mother was a whore." I looked around, realizing how loud I was, even in the din of the restaurant. "Now you want me to be part of the family?"

"Regardless who likes it or not, you are part of the Reilly family. Part of my family. As I'm the head of the family and organizing the reunion, I would like you to be there."

I opened my mouth to speak, unsure if I'd go with calm and considered or outright rude. I thought better of both. "I'll think about it. That's all I can do right now."

He waited until we were in the car to raise the other topic that made me angry. "I hope you're not actually investigating Billy's murder."

"I hope you're not actually telling me what to do."

"We've been through this. I'm not. But you have to allow me to be concerned for you."

Do I? Do I have *to do anything for you?* I forced my body to relax, loosening my fingers on the wheel.

"You have so much in the works: two sponsors and a transition to a new series. Do you have time to investigate? You can't tell me you *want* to talk to people about Billy."

He had me there. "No, but I'm concerned about the reputation of racing and the preservation of the Long Beach race. I don't want the rest of the world thinking we're a hotbed of crime."

"Why? Why you?"

"Because I can and I care." I looked at him while we were stopped at a light. "This is my career. My *life*. I care that people respect the industry. I'm not saying I'm going to find his killer. But if I can help the police—and people involved with both racing and Frame Savings think I can—then I will." I paused. "Speaking of which, do you know of anyone at the bank or in the family with a grudge against Billy?"

He stared at me in surprise. I shrugged, and we rode the remaining blocks in silence.

Finally, as I pulled to the loading zone in front of the Frame Savings building, my father spoke again. "Please consider both of my requests."

I turned off the car, using the extra moments to reach through my anger for a nod.

He put a hand on mine. "I hope you understand why I ask. I'm concerned about you, and I want you to get to know the rest of the family."

"I said I'll consider it." I bit off the words.

He might have wanted to say more, but he left it. "Thank you. And thank you for joining me again. I'll see you at the events over the next few days." He patted my hand in lieu of a hug and got out of the car, then turned and waved as he was halfway across the plaza to the main entrance doors.

"Sorry, James," I muttered. "Not going to happen. I'm still going to ask questions about Billy. And you'll see me at the big, happy Reilly family reunion when hell freezes over."

Chapter Twenty-one

I sat at the curb for a few minutes, calming down. I'd started the meal in a decent place with my father emotionally. But by the end, I was back to being frustrated with his demands and assumptions. He always asked for more than I could give. Not for the first time I thought my life would be less complicated if I hadn't encountered him as an adult.

I idly watched the people in the small plaza in front of the bank headquarters. Two large planters with wide edges, perfect for sitting on, flanked a central walkway. It was one o'clock, and half a dozen people sat alone or in small groups finishing lunch, smoking, or reading. Still others entered and exited the building, walking with purpose. I couldn't categorize the bank's patrons or employees in any way, they were all sizes, shapes, genders, and ethnicities. Like Los Angeles.

One woman caught my attention because she walked more hesitantly than most and carried a bag that looked like a folded blue tarp under her arm. She walked to the middle of the plaza, paused, and went to a planter to sit down. Then she popped back up, moved to the center again, and sat down on the ground.

I looked around, wondering how a normal L.A. resident reacted to this kind of behavior. No one seemed to notice. Two people leaving the bank walked around the new obstacle, never missing a beat of their cell phone conversations.

I studied the woman. She was petite, dressed in khakis, tennis shoes, and a long-sleeved, knit top. Her short, brown hair wasn't unkempt, and she didn't look homeless.

She set out a small sign, a triangle of cardboard that proclaimed, "Shame on Frame Savings." A protest? I wondered if that happened a lot here. But she'd timed her statement poorly for maximum attention, given the number of people leaving the plaza to return to their desks. She pulled more objects out of her bag and set them in front of her. She seemed to be shaking, but I didn't understand why, since the temperature was in the high seventies with no wind.

I glanced in my mirrors, unwilling to leave before seeing how this scene played out. I looked back at her and took five seconds to understand what I saw.

Red can. Pouring liquid on herself. What? What?! Gasoline?

I glanced around to see who else was watching. As unbelievable as it seemed, no one stopped to ask her what she was doing. No security guard from inside the bank building ran out to investigate. I was jittery with adrenaline and indecision.

That's when it hit me. *I'm in L.A. Someone's filming this, right?* I relaxed and craned my neck for cameras, crew, and those midsize white box trucks I'd learned signified a nearby shoot, certain I'd spot them in clever hiding places. Nothing. No one.

I glanced back at the woman. She carefully capped the red gas can and set it aside, on top of the folded blue bag. I saw her shoulders shaking more violently, and I thought she was probably cold now she was wet. *Gasoline?* Gas would mean this was real. I still voted—desperately hoped—for made-for-television or -film. Or a prank. Anything other than the logical conclusion of a protest sign and a dousing with flammable liquid.

I unbuckled my seatbelt and turned around, frantically looking for a director to yell "Cut!" or anyone else observing the situation. *It's the middle of the day in a financial district, how can no one notice this?!* The logical part of my brain knew I was the only one to witness the whole chain of events. Any single action might be explainable and something a busy passer-by didn't want to deal with. Except maybe the gas can.

I turned back to the woman. She was hunched forward, curled around herself. Fumbling with something. She made a sliding motion with her right wrist. *Like trying to light a match.*

I didn't think. I yanked the keys from the ignition as I leapt from the car and scrambled through the plaza. *Don't light. Let me be ruining a scene. Please don't set yourself on fire.*

Neither of the matches she tried ignited. I reached her and slapped the wooden box out of her hand, sending it skidding toward one of the concrete planters. My eyes stung from the fumes.

She sobbed, her body jerking back and forth from the force of it. "Why? Why?" she wailed. "Let me…" The rest was lost in the cry of a newcomer to the scene.

"Jenny!" A distraught woman stumbled through the courtyard and threw herself on the gas-soaked woman.

I took a step back, not ready to leave, but happy to be away from the smell. I saw what must be the new arrival's car stopped behind mine, her driver's door hanging open into traffic. I looked back at the women, both on the ground now, both crying. I carefully picked up the two matches that hadn't lit from the pool of gasoline, carried them to the planter, and set them on the lip, above the box on the ground. My knees shook, and I sat down.

I heard sirens. Within moments, an ambulance, a fire truck, and two police cars surrounded my car at the curb, all with lights flashing.

I watched the action: frantic while the paramedics determined the woman wasn't injured, and calmer as they assessed her and figured out what they were dealing with. I told my story to two different police officers and pointed to the matches on the ground near my feet. At one point, I fetched my purse and a bottle of water from my car, locking it while I was there. I studied the woman who'd rushed in, wondering why she seemed familiar. When I trusted my legs to hold me, I approached her.

She turned to me with a stunned expression, and I remembered where I'd seen her. "You were at Media Day for the Long Beach race. With the pink scarf."

She clutched the pendant of the necklace she wore. "I don't…"

"Never mind." I gestured to the gas-soaked woman. "She's a friend?"

Her shuddering breath told me she was barely holding herself together. "My sister."

No wonder she was a wreck. "I'm so sorry. Can I do anything to help?" They felt like stupid questions, but had to ask. "I'm Kate Reilly."

"Tara Raffield." Neither of us made any move to shake hands. Instead, she narrowed her eyes at me. "Why do you care?"

I reminded myself Tara had almost seen her sister go up in flames. "I dropped someone off, and I saw—I couldn't let her…" I stopped, not wanting to say the words. Not wanting to think them either.

Tara closed her eyes.

"Sorry again." I dug a card out of my purse and handed it to her. "Please let me know if there's anything I can do to help. I don't like to see anyone in distress."

One paramedic stripped Jenny to her underwear while another held up a blanket to shield her. A third held a plastic bag open to receive Jenny's clothes. All three men were remarkably nonplussed by the smell, though even the residue of the gas on Tara made my eyes water.

Tara started to move away. "I've got to go with the ambulance."

I put a hand on her arm. "Can I check in with you sometime and see how she's doing? I don't mean to intrude, but I'd like to know."

Tara glared at me. "I still don't understand why you care."

"It scared me. I'd like to know she gets better." *Since I just saved her life.*

This time Tara sneered. "This is a first. Someone from the corrupt Reilly family actually giving a damn? I find it hard to believe."

I was stunned into silence.

"That's right," she taunted. "I know exactly who you are. Your family and this miserable excuse for a banking institution can stay the hell away from me and my sister."

She stalked to the ambulance and climbed in.

Chapter Twenty-two

I scrapped my afternoon of shopping. After watching someone distraught enough to set herself on fire, I wasn't in the mood for looking at multi-thousand-dollar outfits.

Instead, I went back to the hotel, showered, and changed clothes, needing the psychological cleansing, as well as the physical. Then I did something unusual for that part of town, or maybe the whole city. I took a walk.

In the neighborhood behind the hotel, I admired flowers, shrubs, and beautiful houses while I tried not to think about what the bank had done to make Jenny suicidal or what Tara had meant. I'd had no time to explain to Tara I wasn't corrupt. That I was barely part of the Reilly family. Barely part of the bank.

I sighed. I didn't have much of an argument. *Except, dammit, I'm not a bad person!* I went back to studying landscaping, listening to birds, and wondering how lost I'd have to feel to be driven to harm myself. I thought about the times in my life I'd felt trapped and unhappy, and I focused on what made me happy.

Getting in a racecar. Being part of a community of focused, talented women, like the Beauté campaign. Talking and working with genuine, caring people. I needed to concentrate on those activities and not let expectations about my investigative talents weigh me down. I hadn't let Billy bring me down in life. I wouldn't let it happen now.

By evening, I'd managed to shake off my subdued, introspective mood, and I waited for FBI agent Ryan Johnston on the red carpet of the hotel's entry, watching a parade of expensive and exotic cars. I appreciated the new, black Corvette Stingray, the street version of my racecar, that rolled up, and I burst out laughing when Ryan climbed out of the driver's seat.

He grinned. "It's my fun car. Want to drive?"

"No, thanks. I get enough at work."

I studied him as he drove us to an Indian restaurant. When we'd met, more than a year ago at the 24 Hours of Daytona, I thought he was a bad guy, a hatchet man for a shady businessman and team owner. I was still skeptical when he turned out to be an undercover FBI agent, since I'd been the one to intervene and foil a kidnapping of my half-sister, not him. But I'd mellowed with time. I wasn't angry with him anymore.

In the meantime, he'd grown his short, dark hair longer and trimmed his sideburns. A day's worth of beard growth added an edge. That, combined with the humor and intelligence in his eyes, made my insides jump around. I no longer thought he looked like the perfect henchman to an evil overlord.

Our conversation stayed light and amusing until we were seated at the restaurant and had ordered. Then Ryan asked me what I'd done that day, adding, "It seems you've got a lot on your mind."

"I was trying not to bring it with us."

He took a sip of his beer. "Must be pretty bad."

"Surreal." I described Jenny's attempted suicide, Tara's reaction to me, and the basics of my relationship with Frame Savings, without going into the complexities of my relationship with my father. But I'd forgotten Ryan knew many of the players.

"I can see her calling some of the family corrupt, like Ed Grant—I mean, Edward Reilly-Stinson—his son, and his son's BFF."

"Billy and Holden. Except that Billy was killed the other day."

"Doesn't mean he wasn't corrupt." He chewed a piece of bread. "But your father—James?—seemed honest. It's rude of Jenny's sister to fling that at you."

"I can't stop thinking about how powerless Jenny must have felt. How meaningless life must be for someone to do that. And seriously, who chooses self-immolation?"

"It's a pretty rare method." Ryan covered my hand with his. "It's impossible to know what brings people to different choices. She's probably got a reason, or reasons, and you'll never know what they are. You can offer help, but you can't force it on anyone."

He sat back and I moved my wineglass out of the way as our food was delivered, plate after plate of it. I was about to dig into the rice when I felt my phone vibrating in the purse tucked against my hip. I ignored it. Ignored the second buzz. By the fourth, I apologized to Ryan and looked to see who was trying to reach me.

My mouth dropped open.

"What is it?"

"It's Tara, the one who was so angry at me today. She apologizes for what she said. She didn't realize I saved her sister."

"You left that part out."

I shrugged. "She says if I come to the hospital she'll tell me everything she knows about the Reillys. The secrets she's uncovered from twenty years of working at the bank." I looked up at Ryan. "She'll also tell me what Billy was up to that probably got him killed. How would she know I'm curious about that?"

Ryan nodded to my plate. "Eat up, it's hot."

"I should respond. I should go there." I set the phone down. "I also should remember this is a date. I'm sorry."

"It happens. You can make it up to me another time. Let's figure out what you're going to do about this. But eat while we do that."

I shoved away my guilt and started eating.

"Do you want to know secrets about the Reilly family, Kate?"

It was a great question. "Yes and no. I feel like I need to hear what she has to say." *Even if it cracks open a can of worms.*

"Why's that?"

I shoveled a huge bite of food into my mouth and gestured apologetically.

"Tell me you're not investigating Billy's murder."

I shrugged, still chewing.

"Facing down a quartet of enormous men with guns—and knives, let's not forget the knives—at Daytona wasn't enough for you?"

"I've got reasons." But explaining the pressure put on me by the race organizers and my new sponsor didn't impress Ryan at all.

"You need to leave this to the pros. As you've seen in the past, you can get hurt."

I ate another bite of food to avoid talking. I didn't mention the other two murder investigations he didn't know about.

"Why do I have a feeling you're going to ignore my advice?" he asked.

"I have access to people and information the professionals don't have. Unlike last time, I have no skin in the game, as Gramps would say. I'm not emotional about Billy's death." I paused. "Useful information goes to the pros. I'm not going after anyone."

His nod was grudging. "Are you going to talk to Tara?"

"Will you forgive me for how rude it is?"

"If you'll let me go with you and give me a raincheck on a date."

"You want to go?"

"You've got me curious. And maybe I can help you stay out of trouble."

We finished the food quickly and made the short drive to Cedars-Sinai Hospital. Ryan walked around to shut the passenger door after I got out, and he stopped me with a hand on my arm. "One thing first." He leaned in and kissed me.

I didn't feel instant fireworks. What I felt was a slow burn, a wave of heat that spread throughout my body. My hands were full of my purse and jacket, so I didn't touch him, but I might have moaned softly as he pressed soft kisses to the corners of my mouth. He pulled away and smiled again, releasing me, then grabbed my shoulders as I swayed. His smile got wider.

"That's embarrassing," I mumbled.

"Kissing me?"

"No. After..." I gave up. Filed that sensation away to think about later. "I have to tell you something."

"You're Lucas Tolani's new girlfriend?"

"And that's more embarrassing." I sighed. "We're supposed to go on a date in a couple days, that's all."

He took my hand and headed toward the hotel entrance. "You've agreed to a second date with me already. Besides, I carry a gun. I'm not worried."

Chapter Twenty-three

We found Tara alone in one of the waiting rooms. She was calmer than when I'd seen her last, but her red eyes stood out in a face otherwise devoid of color. She set down her cup of coffee as we entered and, with an uneasy look at Ryan, rose to shake my hand.

"Kate, thank you. I hope we can start over. I'm Tara Raffield. Jenny Shelton is my younger sister."

I introduced Ryan. "He's a friend of mine. We were out to dinner."

He stepped forward. "I'm sorry for your sister's troubles, and to intrude on yours. I can wait out in the hallway while you two talk."

"He's FBI," I added, "so he knows how to keep a secret." Tara caught her breath, and I reassured her. "He's here as a friend, for me. Not as an agent."

Her shoulders slumped. "I don't mind. What I have to say is more about your family anyway. I can't keep my secrets anymore. Not with all this."

We sat down, and I leaned forward, focused on Tara. "How's Jenny? Was she hurt today?"

Tara looked at the floor. "Physically, she's okay. They're keeping her overnight because she was having breathing issues—she had asthma as a kid, plus the fumes today. Then they'll hold her at a different facility for seventy-two hours."

"A fifty-one-fifty?" Ryan asked.

"Right. An involuntary psychiatric hold. I suppose you'd be familiar with it." She dropped her head into her hands. "I knew she needed help, but I didn't know it was this bad. I can't imagine what might have happened today..." Tara started to cry.

I patted her back. Despite having six inches on me and looking like a thirty-five-year-old fitness model, she felt fragile.

Tara sat up and pulled a tissue from her pocket. "I swore I was done with tears, moving on to anger."

Being upset seemed reasonable to me. "You said you had information about Billy."

She got up to pace. Took two deep breaths in and out. Cleared her throat. "Information about Billy and others. I should start by explaining why Jenny—no, I'm not sure I can explain that." Tara gave a self-conscious laugh. "I can explain what drove her to it. And who."

She stopped, hands on her hips. "Right now, I don't care where or how you share this, but that's my anger talking. Tomorrow I'll probably want you to keep it quiet."

"Of course," I replied.

"Unless there's something criminal, which I'd need to report." Ryan paused. "You can always ask me to go get another cup of coffee at that point."

Tara smiled. "I like you."

I did, too.

Tara blew out another long breath. "Jenny and I both worked at Frame Savings. I'm still up in the corporate offices, in human resources, and Jenny was one of the assistant managers in the branch office downstairs. She's been diagnosed with breast cancer. She's just started treatment."

"I'm so sorry. Is it going well?"

"Good so far. Stage three cancer, but they're happy with how she's responding."

After a moment's pause, Ryan picked up the conversation. "Was there more going on in your sister's life?"

"Quite a bit." She looked at me, hesitantly. "This is where your family comes in."

"I may share a name with them," I said. "But there's only one person I care about. I can't imagine he's part of the problem, but if he is, I'd rather know."

Tara took a deep breath. "What I didn't know about Jenny was, for the past year, until a couple months ago, she'd been having an affair with a married man working at Frame. Right before her cancer diagnosis, he dumped her and threatened her physically to keep it quiet. Belittled her, telling her no one would believe her even if she did talk. Told her he'd come after her if she complained. Can you believe, in this day and age, he could threaten that and she'd believe him?"

"No evidence other than her word against his?" Ryan queried. Tara shook her head.

I asked the obvious question. "Who?"

"Coleman Sherain." My jaw dropped as she kept talking, disgust clear in her voice. "What makes it worse is I work with him. Sure, we've all known for years about his second family out here in L.A. Even about other affairs. But I never thought my sister would be dumb enough to fall for his act."

I met Ryan's eyes and answered the question in them. "Married my father's sister, worked for the bank his whole career. Holden's father." I turned to Tara. "That's enough to make your sister upset."

"I'm not done. Then there was Billy. He propositioned Jenny, apparently at Coleman's suggestion."

I was quickly heading toward outrage. Ryan took my hand.

Tara started moving again. "Billy was the last straw for Jenny. When he got aggressive, she slapped him and shoved him into a filing cabinet. Hard."

"She could bring charges of sexual harassment," suggested Ryan.

Tara's mouth twisted. "By the next morning, Billy had a restraining order against her. That afternoon, he fired her on charges of theft, which I know he made up. Billy told her he'd skip formal charges if she left immediately. She was hysterical, threatening him and Coleman. Security had to escort her out of the building."

I turned to Ryan. "It's outrageous. Can't she do something?"

"Of course she can," he replied. "But as I'm sure Tara knows, it would be a long, difficult road to win a judgment. She didn't help her case with the violence against Billy, though it's completely understandable. Unfortunately her violence is easier to prove than the men pressuring her into a relationship."

I turned to Tara, disgusted. "She could go after them."

She sighed. "What your friend here sees is how much Jenny would be on trial, how it would expose her and hurt her, because they'd throw everything money can buy at her. And we can't fight that. Not the money, and not while Jenny's fighting cancer."

Ryan finished the thought for her, his voice gentle. "And not now she made an attempt on her own life, publicly, in an effort to shame them."

Tara dropped back into the chair across from me, rubbing her forehead. We sat in silence for a minute, and Ryan asked a great question.

"What do you expect Kate will do with this information, Tara?"

She was amused. "I don't expect you to avenge Jenny. But I wanted you to know about Billy, since you were asked to investigate his murder."

"Looking into, not investigating…but how do you know?"

"Office grapevine. Part of me hopes you can get Jenny's story to someone cares and might do something about it. I've worked for the bank for fifteen years. I know not everyone is an unethical slimeball. Your father's not, but he's hard for someone in my position to reach. Your father will listen to you, where he might not listen to me." She hung her head again. "Which makes me sorry all over again for lumping you in with them earlier."

"I can't promise anything, but I'll talk to my father about Jenny and Billy and Coleman. What else can you share?"

For the next twenty minutes, she told us everything she knew. First, the clues that led to her figuring out Coleman had a second family locally, in addition to the official one back east. On his weeks-long visits to L.A., he split his time between "a friend's house"—the second wife's—and the corporate apartment—where he entertained other mistresses, including her sister. When Coleman wasn't making use of the apartment for affairs, Edward Reilly-Stinson was. The two men were cut from the same cloth, it appeared, at least as far as marital fidelity went.

Then Tara told Ryan and me about Billy, who'd been put in charge of the branch office a year ago, after his and Holden's debacle at Daytona. As the HR manager assigned to issues with the home branch, her workload quadrupled when Billy showed up. He was a worthless leader, delivering only half-baked direction and blaming employees for resultant failures. She'd spent the last six months documenting employee complaints to create a paper trail implicating Billy, while simultaneously being yelled at by him for employee performance and blamed by the executives for Billy's own shoddy work.

"It's hard for me to be sorry he's gone," she concluded.

I remembered something. "Were you at the Media Day for the race because you were following him?"

She flushed. "Stalking is probably a better word. I'd been tailing him and Coleman, even Edward, for weeks, whenever I could. I was trying to find Billy's weak spots, to find some leverage. At that point I knew he'd fired my sister, and she'd reacted inappropriately. But I didn't know about the sexual harassment and faked theft charges."

Ryan shifted in his chair. "Probably good you didn't."

I believed her and didn't actually think she'd killed Billy. But the fact she'd been in Long Beach that day meant she could have. "I assume you didn't come up with anything you could use against him?"

She frowned. "Vague pointers and ideas. Billy had started to run with the big dogs—"

Ryan broke in. "Those being?"

"Coleman, for sure. Edward, sometimes. Also other influential, local businessmen. Billy was joining the club, literally. There's a group of businessmen that meets every Thursday morning for breakfast. Coleman always attends, and he comes back more full of himself than ever, bragging about knowing the real movers and shakers of the city. He'd been taking Billy with him lately."

Ryan sat forward. "Do you know who else is in that club?"

"I could go through call logs and make some guesses, if you wanted, but for all his loose lips about his homelife, Coleman didn't talk about that group, except in the general case. 'The real money-makers' and 'big-time wheeler-dealers,' that sort of thing."

"Coleman and Billy weren't the most likely combination."

"Coleman's son Holden is in San Diego—though he was part of the group when he visited. And Billy's father isn't out on this coast as much as Coleman. Billy and Coleman were here. But their relationship wasn't going well."

"They didn't get along?"

"I think Billy didn't listen to Coleman the way Holden does. Billy didn't respect Coleman. He thought he was entitled to authority. And salary and deference."

"Did you see Billy and Coleman argue?" Ryan asked.

"All the damn time. Especially over branch management. Coleman tried to tell Billy what to do, but Billy talked back and did what he wanted."

That sounded like the Billy I'd known and hated.

Chapter Twenty-four

A short time later, Ryan and I left Tara alone. I was drained from the revelations, and Tara was paler than before, clearly exhausted. We agreed to talk more soon, and I'd made her promise to let me help with anything she or Jenny needed, whether legal issues or the cancer treatment.

Ryan took my hand again as we exited the hospital for the parking lot. This time it was more comforting than romantic.

"Sorry again, this was a terrible date."

He smiled. "I understand. You need questions answered, and I'm not talking about a murder investigation."

"I'm not sure what to do about this family."

He dug his keys out of his pocket as we reached the parking lot. "This obviously isn't the time to ask about your history with them. Maybe you'll share that with me sometime."

I was relieved he didn't push. I thought through my schedule, and had an idea. "Do you have a black suit?" I remembered who I was talking to. "A dressy one, not a special-agent one?"

He nodded, his face showing no surprise or curiosity. Must be FBI training.

"How about I make this up to you tomorrow night? And I'll answer your questions." I reconsidered. "Except I'm not sure it would be fun for you. Maybe it's not a good idea."

Still holding my hand, Ryan pulled me to a stop. "Ask me, don't decide for me."

"There's a gala tomorrow night celebrating the partnership between my primary sponsor, Beauté, and the Breast Cancer Research Foundation. We've got a fundraising walk in the morning through downtown and a party at night. Boring chicken, speeches, a live auction. Would you like to attend with me?"

He stepped closer. "Be your date?"

Something about his scent—woodsy, spicy, male—made that slow burn start up again. "You might be bored."

"Would you like me to be there with you?" He watched me, and I had the distinct feeling this was the cop reading the suspect for truth.

"I would."

He smiled and unlocked the Corvette. "I'd be happy to attend."

As he drove me back to my hotel, I asked if he had any thoughts on Tara's story. "Or maybe you know something about the people involved? You've been based here a while now."

"I can't share information about active investigations."

"You do know something about someone?"

He laughed. "My job is finding out things about people. I can't tell you who or what. But I'd appreciate it if you'd let me know what you're hearing."

"I'll take all the insight I can get."

"Officially, I can't help. But I can talk things over with you, give you some advice, as long as it doesn't touch on active investigations." He stopped at a light and turned to me. "You need to be careful. There are always rumors of backroom deals, political corruption, and money laundering that float around the West Coast. I don't know if your family members are involved, but they could be, so be subtle."

"Now you've got me worried."

"That'll keep you careful." The light turned green, and we started moving. "Do you believe that neither Tara nor her sister killed Billy?"

"I want to." I frowned, looking out the window at the massive, impeccable Beverly Hills homes we passed along Sunset Boulevard. "They both could have. I saw Tara there myself, and she admitted stalking Billy. Plus if her sister's that unbalanced, she could easily have struck out at the person responsible. So no, I don't entirely believe her."

"I'm glad to hear it. You might make an investigator yet."

If he only knew.

Ryan let me off at the Beverly Hills Hotel with a simple kiss on the cheek and a promise to pick me up the next night in black tie. I wandered the lush hotel grounds for a few minutes, trying to make sense of everything I'd heard. I'd believed terrible things of Billy and Holden. And of Edward, Billy's father. Hearing the same about Coleman, Holden's father, shouldn't be a surprise, but it was.

A series of questions played over and over in my head, like an earworm. *Did my father know what was going on? If he did, how could he live with it? If he didn't, how could he miss it?* I had no answers, yet. But I knew I'd have to talk to him about what I'd learned.

The next morning, I felt as dismayed and saddened as the night before. But I was at least more optimistic, thanks to the five thousand supporters of breast cancer research who turned up at the Bonaventure Hotel early on a Saturday morning to walk a 5K through downtown Los Angeles. After the walk was completed, the final speeches had been made, and the last sample packs of Beauté's products had been handed out, I settled into a thirtieth-floor conference room in the Beauté corporate offices with some of the executives.

My two-year contract with Beauté was in its last six months, and I'd expected the meeting to be a standard check-in. Instead, they told me Beauté was interested in continuing to sponsor me after my initial contract expired, especially if I moved to NASCAR or IndyCar. They asked me to compile estimated costs and options for different tier teams in both new series. And they wanted a contact at Frame Savings, to discuss coordinating approaches.

I felt numb and sat down on a bench outside the skyscraper, trying to process my good fortune. With the Frame Savings money, I could bring much-needed funding to Sandham Swift for the next year, as well as secure a ride in the Indy 500. Plus eek out an Indy Lights race or two. If I performed well enough, the amount would increase for the following year. The two sponsorships together would be funding enough for the Indy 500, other IndyCar races with a mid-level team, *and* testing with a NASCAR team. Maybe even running races in a feeder series to NASCAR.

Beauté and Frame Savings together could make all of my racing dreams come true. I took deep breaths to stop the world from spinning and called Holly.

"Why do you sound strange, Kate?" I heard clanks and whirring noises in the background from Miles' garage.

"Lightheaded."

"What's wrong?" The background noise faded away. "Is everyone okay?"

I started laughing. "Fine. Better than fine." I explained Beauté's offer and the different possibilities that had occurred to me.

"Hooo-leeeee shit, sugar. Seriously?"

"Seems like."

"Well, then. Think carefully about what path you want most. We'll round up the numbers and give them a tempting package for the direction you want to go." She paused. "Now, as your friend. Go celebrate a little. You're in Beverly Hills! Splurge on something outrageous. Do some recon for when I get there Monday."

I took Holly's advice and headed for Rodeo Drive, three blocks of shops with every imaginable luxury brand. I resolved to enter at least every other store, despite feeling out of my depth in both price and style. I browsed patterned leather sneakers, gold leather jackets, skimpy sundresses, and fringed handbags, trying to keep a nonchalant expression on my face. As if I spent $1,640 on a handbag every week. Or $780 on a scarf.

I was one in a long stream of tourists strolling up and down the line of shops, and I enjoyed letting the colors and textures of the goods wash over me. Thinking of which outrageous outfits to tease Holly with. Waiting for something to catch my eye. Wandering in total anonymity.

Until the fifth store. A little white puffball of a dog ran toward me at the front of the display area, where I stood stroking cashmere tank tops. The dog made a beeline for me, yapping and snarling ferociously. It stopped, sniffed my shoes, and propped its front paws on my shin.

I saw a pink tongue and a bejeweled collar. "Pookie?"

A shriek came from the back of the store. "My baby!"

I recognized the voice. With a sigh, I scooped Pookie up to reunite her with her owner.

Even more surprising than finding Nikki Gray in a store on Rodeo Drive—maybe not surprising after all—or finding she'd brought Pookie-bear with her, was discovering her other companion. Elizabeth Rogers, Ms. Totally Bland, herself.

Elizabeth sat in a plush chair and typed on her cell phone, not worried about the dog. Nikki was looking under clothing racks.

"I think you lost something," I announced.

Elizabeth's head whipped up, her scowl at her phone turning to a smile.

Nikki emitted another shriek and extricated herself from the merchandise, revealing leopard-print leggings and a purple silk blouse. "Sweetums!" She waved her hands.

I handed the dog over as Nikki scolded her. "Bad doggie. Why Pookie run away from mama? Silly Pookie-bear." Finger shaking gave way to nuzzling from both parties.

Elizabeth stood up and gave me the celebrity hug—hand lightly patting back, air kiss to one cheek. "What a surprise! What are you up to, Kate?" She laughed. "Shopping, of course."

"Seeing the sights."

"They are something." We shared a smile as Nikki stopped communing with her dog and turned to me.

"Kate, thank you for rescuing Pookie." She was dressed down, not quite as much eyeliner and maybe only one set of false eyelashes. Minimal diamonds.

"Where's the camera crew?"

Nikki tucked the dog inside her Hermes Birkin bag open on a chair. She tapped Pookie on the nose one last time. "Stay." She turned to me. "Day off for them. Shopping day for me."

"Plus a little business." Elizabeth retook her seat.

"I'm interrupting."

"No, no." Nikki wrinkled her nose without moving her forehead. "We're shopping *and* talking *and* getting to know each other. And a teensy bit of business. Mostly a girls' afternoon out, so say you'll join us!" She clapped her hands.

"Sounds like fun." *And a cultural experience.*

Chapter Twenty-five

Nikki threw questions over her shoulder as often as she pulled items from the rack to hand to a discreet saleswoman.

"So Kate," she began, "have you found anything out to help us?" Without letting me respond, she spoke in a loud, fake whisper to Elizabeth. "Kate's going to help me and Donnie make sure poor Billy's death doesn't hurt the race."

"What exactly does that mean?" Elizabeth asked.

I shrugged. "Ask around about who might have wanted him dead. Give Nikki and Don a quiet heads-up if the result will reflect badly on the race organization. Or the race itself." Nikki focused on a blouse, and I leaned toward Elizabeth and lowered my voice. "I'm not really sure, but it's making her happy for me to ask a few questions."

"I understand."

"Figured." I raised my voice again. "I don't have a lot of information yet, but maybe you can tell me more about him."

"He's dead. Why do you need to talk about him?" Nikki asked, as Pookie barked punctuation from her purse-perch.

I managed not to roll my eyes, but it was tough. "Figuring out who killed him means figuring out why it happened. That usually has something to do with who he was."

"Unless it was a random event," Elizabeth suggested. "But that's pretty unlikely."

I was grateful Elizabeth seemed to understand, and I appreciated the glint of humor in her eyes as she watched me deal with Nikki.

"Okay." Nikki stared into the distance, a lurid yellow silk blouse drooping unnoticed from a hanger in her hand. "Billy."

It was the first time I'd seen her show any reaction to his death. "Sorry. It must be difficult for you. How long had you been dating?"

She snapped to attention, frowning at the blouse and replacing it on the rack. "A few months."

"How did you meet?"

"A party for race sponsors and executives."

Would I have to pry every tidbit loose? "What made you get involved?"

Nikki swiveled to look at me, incredulous. "To start with, hot. Hot, hot, hot. I mean twenty-four-year-old body hot."

I tried to quell my nausea. "Was that it? Sex?"

"Not that it wouldn't be enough," Elizabeth noted, amused.

Nikki flicked through hangers. "He was going to help me understand the racing world. I hadn't been involved before, since my husband ran the event. But now that it's my responsibility, I wanted an insider's help, and he convinced me he had all the connections I'd ever need."

I opened my mouth to ask the next question, but Nikki whipped around. "I'm going to go try things on." She stalked off to the dressing room.

I exchanged shrugs with Elizabeth and sat down in the remaining chair. Another shop worker appeared and offered us glasses of water, then held a tiny dish to Pookie's mouth and waited while the dog lapped it up.

When she left, I turned to Elizabeth. "I didn't know you were friends with Nikki."

She held up a hand and wiggled it back and forth. "Friends? Colleagues? Business associates? I contacted her on behalf of the series, to help her grow into her new role. Plus, I've been out on this coast a lot, seeing Holden. Nikki would call and want me to talk to her about racing. Or want me to go shopping with her." She paused. "That is, watch her shop."

We smiled at each other, and I felt a connection with her for the first time, which emboldened me to bring up my family. "I know that my looking into Billy's death is odd, since it's no secret he and I—and Holden—haven't been friends."

"So I understand."

"Nikki and Don asked, for the sake of the race." I didn't mention Frame Savings or Coleman's additional pressure.

Elizabeth wasn't as judgmental as I'd expected anyone allied with Holden to be. "It's good of you to want to help. Even if you don't solve the crime, it might bring comfort to people like Nikki to have you involved."

"I'll leave catching a murderer for the cops. I want to do what I can to make sure racing isn't tainted by this."

"That's really great of you." She leaned forward. "I'd also be happy to help you make sure the racing world is still seen as honest and respectable."

Crooks and cheaters were legion in racing's history, so I thought she aimed too high. But I was happy for the support. "Thanks. How much did you see Billy in the last year?"

"About once a month, with Holden, of course. Holden and Billy also spent time together when I wasn't around."

"Did you know what he was doing? How he was doing?"

"Working at the branch here. I'm not sure how it was going. His side of the story was that people didn't respect good ideas or respect him. He was frustrated with the entrenched bureaucracy at the bank, but he was fired up to make changes." She paused. "He felt the branch job was an attempt to marginalize him, to keep him from his rightful role in the bank structure. I remember him saying, more than once, 'I'll show them they won't keep me down long.'"

A job many people would give their right arm for, and he thought it wasn't worthy of him? What a useless sack of—no, Kate, no judgment. I gritted my teeth.

Nikki exited the dressing room in a swirl of green chiffon. She'd put a long, flowing, yet backless top over her zebra-striped leggings. I blinked. No, the other leggings had been leopard.

"What do you girls think?"

Elizabeth winked at me. "You look great, Nikki. The green really makes your eyes pop."

Nikki swept back into the changing room, and I turned to Elizabeth. "Where does she wear something like that?"

"No idea."

"Billy was making big plans and changes at work. Any idea what he did outside of it?"

"Aside from Nikki?"

I'd walked into that one. "Dating her, check. Anything else you heard about?"

"Coleman was taking Billy under his wing in the community."

"Volunteer work?"

"More like getting to know the local business community," Elizabeth replied. "Making connections to bring business into the bank. Breakfast meetings, dinners to entertain people, that sort of thing."

"I heard something about a Thursday morning breakfast meeting of influential businessmen. The local movers and shakers."

Nikki appeared in front of us again, in a screaming, hot pink bustier paired with the same zebra leggings. My eyes watered in response to the color.

"I remember something about the big dogs," Elizabeth said to me.

"You mean the BDBC." Nikki tossed the words over her shoulder as she examined herself in the mirror, hands to hips, curving her shoulders forward to emphasize her breasts.

"BDBC?" I asked.

"The Big Dog Breakfast Club. All the boys who meet Thursday mornings." Nikki met my eyes in the mirror. "That's not the *real* name. That's what my husband called it."

I exchanged equally confused glances with Elizabeth. "Your husband was in it?"

"The boys helped him make all kinds of money. He used to say it was the best club he'd ever joined. That the boys would never steer him wrong." She looked at the rings she wore and smiled. "I liked the group because when he made money from it, he'd buy me more baubles."

Considering the "baubles" she wore represented dozens of carats of gems, I understood her affection for it. "What kind of deals?"

"He wouldn't tell me, which was strange, since he told me more than I ever wanted to know about the catsup factory."

Don't ask.

"Do you know who else was in the club?" Elizabeth asked.

Nikki shrugged. "Coleman Sherain. Billy, sort of. Do you want me to find out more?"

"I'd appreciate it." I watched Nikki shifting back and forth to examine her shoes in the mirror. Five-inch, pink, translucent, strappy heels. "You know Coleman Sherain?"

She spoke first to Elizabeth. "I'm sorry, dearest, for what I'm about to say." She turned to me. "I hate that asshole."

Chapter Twenty-six

Elizabeth made a noise somewhere between a snort and a cough.

Nikki tripped over to the chairs, scooped up Pookie from her purse, and sat down with her on her lap. "I'm sorry, Lizzie, but it's true. I know you love your Holden-baby"—I concentrated on my breathing so I didn't gag—"but his father is a complete jerk."

Elizabeth whispered. "Don't worry, I kind of agree." She and Nikki giggled together.

Elizabeth is turning into Nikki. I've got to get out of here soon. "Why do you say that?" I asked Nikki.

"This stays between us girls, right?" She looked from me to Elizabeth and back, and offered up both pinkies. "Swear?"

We dutifully hooked pinkie fingers with her. "You have to understand, I'm not averse to male attention, but I don't engage with married men. At all. I won't go there. I'm also not fond of men who can't take no for an answer. Coleman was both of those."

"He hit on you?"

"Hard. Twice. Trotted out lines about his lavish apartment in town with its multimillion-dollar views. As if that would get me to break my rules." She harrumphed. "No view is that good. No man is that hot."

"Sounds like he has a routine," I suggested.

"It wasn't his first infidelity rodeo. Honestly, I think Elizabeth might have the only decent one in that family. Not that I've met them all. In fact, Katie, I've heard your father is quite a different breed."

"I guess so." *Should I thank her?* "What about Billy?"

"Let's get something to eat and a bottle of wine, and I'll tell you how that idiot thought he could bully and manipulate me. Be right back!" She tripped away to change.

My shock—and it seemed like Elizabeth's also—lasted until we were seated in a restaurant's outdoor courtyard a block away. Nikki ordered wine on the way in and wasted no time pouring us all large glasses when it arrived. She drank half of hers down and cooed.

"You'd been dating Billy for a few months," I began. "You were happy at first. At least you said he was attractive. What happened?"

Nikki sipped the rest of her wine more slowly. "He was hot. He gave me my Pookie-bear." She reached over and scratched the dog's head. "And he gave me useful information about racing. It seemed like fun having him also work on the race weekend, even if Donnie wasn't all that happy with him." She wrinkled her nose. "After a few months, I realized I'd let it become all about him—not only racing, but everything. Even then, it was easier to let things drift along for a while."

"We've all been there," I assured her.

"He was the first person I'd had a relationship with since my husband's death. For a while, it was nice to have someone else make the decisions, take care of me."

She paused so long that Elizabeth spoke up. "It wasn't nice anymore?"

"When I questioned his actions, he got angry."

I covered one of her hands with mine. "Was he violent?"

Nikki looked blank, then understood. "*Hell*, no. No one touches me if I don't want him touching me. Billy threw tantrums or got sly. Tried to tell me I should be grateful for his attention and connections. That the race and I would be lost without him. He made vague threats about disrupting the weekend."

Elizabeth got angry, fast. "That's outrageous! You should have—"

"No recourse unless he did something." Nikki shrugged. "It was easier to keep him around until the race was over. He couldn't have done anything at that point."

"That must have been awful, staying with him." I felt almost sorry for her.

"Cute little Katie. He was still smoking in bed. It wasn't hard…well, that would be a lie." She let loose a big, throaty laugh as she reached for the bottle.

Elizabeth choked on her wine, and I felt my cheeks flush.

"It wasn't difficult keeping him around," Nikki continued. "I simply stopped listening to his big plans for my money."

"Big plans?" I echoed.

"I remember." Elizabeth flushed, but that had to do with her empty wineglass. "He wanted to start a new team with you."

Nikki pursed her lips. "I'd pay and he'd run it. I didn't bother telling him it'd be a cold day in hell before that happened. He'd have been out on his ass soon enough."

I wondered if Billy might have talked her into it in the end.

Nikki caught my eye. "You see, Kate, I learned important lessons from my cheating husband and Dolly."

"Dolly?"

"Parton," Nikki replied. "Dolly says it takes a lot of money to look that cheap. I, on the other hand, look expensive, which takes even more money. My husband taught me it takes money to make money. Therefore, I'm not going to waste the money I have on something that won't make me enough money for me to live and look the way I want to."

She made sense. I needed more wine.

Nikki raised her glass. "Here's to poor Billy. He wasn't the big prize he thought he was. He saved me the trouble of dumping him by getting himself killed. But he was *outstanding* in bed. Rest in peace."

A strange epitaph.

We got away from the topic of Billy while we ate. Nikki wanted to know what it was like for both of us as women in racing, and she wondered why we didn't have any support groups.

"Actually, I had an idea." Elizabeth turned to me. "I want to start an informal networking organization for women in motorsports, in any role, from hospitality to drivers. Would you be interested? Help me get it going?"

I was surprised by the request—by the person making the request. Before that day, I'd never given Elizabeth credit for anything. Personality, emotion, commitment to a cause, nothing. Now I'd seen hints of all of them, and I was impressed. "I like that idea a lot."

"Great! Let's talk more next week. Think about invitations."

I'd already started a mental list.

A waiter approached and handed Nikki the check and a small, plain brown shopping bag. I made a move for my wallet, and she stopped me.

"No, sweetums, don't be silly. This is my treat for girls' day out." She didn't even look at the bill, but gave the hovering waiter a credit card. She reached into the brown shopping bag, removed two small, white boxes with enormous black bows, and handed one to me, one to Elizabeth.

Nikki put her hands together as if praying and bowed her head over them. "These are my gifts to you both. To remember our afternoon. Thank you for being with me. Namaste."

I stuttered out thanks, confused by the greeting I associated with yoga. Elizabeth was smoother about it, and I wondered if she was used to Nikki's displays of enthusiasm and affection. We opened our boxes to find matching pink balls of fluff, with clasps.

"A key ring?" I wondered, holding it aloft.

Nikki beamed, her fingertips pressed to her mouth. "It's a mink bag charm. You know, to hang on a bag and give it a little style."

"From Louis Vuitton. Nikki, you shouldn't have." But Elizabeth smiled as she said it.

Nikki pouted. "Don't be upset with me."

It was adorable, but mink? Louis Vuitton? Hang it on my bag and wait for it to fall off?! "Thank you, Nikki. It's completely unnecessary, and I love it."

"You're welcome. I thought it might remind you of Pookie and me." At her name, the dog poked her head out of Nikki's bag. "You know, we're silly on the surface, but sweet and tough underneath. You go ahead and put that on your bag, it won't get lost."

I laughed, impressed by her self-perception. That made two of my preconceived ideas about people turned upside down in the past couple hours. I'd need to rethink my approach.

Chapter Twenty-seven

Back at my hotel, I called Tara to ask about her sister, who was healing physically and was now at a different facility undergoing psychiatric evaluation. I thought Tara sounded tired but relieved, and I told her so.

"It feels terrible to say it," she replied, "but you're right. I wish it wasn't happening, but I'm glad she'll get professional treatment. Thank you for helping me by listening."

"I'm glad you had the courage to share the truth. I needed to hear it." I paused. "On another topic, do you know who Coleman's second wife is?"

"Only that she worked for Frame Savings. I'll ask around and find out for you."

"Just be careful."

After that call, I spent thirty minutes updating the list of people who might want Billy dead, reminding myself that putting a name on the list didn't equate to an accusation. I had three columns: Racing, Bank, and Personal/Family. I added Nikki Gray to the four names already listed in the "Racing" column: Don, Elizabeth, Erica, and Penny. I knew enough now to add some names to the "Bank" column, and I steeled myself to play fair and write everyone down. Tara Raffield and Jenny Shelton went on the list, along with "Other?" I didn't trust Billy to only have been a jerk to one person in his branch office, so there had to be more names.

I stared at the blank column for "Personal/Family." My instincts told me to write Coleman's name, and my rational mind kept asking why. *Because he has a mistress? Because he thought Billy acted too entitled and was headed for another demotion?* They were family. I wrote Coleman and Nikki down—even though Nikki was already in the Racing column—as well as Holden.

Then I called Detective Barnes at the Long Beach Police. I told him what I'd learned about Billy's unethical practices at the bank, his association with the "Big Dogs," and how angry he'd made everyone at the race organization.

"I don't expect it's useful to you," I admitted. "But I wanted to tell you what I'd learned."

"I like information. You never know what will be the key."

"How's your investigation going? Anything you can tell me?"

To my surprise, there was. "This is in confidence, but the stick we found at the scene was tested, and it's not the murder weapon. If you know of anything in your racecars or trucks that's about an inch in diameter, smooth except for a ridge on it, please let me know."

"It could be almost anything."

He sighed. "That's the problem."

We hung up and I wrote "murder weapon??" in my notebook and spent a minute feeling stumped. It was five o'clock, and Ryan would pick me up in an hour and a half for the gala. I put the notebook away and turned off my brain until it was time to get ready.

The start of the evening was a near repeat of the night before, as I waited on the hotel's red-carpeted entryway for Ryan. The difference was we'd both upgraded from casual wear to black tie. Even the valets noticed, one of them complimenting me as I waited.

I fidgeted in my full-length gown—navy, with a curlicue pink pattern at the sides, and mermaid style, fitted to the knees—and wondered how I'd get into the low-slung Corvette. But I needn't have worried. Ryan pulled up in a sleek, black BMW 5-series.

I did a double take. "How many cars do you own?"

"Borrowed it from a co-worker so you could get in and out more easily." He waved off the valet and walked around the car to open the door for me. "You look spectacular, Kate."

I looked him up and down, an athletic, handsome man wearing a tuxedo and a confident smile. "We both look pretty great."

He helped me into the car and kissed the back of my hand before closing my door. He glanced at me as we drove down the hotel driveway. "Any more family bombshells today?"

"No, thank goodness. But it wasn't without its surprises. And entertainment." I explained I'd had positive news about future sponsorship possibilities, but didn't go into details. I also described my shopping experience with Nikki and Elizabeth. And Pookie.

"You gotta love Beverly Hills." He grinned as he swung from La Cienega onto the freeway and floored the throttle.

"I feel like I'm in a movie. I'm sitting there, watching it all happening, talking to Nikki, and thinking no one will ever believe it's real. That she's real." I paused. "Except the obvious parts of her that are fake."

He laughed. "I know how you feel. It seems like most of it should be fake here. You know, they make movies, which are fake reality, so why should they feel reality is sufficient? Are they trying to avoid reality, improve on it, or be better than the reality next door? Hard to tell."

"I'm confused because I can't figure out Nikki. She's nice, and I think she's smart. But she sometimes talks like she's out of breath, hauls pocket dogs around everywhere, and only dresses in tight, cleavage-baring clothing. Is she playing me? Or is all of her for real?"

"I can't speak to her motives, but I can tell you she is what she seems: a very, very rich widow. And despite the look and behavior you've described, she's not stupid. I'd suggest not judging the book cover."

Point taken. "Do you know her?"

"I checked her out to be sure she wasn't dangerous."

"That's…sweet."

"I'm not telling you anything officially." He sighed. "If I'm being honest, which I understand may seriously jeopardize the outcome of this date, I wanted to be sure you wouldn't stumble into trouble."

"For that, I'm not sleeping with you tonight." I couldn't believe I'd said it. Kate Reilly, flirting. I wasn't usually good at that.

"Not tonight?" Ryan slid a glance sideways.

I studied his profile. He got more and more attractive the better I got to know him. The tuxedo helped. *What had he said?* "Did you look up anyone else?"

He smiled and waited a beat before responding to the change in subject. "Tara and Jenny are also who they say they are. Your friend Don Kessberg has a history of violence."

Remembering his outburst by the pool, I wasn't surprised. "He admitted to a temper."

"He was convicted once for assault, for severely beating a man who taunted him about losing a race. A long time ago, but you never know."

"Can you tell me that?"

"Those records are public, plus there are a couple newspaper articles. You can find the information yourself online."

"Good to know. And thanks for looking out for me."

He reached over and laced his fingers with mine. "Your turn. What am I in for tonight?"

"Your basic expensive-ticket fundraising dinner. We'll be seated at the table of a big BCRF donor. Some of my family will be there, as Frame Savings bought a table. Some speeches, introduction of the Beauté campaign spokeswomen—that's me and five other women—and a live auction."

"Anything good up for grabs?"

"That's why the bank is there. They helped me put together a package for a VIP trip for four to Petit Le Mans this year, including accommodations at Chateau Élan, tasting at the winery, transportation to and from the track, pit access during the race, meetings with all of the Sandham Swift drivers. And, if they can stay another day after the race, an afternoon of go-kart racing and coaching with me."

He released my hand as he prepared to exit the freeway. "You should know something about me, Kate."

"What's that?"

"I do love a good live auction." He winked at me as the light at the bottom of the ramp turned green. "And I miss going racing."

Chapter Twenty-eight

Two hours later, in the Bonaventure Hotel's California Ballroom, I stared at Ryan, dumbfounded. "You bid on that."

"And won." He was smug.

"How much does the—your job pay?"

"I have some family money." He patted my hand. "Don't worry about it. It's a donation to a great cause."

"You're right. Thank you."

I abandoned him to the approaching auction helpers wanting his credit card. The live auction continued around us, and I studied the man of mystery I'd brought as my date. When others asked, he referred to himself as an operational efficiency consultant, which didn't invite follow-up questions. I guessed that was the point. I hadn't asked why he didn't say he was with the FBI, but I started to wonder if I was sitting next to James Bond.

The auction helpers left, and Ryan fielded congratulations from others at our table. Two auction items later, the formal part of the evening was over. A ten-piece swing band resumed, and the small dance floor at the side of the room saw its first couples.

"Come on." Ryan hauled me to my feet.

"What? No, I can't."

"I'll teach you." He swung me into his arms. "Step, step, step-step. Repeat. Kate." I looked up from my feet to see him smiling. "If you can heel-and-toe downshift, you can do this. Feel the rhythm of the steps, like you'd feel the rhythm of an engine. Follow me, and don't look down."

"You *are* James Bond."

His chuckle made heads turn. "Not exactly. I went through cotillion as a kid."

Halfway through the next spin around the floor, Ryan led me to the nearest table. "I got a 'Come here' look from your father," he said into my ear.

We were only a few feet away from my father's table when I saw red. Edward sat between Holden and my father's wife in a chair that had been empty when I'd visited earlier in the evening. I struggled to stay calm. It wasn't enough that my father, his wife, and Coleman and Holden were all in attendance—plus Elizabeth Rogers, though she wasn't as problematic—but now the man who never passed up an opportunity to harass me? Why would my father let that happen?

Edward was red-faced and scowling, but it wasn't the sight of me that made him furious. He struggled to his feet, glaring at Ryan. "What are *you* doing here?"

My father knew Ryan from the Daytona race where we'd met more than a year ago, but of course, Edward knew him better, since Edward had driven on the team Ryan worked for undercover.

Ryan extended a hand to my father. "Mr. Reilly, good to see you again. Ryan Johnston."

My father's eyebrows went up. "Are you here officially?"

"He's my date."

"I'm based in Los Angeles now," Ryan added.

"How interesting," my father replied. "It's good to see you again. I think you know some of the people here." He led Ryan around the table to meet my stepmother, Amelia.

Elizabeth watched them, as she held Holden's hand in both of hers. Holden, meanwhile, glared at me, stony faced. Coleman, hand on his bowtie, stared disdainfully at Elizabeth and Holden before turning my direction. Edward seethed, and the two other guests at the table acted like timid rabbits, shrinking into themselves and darting frantic glances back and forth.

Edward moved toward me, stopping three inches too close for comfort. I held my ground, lifting my chin higher and trying to convey indifference.

"You are a fraud," he hissed. "Think you're an investigator? I'm going to enjoy watching you try, so I can see you fail. Again. Think you're a driver? You're not good enough. Worthless, and I'll expose you. Why didn't you die instead of my boy?"

Ryan and my father returned in time to hear Edward's last question. Ryan put an arm around my waist, holding me up as much as offering solidarity.

My father clenched his jaw. "Edward, I told you to stay away from Kate."

Edward bent forward, his shoulders shaking. "My boy," he choked out. I was almost moved by his emotion, but Edward looked at me from the corner of his dry eyes and smiled.

I crossed my arms over my chest, trembling. He'd wounded me with his words, but I refused to let it show.

My father gestured to Coleman to help Edward.

"I'm not doing this. We're out of here." I moved away.

"Kate..." my father began.

I took a deep breath, but I didn't speak.

"Please, wait. You need to speak with the others. Amelia and our two friends are very interested in your future plans."

I didn't even process his underlying message of potential sponsors. I got stuck on him telling me what I was required to do. "You think you can tell me what to do when you obviously don't care about me at all?" My voice rose by the end. I was breathing hard.

"Steady," Ryan murmured, stepping forward to put an arm around my waist again.

My father looked shocked. "Don't be ridiculous."

I drew a deep breath and might have screeched something damaging, but Ryan stopped me, herding my father and me to a doorway the servers had been using. "How about you two discuss this in a more private space?"

He guided us into a serving corridor, around a corner, and through a door into a small, unoccupied meeting room. He squeezed my hand before he left. "I'll be nearby."

When we were alone, my father started to pace. "How can you think I don't care about you? I brought potential sponsors tonight. How can you be that blind?"

"How dare you hold the sponsorship over my head to make me deal with your family? Is that all family is to you? People to do your bidding? If so, I want no part of it." My voice shook. "How could you bring him here?"

My father stopped moving and looked at me. "Edward?"

"He hates me. Why would you make me deal with him?" I refused to cry.

He frowned. "I'm sorry. He's part of the bank and part of the family, and the family always shows up to support bank initiatives. Always."

"Maybe you should have told me interacting with him at every turn was a condition of the sponsorship or of being part of your life. Then I would have had a choice." I hoped I sounded as bitter as I felt.

"I know we've all had our differences in the past, but we need to put it behind us."

"Are you *kidding* me?" I shouted it.

My father stared at me, silent and shocked.

Now I was the one pacing. Ranting. "How can you be that oblivious, James? You say I'm part of your family, but you don't think about what I need. You don't care that he hates me and takes every opportunity to tell me so. We talked about this and you said you're also mad at him for thinking I'm a whore like my mother. But now you're not? Then he tells me I'm—" I didn't want to repeat what Edward had whispered. I leaned my forehead against the gold-patterned wallpaper of the conference room, welcoming its cool, scratchy feel.

"Kate, what he said just now, comparing you to Billy. That's his grief talking. I'll address it with him." My father's voice was quiet. "He and I talked earlier today about the things he said in the past about your mother. He apologized. He was acting out of old information and habit. He doesn't think that now."

Yes, he does. "Did he apologize for paying my grandmother off, too?" I laughed. "You really think he's changed his mind? Then why did he tell me just now that I'm worthless? That he'll expose me for a fraud? Why did he look at me like I'm dirt?"

My father gritted his teeth. "I'm sorry. I'll speak to him."

I pushed away from the wall. "What good will that do? Are you the school principal about to discipline the bully? Except you're not. Or maybe you'll try, but he'll ignore you. You'll roll over, 'put it behind you,' *like you've done before.* He's already screwed up your life once. And now you think talking to him will make him stop going after me?" I shook my head. "You know what I still can't believe?"

My father grew more still and self-contained the angrier I got. "No."

I stepped close to him and looked him straight in the eye. "I can't believe with all that your precious brother Edward and his pal Coleman have done, you still choose them over me. You choose the family over me. You've done it for twenty-six years now. You're still doing it. You've never chosen me."

"What do you mean, what they've done? What does Coleman have to do with this?"

I unloaded, telling him everything I'd learned about Coleman's second family, Billy and Coleman's unethical and illegal dealings with Jenny, the apartment Edward and Coleman used for affairs, and the "big dog" businessmen that Edward and Coleman ran with. I told him the information came primarily from one source inside Frame Savings, with verification from outsiders. I didn't—and wouldn't—tell him my sources.

I could tell the news shocked him and made him as angry as I thought he should have been on my behalf. He spent a minute sifting through the information, a muscle in his jaw twitching, before he regained control. "I'm having a hard time believing this."

I'd heard enough. "Of course you don't believe me." I forced out a laugh. "Why would you believe me? I've never been good enough for you. Never in my life. Never been *enough*. Just once I'd like to be enough for you. For someone."

"I believe you. But I need to look into the accusations. Have proof before doing something about it. Before talking to my sister."

I fumbled for the doorknob, my vision blurred by tears. He put a hand on my arm, and I shook him off.

He kept talking. Pleading. "You're good enough. Don't let that into your head. I do choose you. I want you in my life. Stay, please. Talk with me and Amelia. Let's work this out."

I stopped in the open doorway. "There's nothing to work out. You find your courage and trust me—pick me—for once in your life. Or nothing."

I straightened my spine and raised my chin. Wiped the tears from under my eyes. "All I know is I won't do this anymore."

Chapter Twenty-nine

I had my game face back on by the time I found Ryan inside the ballroom. I slipped my arm through his. "Thank you for your support."

"Is everything all right?" He led me around the edge of the ballroom, away from the Frame Savings table.

"Family: easy come, easy go."

"I heard some of what Edward said—"

"Not now, please."

My mask must have slipped, because he curled an arm around my shoulders. "Another dance? It's a slow one, so I can kiss you on the dance floor."

"Tempting."

"Or we find a dark corner where I tell you how smokin' hot you are when you're angry."

I laughed, grateful for his efforts. "I'd like to find a couple people and leave, if you don't mind."

"I'm with you. Lead on."

We'd retrieved his car from the valet and gotten in when I saw Coleman exit the hotel and hand over a ticket for a car. He was alone.

I stopped Ryan when he put the car in gear. "I have an idea."

"Why do I think I won't like it?"

"It's nothing illegal, Agent Johnston."

"Except it could be considered stalking, harassment, or invasion of privacy."

"Not if he doesn't notice. I'm not going to talk to him, I only want to see where he goes."

"What's that going to tell you?"

"I don't know. But I want something useful to come out of this mess tonight. Especially after Uncle Edward told me he can't wait for me to fail."

"I never did like Edward. Okay, give me a kiss." He tapped his cheek, so I leaned over and pecked. He spoke again. "Since you begged me to show you how we do car-to-car surveillance, I'll demonstrate. You pick a car. Any car."

I grinned at him as Coleman pulled his vehicle around us and exited the hotel's driveway. "That silver Mercedes."

He really did give me a lesson in tailing someone as we followed Coleman west to Santa Monica and into a neighborhood of small bungalows. We didn't make the last right turn Coleman made, but pulled over to the curb and doused the lights. Fortunately, Coleman wasn't hard to find. He'd pulled his car into a driveway halfway down the block.

After he'd gone inside, we cruised down the street, and I noted the address. "I'm betting that's the second wife."

"And kids," he added.

"What?"

He navigated out of the neighborhood toward Wilshire Boulevard, to take us back into Beverly Hills. "I don't think Second Wife is playing hopscotch on the sidewalk or riding the two kids' bikes."

I turned to him. "You're good. I saw the bikes, but they didn't register. And I missed the sidewalk chalk."

He smiled. "Flattery will get you everywhere."

"How many times do I have to tell you how attractive you are before you'll look up ownership of the house for me?"

"You can't put a number on...wait, no. I'm not doing that."

"Tara was going to find out Second Wife's name. What if you simply look up who owns the house and tell me yes or no?"

Ryan pulled the car over on one of the wide, quiet residential streets below the Beverly Hills Hotel. He turned off the ignition. "You know that information is public record."

"It is?" *Learn something new every day.*

"How about this? I'll look it up for you, and you cut back on playing private investigator."

"I thought you understood why I was doing this."

"I do. But I want you to be more careful. No stunts like tailing someone. No asking random people questions about the cabal of local businessmen." He held up a hand. "I'm not telling you not to ask questions. I'm not trying to run your life. But leave anything active or dangerous to the pros. Turn the leads over to the cops and let them follow up. Tell me, and I'll see if I can help."

He reached down and unfastened my seatbelt, then took hold of my shoulders and pulled me closer. He spoke the next words a couple inches from my face. "You're good at handling danger on the track because that's what you're trained for. You're not trained for handling danger in the criminal world. Leave that to the experts. That's all I'm asking."

I couldn't argue with his reasoning, nor, with his eyes staring into mine and his lips that close, did I want to. *But I don't always know what questions might get me in trouble.*

Ryan moved closer, whispering, "Agreed?" with his mouth an inch away from mine.

I ignored the voice in my head and kissed him. Enthusiastically.

A few minutes later, I wandered the hotel again, finally settling on a chaise at the deserted pool. I felt too unsettled to prepare for sleep, but I wasn't sure what weighed on me. I shifted my feet up onto the chair and reclined, looking up at the night sky and admitting I was lying to myself. I knew what caused my unease. I was still furious at my father.

I frowned at the sky. *Be honest. You're angry, but you're also hurt.*

I had to get my pride out of the way and admit it. I was hurt by his actions, current and past. My grandparents had done everything they could to make me feel loved. But having no father and no mother, even though she was lost to death, left a hole where the doubting voices whispered, *You're not good enough.*

I wrapped my arms around myself. Edward's words had ripped open the protective covering on that hole inside me, and I'd lashed out in defense at both him and my father.

Your father isn't handling things well, but neither are you.

I felt sorrow deep in my chest. I hated disappointing myself. I felt good about expressing the anger I'd harbored for years and still believed he asked too much of me and not enough of his brother. I couldn't deny how exhausting every interaction with my father and his family was. Something had to change. I couldn't stay on the emotional rollercoaster.

The next morning, I got myself on a more even keel, working out, eating breakfast, and downing my first cup of coffee before dealing with the world, starting with Holly's voicemail.

"Good news is you looked spectacular last night, and so did Ryan. Bad news is, you're all over the Internet. I'll send links."

I didn't bother looking for her e-mail. The stories weren't hard to find.

"New Girlfriend Cheating on Lucas Already?"

"Girl Driver Two-Times Movie Heartthrob"

"World's Sexiest Man Not Enough for Her?"

Each was accompanied by the same photo of me and Ryan on the dance floor, looking at each other and laughing. I enlarged the photo. Holly was right, I did look great. So did Ryan. I scanned the articles and tried to be calm about what I couldn't fix. While I didn't like the notoriety focused on my love life instead of my driving, and I really didn't like "girl driver," they'd gotten my name right and accused me of nothing worse than dating two men. One even included a photo of me and Alexa with the Beermeier Racing car. Ryan had gotten off lightly, being referred to as "an unidentified man."

While I was online, I clicked over to my nemesis, Racing's Ringer, a racing gossipmonger who was anonymous to most of the world. I knew his identity, but the knowledge rarely helped me. Not only did he have a tidbit about the supposed love triangle of me, Ryan, and Lucas, but he'd also posted an item titled "Kate Reilly: Racing's Problem Child."

In it, the Ringer detailed the crimes—from cheating to murder—I'd been "involved in." He mentioned I'd been responsible for clearing them all up, but wondered why all the bad news swirled around me. He even mentioned Billy's murder, though he was good enough to skip the family connection, labeling Billy only "a key player at her newest sponsor."

But the worst was the feedback he included from unidentified members of the paddock. That chaos followed me around. That my driving wasn't worth the problems that accompanied it. The article intimated the opinions were widespread and continuing to proliferate.

I slumped back in my chair, closing my eyes, giving in to self-pity for a moment. I could deal with complicated family problems. I could handle a racecar. I could even manage to look for murderers. But I wasn't sure I could cope with the loss of my reputation and my sponsorship in a single evening. All of it together was too much. *It's quite a talent you have for chaos.*

Chapter Thirty

The endorphins from my Sunday morning workout didn't diminish my ability to go from self-pity to anger very quickly. I texted the Ringer, thanking him for the one-sided smear campaign on my reputation.

His reply came back promptly, apologizing but claiming he had to report the sentiment, as he'd heard it from too many directions. He did promise to write a follow-up any time I wanted to give him an official interview. I threw my phone on the bed in disgust.

I made more coffee, then reviewed the rest of my e-mail and social media notifications. I called Holly for a strategy session on how to handle it all.

She picked up immediately. "If it isn't my favorite femme fatale."

"Funny." I told her about the Ringer's response to my message.

"That's all right, Kate, don't you worry. That boy's going to owe us one."

"Which doesn't help me now." I filled her in on the blowout with my father. "I went to bed wondering if I'd lose my sponsor. But hey, I wake up wondering if anyone will ever put me in a car again, so maybe it'll all work out."

"Overreact much? Sugar, get a grip. It's good press, and you'll ride out the negative aspects. Ignore the posts. If you can't, refer to Ryan as a friend with his first name only, and talk about the money the gala raised for breast cancer research."

"Give them my message, don't respond to theirs." I started to return to my senses.

"I'll be there tomorrow. Try to make it one more day without finding anyone dead."

"You're hilarious. Did you find someone to give us costs for racing in NASCAR?"

"Two sets of data coming later this week."

"Great. I'm going to e-mail Alexa this morning to start getting IndyCar numbers."

We disconnected after confirming Holly's arrival time the next day. In a calmer frame of mind, I composed and sent a message to Alexa Wittmeier, asking for Beermeier Racing's costs for a full-season IndyCar effort, as well as an Indy 500-only package. I also included a link to the national entertainment magazine article featuring her and her car.

She called me within fifteen minutes, in top spirits. "I'm happy to hear your sponsors are coming through." She chuckled. "I expect it wouldn't ever be dull with you on the team."

I gathered my courage. "I was concerned I'd already added to the team's workload, dealing with this nonsense. It's not a problem?"

"Exposure always takes effort. The team liked working with you."

A variety of emotions flooded my system, warming me. Relief was paramount, followed closely by pride and a trickle of excitement. "I'm so glad."

"If you don't mind some advice, ignore the crap."

"Which crap?"

"The horseshit about people thinking you don't belong in the paddock. Ignore it. Trust me when I tell you it's a bunch of small-minded assholes feeling threatened. All they know to do is lash out at anyone who doesn't fit their idea of normal."

"I appreciate that. You know who's saying it?"

"No idea."

I clued in. "You got the same thing when you raced?"

"Got, am getting, will continue to get. I wish I could tell you it stops when you climb out of the driver's seat for good, but it doesn't. We're still partially outsiders."

"How do you deal with it?"

"Brace yourself, and ignore it." She laughed again. "That's a contradiction. Be prepared to hear questions about taking a man's job, deserving something less, and being a problem because you're different. That way you're not blindsided when an ignorant idiot spouts off. But ignore them. Have a small group of close, trusted associates you go to for reality checks. Ignore everything else."

I spent a moment coming to terms with the idea I would never feel like I fully belonged. That I'd always be different. *You're used to it now, aren't you?* "I appreciate the advice. It's hard knowing who to listen to."

"Kate, if you drive for me, I'll always be straight with you. No politics, at least between us, and no B.S. I know our operation isn't the same scale as the big boys in IndyCar"—she referred to the three best-funded and biggest teams in the series—"but we've got smart, good people, and we're on the cusp of bigger things. Plus, I can promise you, we'll never treat you like you don't belong. Or like you're less than any male driver."

I thought about her words after we'd gotten off the call. What surprised me was Alexa selling me on Beermeier Racing. With funding from one sponsor in hand, and money from a second under discussion, I would have options. I might even be courted by teams. The idea was heady, and I let myself daydream about driving for the mythic names in open-wheel racing, piloting the best available equipment to poles and podiums. And then I thought about having a real connection to my team. A mentor, like Alexa. I'd have to find the right balance.

As I spun a fantasy about drinking the iconic milk in the winner's circle of the Indy 500, my phone signaled a text message. Tara Raffield brought me back to earth with two women's names: Lucille Tremmel and Rachel Krimmer. Both were former Frame Savings employees, Tara reported, and both had affairs with Coleman Sherain. But she didn't know if either had stuck with him for the long term.

I thought of Coleman in unflattering terms as I texted Ryan, asking if he'd looked up the house information. He, too, called instead of replying.

"I had a good time with you last night, Kate. Thanks for including me."

The evening's events flashed through my mind, from mediocre chicken to Ryan winning the auction, from my meltdown over family to his sizzling kisses. "It was memorable."

He laughed. "I have to admit, I've never had a date so well-documented and publicized."

I sucked in a breath. "Is that a problem for you at work?"

"Only for the teasing." He paused. "The photo was great. You looked radiant."

It was an old-fashioned word, a compliment I'd only ever heard my grandfather use. I liked it. "You looked pretty good yourself." I refocused. "About the owners of that house."

"I suppose I can't distract you."

"Did you look it up?"

"I did. And as I said, it's a matter of public record."

"Tell me if it's Lucille Tremmel or Rachel Krimmer."

He sighed. "I don't want to know how you have those names, do I?"

I jumped up, feeling a surge of triumph, and started to pace. "I knew it! Is it Lucille?"

"Yes. You're going to stay away from her and that house, right?"

"I promised you I would. Nothing active or dangerous. Careful questions only."

I heard him exhale. "I'll hold you to that."

A few minutes later, I got another text. This time it was Lucas reminding me to ignore the tabloid press and telling me he missed me. I sat down for a minute, flustered. I should be over the movie-star freakout reaction. *But he'd played romantic comedy leads, action heroes, and Mr. Darcy. And he* misses *you!* I reminded myself he wasn't his screen roles, that I didn't really know him. Yet. Until our date the next night.

I pushed those nerves away and collected my gear. Time to meet the other movie star in my life, but on my turf.

Chapter Thirty-one

I saw Penny as soon as I walked into the K1 Speed karting center in Torrance shortly before noon. Maddie's assistant stood near the registration desk, head bent to her phone, as always.

I went to her before checking in. "Everything all right? Is Maddie here?"

She slipped her phone in a pocket. "We're checked in, and we've paid for you. You need to set up your account. Maddie's tucked in a back corner."

I created my username, "Kate28," to display on the screens with my session times, and I joined Maddie, Penny, and two young women I didn't recognize. Penny introduced them as her cousins, Ellie and Andrea Iwen. They were twins: eighteen, tall, slim, and gorgeous. Every male eye in the place was on them, while they seemed totally unaffected.

"They're my diversionary tactic. No one notices me next to them." Maddie smiled at me. "I'm only going to throw a diva meltdown if they beat me on the track."

I glanced at the two girls. "Any go-karting experience?"

"Never been in one," one of them replied.

I turned to Maddie. "Piece of cake. Let's go."

The fourteen-turn, slick, indoor track wasn't much like the Long Beach street circuit, except that both were flat, with little banking in the turns. An electric go-kart also wasn't anything like the Toyota Scion Maddie would race next weekend, but seat time was seat time. The more minutes Maddie spent in a vehicle thinking about how to maximize speed and make every turn more efficient, the better a driver she'd be.

We did two on-track sessions, took a break for water and track talk, and went back for two more sessions behind the wheel. After that, Penny produced deli sandwiches, fruit, and chips from a tote bag, and Maddie and I sat at a booth to eat lunch.

While we ate, I asked how the movie shoot was going. Maddie's eyes shone with pleasure. "The shoot itself is fine. Long hours. But I'm having so much fun with the transformation my character undergoes."

"Lucas told me you play an investigator."

"A real by-the-book, stick-up-her-ass type. But what's great is how she changes. See, she starts as prim and proper, but she falls for Lucas' character and gets sucked into his world."

"He's a bad guy?"

She wiggled her free hand. "It's not black and white. He did a bad thing. He's done a lot to make up for it in his life, done good for a lot of people, but he can only run so far. That's what he learns: karma will find you. Whereas I learn to have more understanding for what people are going through. To let go of requiring perfection of other people. Of myself. And to work with what life hands you without complaining it should be something else." She took a drink of her diet soda. "Basically, I get to solve a crime and show the character maturing into a more reasonable human being. And that's fun."

"Do your characters end up together?"

"Come see the completed film." She grinned. "I'll get you tickets for the premiere."

"As long as it's not a race weekend, I'll be here."

Maddie had done nothing but eat, sleep, and shoot the film for the five days since she'd been in the car on the Long Beach track, and she wanted to know all the details of my L.A. adventure. I told her about the good bits: my oval test, potential sponsor news, shopping on Rodeo, and my delight in the Beverly Hills Hotel's luxury.

"What about your cousin's death? How's that going? Do you have suspects?"

I blew out a breath and gave her the bare-bones outline of who I'd talked to and what I'd seen, including Jenny Shelton's attempted suicide.

Maddie grew somber. "That poor woman. What terrible things drove her to feeling so hopeless?"

"From what I understand, she's been dealing with a mix of personal, professional, and health problems. I've been talking with her sister, Tara." I hesitated, then plunged in. "Tara works for the bank, and she's mad enough—at how her sister was treated while she worked there—to spill a bunch of family secrets. Those might help me investigate Billy's death."

Maddie watched me, but I got the feeling she wasn't exactly seeing me. "I'd like to meet Tara." She noticed my confused expression and bit her lip. "I know how she feels. My brother committed suicide when we were teenagers, and I've been active in the American Foundation for Suicide Prevention for many years. I'd like to help if I can."

I promised to connect them, not sure what an Oscar-winner could do to help a bank teller. Then again, if I'd learned anything during my brief association with Maddie, it was she didn't fit any stereotype I'd ever heard of.

She folded up her empty sandwich wrapper. "Enough sadness. We've paid for two more sessions. Let's go beat these other yahoos."

Back in my rental car later, I fielded a call from a hated relative's personality-challenged girlfriend. Who was growing on me. *That'll teach me to judge without getting to know someone.*

"Hi, Elizabeth."

"Hi, Kate." I heard rustling sounds and a door closing. "I felt you should know something I didn't bring up yesterday."

"About what?"

"Billy." She sighed. "We spent so much time bashing him, but I wanted you to know he wasn't all that bad."

If her standard was Holden, I didn't trust her judgment. "Mmmm, 'kay."

"I know he was terrible to you. But—oh God, it sounds like a cliché—he really had a thing for animals. Dogs, mostly. He wanted to save them from all those kill shelters. He bought land and opened his own doggie retirement community, out east toward the desert somewhere. He wanted to save every dog he could. Even used to go around to the L.A. shelters and find homes for the dogs about to be put down."

I tried to reconcile the self-centered, entitled jerk I'd met with that generosity.

She kept talking. "He'd train any dogs he could get young enough to be service dogs. Probably trained three or four in the time I knew him."

I remembered the trio of non-purebreds at Nikki's house. "How many dogs did he have?"

"Three. A big, old chocolate Lab, a black-and-white Terrier mutt, and a puppy that was his latest service dog trainee."

"Nikki has his dogs now."

"She does, but I'm going to take the puppy. Nikki doesn't want to do the training, and besides, it was my idea Billy acted on. I've always wanted to raise guide dogs." She sighed. "It's the least I can do to make something positive out of this for Holden."

"This is a surprise." I didn't want to feel sympathy for Billy. Still less did I want to feel any admiration. "I hope someone will keep his shelter running."

"Holden will, for now." She paused. "I know it's out of character, Kate. But Billy had a good side also. There are people, and plenty of sweet dogs, who will miss him a lot."

Even if I won't. "Do you have any idea why he did all that?"

"He mentioned once making sure no dog ever felt unwanted, which was funny, since he grew up with his own family all around. It's not like *he* ever went into a shelter or foster care or something. Another time he talked about only being able to count on a dog's love."

"You sound like you didn't believe him."

"I believed him," she assured me. "But I didn't understand how he could feel like no one cared for him when he had family. When he had so many advantages in life."

I'd wondered something similar: How he could feel entitled to more when he had so much? "I suppose we can't predict how someone will turn out, based on their environment."

"True."

I couldn't say that her information had changed my mind about Billy. But I'd softened. I felt a smidgen of sympathy, instead of none at all.

Chapter Thirty-two

On my way north on the 405 freeway, I also called Tara to see if Jenny was able to have visitors. She wasn't, but Tara offered to buy me dinner, and I met her near the hospital at an upscale pizza café.

After we ordered, she had more information for me. "I checked online calendars for Coleman, Edward, and Billy," she said, and I could see they'd all marked themselves out Thursday mornings. I couldn't tell for what. There was only an acronym."

"Let me guess, BDBC?" Her eyes got big, and I related what I'd learned about the group from Nikki.

"That explains some of the other folders I saw in the network labeled 'big dogs.' In fact, there was a membership roster I can get you."

"How did you see that information? Did you have to break in somewhere?"

"Would you believe there are totally unsecured files on our internal network? I remoted-in from home last night and found folders for Coleman, Edward, and Billy in a public drive." She curled her lip. "Their calendars have no security on them, either. I can see everything about all of their meetings, including confidential personnel data. I need to tell human resources about that."

I smiled. "Maybe wait a week or two?"

"You bet." She laughed. "Anyway, you want those names? I remember a couple of them, but not all of them."

"You opened the file?"

"I looked at a bunch of files. I was curious if our awful trio would be on the list. They were." She closed her eyes. "I only recall the two names that were crossed out, because I remember the news stories. Bubba Doyle and Richard Arena, local bigwigs busted for insider trading, unfair business practices. Also money laundering."

My eyebrows went up.

Tara misunderstood. "Bubba Doyle is quite a name, isn't it? Or nickname."

"I met Richard Arena."

I shouldn't have been surprised. After all, Edward had driven for Richard Arena's team at the 24 Hours of Daytona. They got connected somewhere. But I hadn't expected their association extended beyond the racing world into the business world.

The waiter delivered our meals, sparing me the need to explain how I knew about Arena's empire of evil deeds. I took a bite of my bacon, pancetta, soft egg, mozzarella, provolone, and black pepper pizza. "If Arena was part of that group, we know they weren't Boy Scouts."

Tara cut into her own mushroom-and-cheese pizza. "That's what I thought. I'll get you the list."

I squirmed. "How about telling me the names on it? Sending or printing the file seems worse than sharing some of the information."

"Whatever you want. Personally, I don't care. I've got to get out of there anyway. I hate them for what they've done to Jenny, and even before that, I was sick of the boys' club."

"Not many women around?" I sipped my water.

"There are plenty in the lower ranks. Only a couple in the upper levels. One woman on the board. It's disappointing."

"Sounds like racing."

"Doesn't it get exhausting? Fighting perception and attitudes all the time?"

I shrugged. "Racing is all I've ever wanted to do. I know I can make my dreams happen if I keep moving forward, keep pushing."

"That's the problem. I don't care about banking enough to fight that hard. It might be easier if I had female friends in the company to talk to."

"Aren't there mentoring opportunities or women's networking groups? We're even talking about starting one for women in racing. Surprisingly enough, that was Elizabeth's idea. She's Holden's girlfriend."

"I wouldn't figure her for girl power."

"You know her?"

Tara finished a bite of pizza. "Seen her around the office a few times. Saw her more in her element, I guess, at the Media Day."

"When you were following Billy."

She looked embarrassed.

"Did Elizabeth talk to Billy much that day? Who else did he talk to?"

Tara didn't know all the names, but she clearly identified Nikki, Maddie Theabo, Maddie's assistant Penny, and Don Kessberg and Erica Aarons from the Grand Prix Association. Then she surprised me. "Coleman was even there."

"What was he doing?"

"I have no idea. I was sitting in one of the empty grandstands, and I saw Coleman get out of a Town Car, cross the footbridge over the track, and find Billy. Coleman literally dragged Billy out of a conversation. They headed out of the main area, toward the convention center."

"Toward the parking structure. What time was this?"

"About two."

"Did you see Coleman leave?"

Tara shook her head and played with the pendant she wore. "I was so concerned with Coleman not seeing me I left the track, got some food, and walked around on the city streets to the plaza. I never saw when Coleman left. I never saw Billy after that either."

"You watched him for weeks, but got scared off in the last hour of his life and missed his killer."

She gave me a weak smile. "Oops."

"I can't blame you, after you saw Coleman show up, but it's too bad."

"That's why I'm trying to help now. I'll see what else I can dig up on the network at the office."

"Be careful." I wanted to tell her not to risk herself, but I wanted her insider information more. Maybe I could help her in return. "You know I've been coaching Madelyn Theabo for the celebrity race?"

"I saw you with her the other day. She seems so nice."

"She's as great as you think. I was with her today, and I told her what happened with your sister—what I saw, not the background. Maddie's been through the same thing. Or worse. She's involved with a national suicide prevention organization, and she wants to meet you. To talk to you."

Tara's eyes were big. "I'm not going to turn down the chance to meet Madelyn Theabo. But I'm not sure what she'd want to talk to me about."

"That's between you two. I'll give her your cell number. Maybe you can talk at the race next weekend."

Tara looked confused, and I barreled on. "Have you heard of grid girls? Women, always wearing tight clothing, holding flags next to a car on the pre-race grid?"

"I've seen them. Haven't really cared, since they're there for the men."

"Right? It's annoying. But we're going to turn the concept on its head next weekend."

"Grid boys?"

I laughed. "Better. My sponsor, Beauté, is partners with the Breast Cancer Research Foundation, and Beauté is running a contest to find three grid girls for my car for this race. We're looking for breast cancer warriors, so the contest asks entrants to tell us why they should be picked, whether they've fought the disease or they've supported others in the fight."

"That's wonderful." Her eyes filled with tears.

I tried to keep my own eyes from watering, as they did almost every time I thought about the idea. "If it goes well here, we'll do it for the rest of the races on the schedule this year."

"I'd love to see that."

I smiled. "They're letting me add a fourth person. You, if you'll come."

She agreed enthusiastically. Back at my hotel room, I sent her the information, sent Penny Tara's contact information for Maddie, and changed into my party clothes. It was time to trade movie stars for rock stars.

Chapter Thirty-three

I took a cab two miles to the famed Troubadour club in West Hollywood, where the drums and bass of the current band got inside you even out on the sidewalk. After giving my name to the man at the microscopic box office window, I got a neon yellow wristband with the club name on it, and I entered the front hallway. I bypassed the bar in its own room on the left, and I started to open the interior door to the main room before I backtracked.

Halfway down the bar was Chris Syfert, a successful music agent and accomplished amateur racecar driver. I'd met her and her more famous cousin, rock star Tommy Fantastic, when they drove an ill-fated third Corvette with Sandham Swift at the 24 Hours of Daytona. That first race had been a disaster, but I was pleased they'd joined us again at the recent Daytona 24 to give it another go. Their persistence got them second in their class. As Chris and I bonded in the wee hours of the night, waiting for our stints, she'd insisted I see them when I was in Los Angeles. Lucky for me, Tommy had a gig and Chris got me on the guest list. I tapped her shoulder, interrupting her conversation with a young, bearded hipster.

Chris turned to greet me with a hug. She had to bend down to do it, since she stood five inches taller than me, even without her three-inch heels. "So good to see you!"

She'd been talking to the drummer of the band Tommy would be playing with. After he excused himself, I climbed up on his stool and asked the bartender for a bottle of Corona.

"It's not Thomas' full band tonight?" I asked Chris. Tommy went by Thomas Kendall at the track, where I'd gotten to know him. I never knew which name to use.

"No. The guys are friends of Tommy's, protégés really, and clients of mine. They cooked up the plan to get Tommy to guest with them on lead guitar for a show here. Tommy can't go more than two weeks without being on stage."

"I'm glad it worked out so I could see him play." Tommy was the lead guitarist for a multi-platinum rock band with crazy longevity for the music industry. They'd hit number one with their first album twenty years ago and never looked back. This small club would be a big change from the stadiums Tommy usually played. I said as much to Chris.

"He loves small shows. Really misses that close-up connection to the audience. He does this kind of thing whenever he can." She laughed. "You should see when the whole band plays here, the Roxy, or the Satellite. They do it under a fake band name, but people still figure it out and pack the joint."

The band playing inside the club stopped with a flourish. After a brief silence, we heard recorded music start up at a lower volume. Chris slipped off her stool. "Let's go find Tommy in the green room."

At the far end of the main room, past a security guard, we climbed stairs next to the stage to reach a long, narrow room filled with a brown couch, tons of music gear, and a half-dozen people. Windows on the left wall overlooked the stage. A door at the end led to a bathroom. Tommy sat on an arm of the couch, but jumped up when Chris and I appeared.

"Kate!" He picked his way over four pairs of legs to throw his arms around me. Then he led us past the people on the couch, tossing out introductions and in the same breath telling me not to worry about names. Chris and I sat down. Tommy leaned a shoulder on the wall.

"Tell me how you've been. How are you enjoying L.A.? What have you been doing with yourself out here?" He lobbed the questions at me rapid-fire and didn't stay still for more than two seconds at a stretch, rolling his neck, cracking his knuckles, bouncing from foot to foot.

Chris grinned. "Try not to mind Tommy. This is pre-performance adrenaline. His way of psyching himself up. I've tried to tell him he doesn't need the energy of an arena show here, but he never listens."

He shook out his arms. "Babe, you know I can't play without my ritual."

Now I understood how Tommy could eat the way I'd witnessed, but still remain wiry. He must work onstage like we did in the racecar. I smiled at him. "I understand rituals." I filled them in on my exploits of the past few days, including the identification of Billy's body.

"I always thought those two punks would come to a bad end," Chris put in.

Tommy growled. "No more than they deserved." Tommy had owned the car destroyed by Edward, Billy, and Holden's greed. We'd all been friends with the driver who'd died as a result.

We were silent a moment with our memories. It was almost a year and three months since the tragedy. Losing a teammate would forever weigh on us, despite Tommy and Chris having a successful return to Daytona and the parties involved—Billy, Holden, and the driver they'd paid to run our car off the road— paying for their crimes with community service, monitoring, fines, and even jail time.

Besides, I was sure none of us thought Billy and Holden had paid enough. *Or maybe Billy had? Could his death be due to what he'd done in Daytona? If so, will Holden be next?* Unlikely, so long after the fact.

We caught up in between songs while the next band played their set, and when they finished, Tommy popped up from the bench he'd perched on. "Showtime!" He grabbed a padded guitar case and moved to the door. The room got busy for the next five minutes, as the previous band stored instruments in cases or collected their gear and left.

I thought about the musical history that green room had seen. Since the club's opening in 1957, everyone from Bob Dylan, Joni Mitchell, and Elton John to Led Zepplin, Pearl Jam, and the Red Hot Chili Peppers had played there. And Johnny Cash. And Prince. The club was legendary, and the green room had held them all.

Chris turned to me with a bottle of water she'd fished out of a small cooler under the windows. "Are you investigating Billy's death?"

I wrinkled my nose. "I'm asking some questions, but I don't have any idea where they're leading me. I'm looking into things only because people have asked me to do what I can to keep the racing world from looking like a group of murderers and crooks."

She almost spit out her water. "There's no denying it's true, especially the crooks."

"We don't have to emphasize it."

She laughed. "What have you come up with?"

I explained what I'd learned of Billy's life and what I'd uncovered so far. "What's amazing is how he seemed to have found a new set of shady types here, in a new business environment, like this club of local businessmen who had to be up to no good. Get this, one of the club's former members was Richard Arena. He was part of this 'Big Dog Breakfast Club' Billy had joined. Along with his father, Edward, also known as Ed Grant, and his uncle, Coleman Sherain. Coleman is Holden's father."

"That's quite a family you have there, Kate."

"Trust me, I want no part of it, although somehow I keep getting sucked back in."

"The name of that club rings a bell." She tapped an index finger against her cheek. "I've heard of them. Never knew who was in it, but it doesn't surprise me to hear Arena was."

"What had you heard?"

"Whispers. The sort of thing where everyone has an idea, but no one wanted to admit to knowing for sure." She eyed me. "That's the group to go to when there aren't normal people you can hire. And by 'normal,' I mean legal."

I hadn't expected that response.

Chris nodded. "Whether you need money laundered, insider information on a deal, or someone gotten rid of, that's the group to see."

Holy shit, like the Mob? "They *do* that kind of thing?"

"Or hire out. That's where to make the connections you need."

I dropped my head into my hands as Tommy played a riff on stage and fans screamed. *What did I get myself into this time?*

She shrugged. "Like I said, some family you've got there."

The two sets Tommy played with his protégé band were amazing, and I felt special being an obvious friend of the rock star in the room. Chris and I left the club together sometime after one in the morning, half an hour after Tommy had finally stopped playing. Tommy had encouraged us both to join him and the band for a meal at an all-night diner. We'd both declined.

I was tired enough as it was the next morning, but fatigue didn't stop me from giving everything I had to the morning's activities: a visit to breast cancer patients with the Breast Cancer Research Foundation.

I'd made plenty of hospital and care center visits in the year and a half I'd been working with the BCRF and Beauté. This one had extra impact, due to two women in their thirties.

Erin Charlton had been selected to be one of my "grid girls" for the race. She'd gotten the all-clear on her own bout of breast cancer, but she was back at the hospital supporting her sister-in-law, Janel, through a first round of chemo. We chatted about their excitement that Erin would be at the race and about their treatments. I asked Erin how she'd gotten through her own last rounds, knowing Janel had been diagnosed with the same disease.

"I won't tell you it was easy. But Janel—" Erin gestured to her sister-in-law, currently hooked up to an IV "—was my rock through my own treatment. She got me through, and now I'll be here for her."

"It must seem like life is too unfair."

Janel smiled at me. "There's a lot of anger. Unfocused, since there's no one to blame."

Erin took Janel's hand. "We've both come to the point of…
what is it? Acceptance?"

"Forgiveness," Janel said quietly.

Erin smiled. "Getting mad at God or the universe doesn't
help. But you're still angry. Janel and I both had to let go of it and
forgive. Accept. Know the anger didn't do anything to anyone,
it only hurt us. Letting go of it actually made us stronger."

Her words resonated deep inside me. I absorbed the idea
of forgiveness. Of acceptance. I might not be fighting a deadly
disease, but I had my own troubles. And I felt the truth of her
words. Fighting only caused me more pain.

Chapter Thirty-four

I pulled myself together and finished my visits, looping back to wish Janel well and tell Erin I'd see her on Saturday. I drove toward Los Angeles International Airport in a daze. I was at least an hour early to pick Holly up, but I needed a quiet place and some air. I found a surprisingly lonely stretch of beach and walked it, hands in my jacket pockets, bare feet in the sand, mind in turmoil.

Anger. It's anger I have in common with Erin and Janel. I'm so angry at my father and his family, I sometimes can't think straight. Mostly at my father.

I had to evaluate it logically, as Erin had, and ask myself if my anger helped anyone. *It helped me feel good, righteous.* Until I felt like a fool or a brat. Or felt weak.

My being angry didn't help my father or my relationship with him. Didn't make a difference in how anyone else in the family treated me. Though it might hurt my sponsorship.

Did feeling angry help *me*? I pondered that question as I watched seagulls and even pelicans swoop over the sand and waves in front of me. I turned to the north and saw the Santa Monica pier with its Ferris wheel. I quit stalling and looked inside myself again.

I might think being angry makes me feel good, but it doesn't last. What lasts is my frustration and my...petulance? Am I acting like a child? I'd been participating in a cycle of behavior with my father and his family: engage, take offense, get mad, and sulk when they didn't agree with me. Repeat, over and over. *Sounds like a child to me.*

I walked down to the edge of the water and kicked at the cold foam that swept over my feet. Now I was angry at myself. And at my family for making me this way.

I laughed out loud. "Way to go. Keep pushing the blame away."

I'd never liked how I reacted to my father and his family. I'd never felt in control of my reactions, which were based in fear and vulnerability. Based in my own insecurities.

I'm afraid they'll reject me. Again. Afraid they won't like me. But I know most of them don't like me no matter what. Why expect anything different?

I stared at the waves for a while, coming to terms with my faulty expectations. Trying to readjust them. I sighed.

"Fix this, Kate. First, stop reacting. Don't let them control you. Only *you* control you." I said it out loud, even though only the seagulls could hear me.

In racing, we talked about running our own race and not responding to what our competitors were doing—we'd change tires on *our* schedule, not because another team took new rubber. I hoped I could function like that with my father and his family. Stick to my own agenda and ignore anything they tried to lure me into. Especially bad behavior.

"Second, decide who you will allow into your emotions. The rest of them become business." I usually knew better than to allow my emotions to interfere with business. Or to let them intrude while behind the wheel. But my father and his family blurred the line. I had to draw and enforce the line myself.

Should I cut them all off? Should I drop the sponsorship? As much as the idea of losing my ticket to the Indy 500 pained me, I considered it. I'd have to scramble more for money and rides, though I still had the possibility of Beauté's sponsorship. I'd have to cancel meetings and contracts, disappoint my father, and possibly damage my career by stopping what had been set in motion. But it could be done. If I needed to.

I shoved my career-panic aside and really thought about my life with and without Frame Savings' backing. My future looked bleak without it and horrible with it, if I kept going down the road I'd been on. But I thought I could stick to the third option: change my approach.

Relief flooded my system, and I felt cold thanks to the freezing ocean water. I backed up to the softer sand that still held some warmth from the sunny day, seeing a fog bank well out to sea, headed landward.

I decided to set my own rules for interacting with the staff of Frame Savings, regardless of whether they were related to me or not. All business, no emotion. I also decided, without examining it head-on, I didn't want to cut my father off. Or his wife and kids, my half siblings.

But they were the only ones I'd let in. The others would jeopardize my career and my reputation. I lifted my head to take deep breaths of the ocean air. I felt like an adult again.

As I leaned against my rental car wiping the sand off my feet, my phone buzzed with a text message. Holly had arrived in Los Angeles at last.

It took a while to collect her and her bags, make our way north, find parking, and wait to be seated for a late lunch. But finally we were seated at a table under the red-and-white-striped awning of the Sidewalk Café, in the center of the Venice Beach boardwalk. We ordered food and iced teas and settled back to enjoy the view.

Many of the people we saw were tourists, but there were obvious locals, including roller-skating women in cutoff jeans shorts and bikini tops, zipping through the crowd sporting big headphones and deep tans. There were also beefy men heading to the famous Muscle Beach, an area of the boardwalk where serious athletes pumped enormous piles of iron on an outdoor patio. Plus the street performers, sidewalk vendors, and homeless. The view was colorful and entertaining, even without the spectacular scenery of grass, sand, palm trees, coastline, and ocean.

After we'd watched for a while, and Holly had sucked down a first glass of iced tea and gotten a refill, I broke the companionable silence. "I saw Miles finished fifth, which he seemed happy about. How did the weekend go?"

"The whole team was thrilled with fifth after struggling all weekend. One of those cars that came off the truck unhappy. And Bristol! What a place."

"I want to see it someday."

"Come back with me to the night race later in the season. You know the saying that it's like flying a jet plane in a toilet bowl? They're not kidding. Nuts."

"How was being The Girlfriend?"

She laughed. "Sugar, that was an *experience*. I haven't been so thoroughly wished to hell by so many people in my life."

"By the team?"

"The team was great. Everyone working with Miles basically knew about us already, so it wasn't a big deal. No, it was the women hanging around trying to bang drivers."

The racing world sometimes called them "pit lizards" or "pit ponies," but Holly and I hated the terms. Of course, we didn't think much of the women either, whose sole mission was to have sex with any racecar driver they could, married or not.

Holly sipped her tea. "There were also women involved in the Series—broadcasters or suppliers—who seemed unhappy I was there. Plus others who were…let's say, suspicious. Like Miles' fan club president."

I groaned. Miles' fan club president hated me for wrecking Miles, as he saw it, two years ago in a race.

Holly shrugged. "He's protective. Thinks no one's good enough for his idol. Certainly not little, old, nobody me."

"Don't say that. You're not nobody."

"In his eyes. Not in mine or Miles', and that's what matters." She smiled. "Miles was great. So happy to have me there."

"You going to go with him more often?"

"When you're not racing, and if I can stand the death wishes. At least if someone does me in for love of Miles, you'll investigate and avenge my murder."

"We've been over this. I look into things, I don't investigate."

"Semantics, sugar." Holly replied. "Speaking of looking into things, tell me about Billy."

I'd been happier avoiding the subject.

Chapter Thirty-five

Over a shared platter of nachos and matching Cobb salads, I filled Holly in on the state of my so-called investigation. I didn't feel much like an investigator, didn't feel like I was getting anywhere. And I was still angry about the whole thing. That reminded me of my beach epiphany, and I fell silent.

"What's in that brain?" Holly asked.

"Right before I picked you up, I figured a few things out… about myself and how I deal with my father and his family. Now I realize they apply to the Billy situation also. Basically, I'm in charge, I don't react or let someone else control me. I keep emotion out of the equation."

She toasted me with a loaded nacho chip. "Outstanding resolutions for both scenarios. What does that mean day-to-day?"

"Mostly it's me turning off the guilt and anger."

"Can you do it?"

"You always ask the tough questions." I stared at the ocean. "I think so. More easily with Nikki and Don than with Coleman and my father. But I'll try, and I'll start by establishing boundaries with my father. Dinner with him and his wife and kids is fine. The family reunion this summer is out. Way out."

"Understandable. Back to Billy, it seems to me you're making progress."

"You think?" I took another bite of my salad.

"You're looking for who has motive and opportunity. Don Kessberg has both." She stopped me before I could speak. "I know he asked you to investigate. That could be a blind. Same goes for Nikki. She was there, she was annoyed with him."

"Does 'annoyed' translate to murder?"

"Does anything make sense about that woman? I haven't met her, but from everything you've told me, she's never what you expect."

"All right." I agreed. "Don and Nikki. I don't want to think Tara did it, but she could have, and she was angry enough."

"Then there's Coleman."

"Turns out he had opportunity. I think. But did he have motive? He'd have to be a reprehensible human being to kill his own nephew."

The busboy arriving to clear our plates overheard my last sentence but didn't bat an eye. I smiled at him, and he responded with a grin.

Holly dimpled up at him. "You look awfully familiar. Have I seen you in something?"

He deployed the smile again. "My new commercial aired last week for holiday-themed marshmallows. Maybe you saw that?"

To her credit, Holly only reacted with delight. "It must be. Congratulations."

He beamed at both of us and whisked our plates away.

"What's next?" Holly asked.

"I keep asking questions. See who else is doing bad deeds Billy might have known about. See if there's anyone else who didn't like him."

"What's next today?"

"Walk along the beach?"

"I want to talk about the elephant in the room."

"The what?"

She clicked her tongue. "Are you going to tell me you haven't looked at e-mail or social media once today?"

"I was giving myself a break. Plus I was out late last night, up early for the hospital visits." I paused, hopeful. "Good news first?"

"The awesome news is lots of publicity already and more requests. Minor items in the national news. Bigger items in

motorsports press. Bad news is it's not all positive publicity…
though it's not catastrophic. Some of it's funny."

I made a "gimme" motion with my fingers.

"A national outlet has a story, sort of a 'who is she?' piece that
picks up on the Ringer's post from Friday."

"The post that says I'm not worth the chaos I attract?"

"Right. This doesn't go into detail about what the chaos has
been, and it does talk about the challenges facing female drivers
in the racing world, but unfortunately, it expands on the whole
'Kate Reilly is high-maintenance' story. They've even got a quote
from some old codger team owner saying he'd never hire you."

My career flashed in front of my eyes. "Who?"

"Winston Carmichael over in IndyCar. But I know him, and
he's really an old coot. He's the most old-school, conservative
owner there is. He never wants anything to change, bitches constantly about the Series, and hates everyone. All of racing knows
it. You'd never drive for him if he begged you to, so ignore him."

"But people are hearing him." I slumped over, trying to push
the hurt away. *All I'm trying to do is chase my dream, and now I'm
ruining things for other women. Fantastic.*

"You can't worry about what people think. Shoot, some
people call dial-a-psychic for advice. You going to worry what
they think about you?"

I shrugged, but sat up straighter. *Meet this head-on. Business,
not emotion, remember?*

"There's only that one article nationally," Holly continued.
"But we're getting lots of interview requests. Remember, that's
a good thing."

I saw the expression on her face and stiffened my spine. "Tell
me the rest."

"I want you angry about this, not wounded, Kate. Can you
do that? You don't cause chaos, you're not high maintenance,
and you're where you are because you're a damn good driver.
Do you believe those things?"

Whatever was coming has to be bad. I knew she was right. I
smiled and worked on relaxing my shoulders. "I believe them.

I also believe I have the best manager, agent, and friend in the world." I took a breath. "What else?"

"It's that son-of-a-bitch Racing's Ringer. He's figured out about your new sponsor."

Oddly, I almost felt relief at her words. "Daddy's buying me rides?"

"Asshole."

I laughed. "Holly, we knew this would come out."

"He didn't have to pile on now. All that bull-pucky about how you only got the oval test and sponsorship because your father owns the bank. It's not true!" She shredded a paper napkin.

"At least I was prepared for that story." Her anger made me feel less awful.

"All right, we'll deal with it, but you should read what he says before you drop blanket forgiveness on him." She pulled out her phone and called up the Ringer's site. Her face lost all color, and my gut churned as she handed me her phone.

"Paddock Questions Female Drivers' Sexuality," blared the headline.

My jaw dropped. Though I didn't want to see it at all, I read the opening paragraph aloud. "While it's undeniably sexist to say women have to act a certain way in the racing paddock, it's true that professional racing women—drivers, engineers, or other roles—who ignore or downplay their gender are often the subjects of questioning glances. More than one paddock insider this blogger has talked to wonders out loud why 'gals want to be on a pit crew and act like men. Do they want to be men?'"

I had to give the Ringer some credit, as he hadn't singled out me or even female drivers as a group, and he never agreed with the misogynist attitude. But the fact that he presented it, side-by-side with a reasonable person's attitude—"Let women do whatever jobs they're qualified for" and "I don't care what's under the firesuit"—implied the sexist view was valid. I started laughing at the absurdity.

"I suppose we should have expected this, too," Holly said. "But I'm blindsided, sugar."

"I can't figure out if the Ringer and others think I'm a lesbian or think I should walk around the paddock in a bikini." I laughed harder at the thought. Then I sobered. "It's like Alexa told me. We're always going to be the outsiders in racing. No matter what. Not because I've found dead bodies and caught crooks. Because I'm female."

"That's flat out depressing. And wrong."

"My options are give up or fight the idiots."

"So keep fighting." Holly paused. "About the bikini idea…"

"You can't be serious."

"I said there was a funny bit. One of the media requests we got was an offer for you to pose naked. To 'show your feminine side,' they said. It's the biggest men's entertainment magazine, if that helps. And a lot of money."

I can't believe this is my life.

Chapter Thirty-six

After jokes about the offer to pose naked—I turned the request down—Holly and I worked on the press inquiries that had come in. I called a journalist for the *New York Times* wanting a comment from me for a longer, serious report on gender in modern sports.

Holly fielded a national network morning show. "They know you'll be on the local show tomorrow, and they want to add a five-minute call to the national program. I pressed them on the topic, and they said they want to talk about an up-and-comer in racing, to find out what the road to get there was like for you. The good and the bad."

"They'll bring up the tabloids and the accusations."

"But probably not to trap you. They said they wanted to explore what you had to go through. I watch them, and the hosts aren't those people. I think you'll be all right."

As we strolled down the Venice boardwalk, watching street artists work with spray paint and kitchen utensils, I focused on the windfall of national exposure I was getting. And tried to ignore the negative spin that had gotten me there. My ringing phone dredged up different anxieties. I checked the display and let Nikki's call go to voicemail. *Time to practice your new approach to business.*

"Hi, Kate!" Nikki sounded animated, but I was coming to recognize the tenacity under her fluff. "Have you figured out who killed poor Billy yet? It's almost been a week now, so I thought you might have. It'd be really great if you could get that worked out before the race weekend, you know? Thanks, sweetums. Oh, and the network left me a DVD of the footage they took during Media Day. I think you wanted it? I'm not sure why. It's not very good television yet, without editing. But it's here. Let me know. Okay, bye!"

Holly turned to me. "That's amazing."

"It was over the top, even for her. What the hell? 'It's been a week, are you done?' Figuring out who killed someone isn't like ordering a pizza…no, she probably wouldn't order pizza. It's not like ordering caviar to arrive on time."

"Can you get caviar delivered here? Probably," Holly decided.

I jabbed at the phone to delete the voicemail and noticed another one. This time it was Coleman's voice. "Please be ready to report to me on the status of your investigation into Billy's death tomorrow, after our meeting. No written documentation required, merely a summary of what you've uncovered and who you suspect." He disconnected abruptly.

Holly took my cell phone out of my numb hand and deleted the message. She patted my arm. "This is where you weren't going to get wound up. Business, remember?"

I sucked in a deep breath, tasting ocean air. I exhaled. Did that three more times. "You're right." I did an internal survey and discovered I wasn't angry. I was annoyed, but I wouldn't march to their orders.

I smiled at Holly. "All good, thanks. Maintaining my calm."

"Great." She took my arm and got me moving again. "Now tell me about the FBI agent and the movie star. Don't leave anything out."

I thought about Holly's amusement later that evening while waiting on the Beverly Hills Hotel's red carpet again, this time for Lucas to pick me up. I had no idea what kind of vehicle to expect, though I half expected a limousine, for privacy. I was completely unprepared for him to drive up in a black Porsche 918 Spyder, one of the fastest, and certainly most expensive, machines Porsche built. A gorgeous, nearly 900-horsepower, hybrid sportscar.

Lucas grinned at me as I got in. "You look great. You're sure casual is okay? You wouldn't prefer dressing up for a fancy meal?" He'd texted me an hour earlier to suggest informal dining.

"My natural state is jeans and tee-shirts, so this is perfect."

"Your natural state suits you." He nodded at the valet nearest his door and pulled away, but he stopped partway down the drive and leaned over to kiss me twice, lingeringly. "Hi, Kate. Thanks for coming out with me."

He scrambled my wits. "Hm, yeah. Thanks."

He chuckled and pulled away. My brain caught up as we waited for the light at Sunset Boulevard and Rodeo, outside the hotel exit. "You stopped in the middle of the drive so no one would see us. But don't you worry about being recognized in this car? They're rare, and aren't people more likely to see you with no lid?" I pointed to the sky through the open top.

He tapped the baseball hat he wore, the Los Angeles Kings this time. "A hat helps. But it's a risk. Most people, even if they recognize me, will be cool. Press might not be. But they're not everywhere, and I'm not always in a mood to slink around trying to avoid them. Hiding from the world is no way to live."

"I understand that. Besides, it's a great car."

Lucas reached over to take my hand. "Is it awful for me to admit I wanted to show off a little? Not my driving prowess, not with you in the car. And not money either, but my love of fine automotive machinery."

"Not awful."

"I'm also not showing off because I think I'm better than you. I've done that before." He shook his head. "This is the embarrassing kind of showing off, just a boy wanting to show off for a girl."

The moment felt unreal, like I was in a movie. Still, I smiled and squeezed his hand. "Then it's sweet."

"Good. It's rare I have someone in the car who really appreciates it."

We made small talk for the few minutes it took to reach the restaurant, a hole-in-the-wall Mexican place. Again, I was surprised. Lucas drove a car that cost nearly a million dollars, but ate at neighborhood joints offering one-dollar taco Tuesdays. I couldn't tell if the contrast was meant to display balance or confuse me. Maybe both.

For the next two and a half hours, we ate excellent enchiladas as we chatted about how we got into our respective careers. When we weren't surrounded by evidence, it was easy to forget his success and fame, to think of him as a regular guy. Walking back outside and admiring how his expensive car gleamed under the streetlights brought it all back.

Lucas dangled his keys in my face. "Want to drive? I'd love to see how a pro handles it."

"You sure?" He nodded, and I felt both excitement and relief. Excitement at getting my hands on the car. Relief because I'd watched Lucas toss back three beers during our meal. A car with this kind of power and complexity deserved a driver's undivided focus.

Not to mention I rarely enjoyed being driven by other people, usually due to ego—and I didn't mean mine. Some of the most terrifying experiences I'd had in a car were being the passenger of a man trying to impress me with his driving skills. None of them, including many dates, ever did. Fortunately, Lucas hadn't felt compelled to show off during the drive to the restaurant— nor had Ryan in his Corvette. But I was always happier in the driver's seat.

"Where to?" I settled behind the wheel, admiring the view.

"A cupcake for dessert?" At my nod, he pointed down the street. "Thataway."

The Porsche handled like a dream. I could tell it had bottled up temper to spare, but it was fluid and controlled even at slow speeds. Five minutes went by before I realized I'd stopped paying attention to Lucas. I turned to him. "Sorry."

"It's educational watching you. Turn here. It's only two blocks down." He must have read the disappointment on my face, because he laughed. "Don't worry. I'll let you drive it afterward also."

I made the turn off of Wilshire Boulevard and spied the giant, neon cupcake sign ahead. I scanned for parking as we approached.

Suddenly Lucas freaked out. "Don't stop! Keep going!"

"What's wrong?"

"Don't stop. Go, go, go!"

Confused, I pressed on the throttle, sending a roar of noise out of the exhaust pipes. Lucas shrank down in his seat as we zipped past the cupcake shop and two dozen parked cars. I glanced in the rearview mirror and saw people scrambling into vehicles and pulling out to follow us.

Lucas turned a frustrated face to mine. "That's the paparazzi. Unless you want to be on the cover of every tabloid tomorrow, drive."

Chapter Thirty-seven

"So much for the press not being everywhere." I drove Lucas' Porsche 918 through the Beverly Hills streets faster than the allowed speed.

Lucas kept watching the side mirror. "They're never there. Maybe Brad has one of the kids out. God knows with all those children, it must be someone's birthday."

I made a last-minute decision to turn left through a yellow-turning-red light. *Who the hell is Brad? Brad?!* I checked the rearview mirror again. "How are they still behind us?"

"They run lights and break every other traffic law. More than we do."

"Shit." At this point, we were headed west on Santa Monica Boulevard again, the same road we'd traveled on our way to dinner. "Why don't we stop and let them get the shots?"

Lucas shook his head before I finished the sentence. "Give an inch, they'll take a mile."

"I can't believe—"

"I've been through this, you haven't. If we stop and pose, they'll have us on the way to Vegas for a wedding with a child due next month." He fished around behind the driver's seat and came up with another baseball hat, which he slapped onto my head.

"That sounds extreme." I looked in the mirror. L.A. Dodgers.

He grabbed my arm. Hard. "We're not stopping. Please, drive."

I could tell he wouldn't hear any arguments, based on his tone and the tightness of his grip. I nodded at him, judged the traffic around us, and nipped around a small white delivery truck, darting in front of it to make a right turn.

"How do we lose them?" I drove down a residential street full of apartment buildings, scanning incessantly for pedestrians. "Don't they already know it's you in this car?"

"Probably. But they don't know it's you with me. Or you behind the wheel."

"You'd rather have stories about fleeing from them than on a date with me?" I heard what came out of my mouth. "I didn't mean like that. Asking a serious question."

"I'm not ashamed about being on a date with you, Kate. It's that they have my public life. I don't want them to have my personal life also."

I stopped at a red light and glanced in the mirror to see two camera lenses pointed at us, clearly visible in the streetlights at the intersection. I saw the driver's door open and someone start to step out.

We were the first car in line. The traffic lights turned yellow for cross traffic. The photographer behind us stood up, camera to his face. I wiggled my left foot onto the brake pedal and set my right on the throttle. Fed on a little gas. The Porsche inched forward.

No cross traffic coming. Yellow light for them. Photographer at his own front fender. *I can't believe he's leaving his car running. Didn't he look at the light? I guess Lucas is right, they don't care.*

I inched us forward more. Photographer at our back bumper. Cross-traffic light is yellow—now red. No one coming. Now! I floored the car and raced through the intersection, leaving the photographer with a shriek of engine noise and no shot. I hoped.

"Waaaaaa-hoooooooo!" Lucas yelled.

I reined the car in from the sixty miles per hour it had reached in three seconds.

Lucas glanced behind us again. "I wish that would stop them for good. But well done."

"Now what? Back to my hotel?"

"We don't want to lead them there either. We want to lose them. Turn left here."

Once again, I nipped through a yellow light, turning onto Wilshire.

"Onto the 405 North," he instructed.

I spied familiar cars only a block behind us. They almost caused two accidents catching up and swerving back and forth across lanes, trying to get beside us. I got lucky at a red light and managed to stay alongside other traffic.

One block to the freeway entrance. The light changed to green. "Go!" Lucas cried.

I turned onto the onramp and stopped at another light, this one regulating flow onto the freeway. Ten o'clock on a Monday night, and the freeway was still full. Five lanes of traffic, moving slowly. It was hard to imagine this many people, even with the evidence all around me.

Finally, we merged into traffic. "Stay in the right lanes," Lucas told me. He continued to fidget, looking in the mirrors, looking behind us, looking ahead.

"What now?" I asked again.

"Skirball exit. A couple miles. When we get off, make one left turn, then stay right."

Five minutes later, I followed his instructions and powered up the hill from the exit, staying right at a split and merging with another road. I'd thought it was dark down on Wilshire, but up here in the hills, there were even fewer lights.

I made a sweeping right turn, and Lucas settled back in his seat, suddenly calm. "I think I still see two or three of them."

I glanced at him. "That relaxes you?"

He grinned and tugged his hat down firmly on his head. "This is Mulholland Drive, Kate. You and this car? No way they can keep up. We'll lose them in a couple of minutes."

The road dropped down and made a quick turn to the left. I responded automatically while I dealt with the surprise. "This was your plan? I break the law to outrun them?"

"They don't stand a chance."

The daredevil part of me wanted to see how the car would perform. The rational part of my brain shouted warnings about police and tickets and other people and injuries and not knowing the road. Yet another part of me was angry with Lucas. *Did he set me up? Why does it matter? You know you're itching to turn it loose. But you can* not *get a speeding ticket. You can* not *injure anyone—especially not yourself. Especially not Mr. Sexiest Man Alive next to you.*

I also couldn't be photographed as the driver of Lucas Tolani's car, having already committed a dozen moving violations.

Lucas got twitchy again as headlights flashed behind us. "Come on, Kate!"

I cycled through my emotions again: excited, worried, cautious, annoyed, angry. I didn't like Lucas in that second, for pressuring me into this. For getting me into this. For being someone the paparazzi would break laws to follow. *Son of a bitch!*

"Go!" Lucas urged.

I went, the car's V8 engine screaming behind our heads.

The road rose and fell, twisted right and bent left, riding along the top of a ridge. Sometimes the land dropped away to the north and the Valley, sometimes it disappeared to Beverly Hills and L.A. to the right. I registered all that after the fact. In the few minutes of the drive, I was entirely focused on the road and the car. Braking and feeding the throttle on or off through turns, feeling the traction control maintain the tires' grip with the pavement. Steering as precisely as possible, and straining my eyes for lights in either direction ahead.

Look ahead, left turn coming. Visibility: enough. No one oncoming. Throttle on. Use all of the road, apex the corner. Rising road, right turn next. Hold on throttle. Hold on throttle. Brake! Careful in this lane. Careful on the brake. Ready to brake harder if a car appears. *I really hope no one is riding a bicycle on this road tonight.*

Through the turn. Car sticking to the ground like glue. Throttle, lunging forward to the next turn. Road dipping down again, off camber left turn, careful with speed. Touch the brakes, easy on the gas. Through the turn. Road still clear ahead. Go!

One time, I powered through a blind, right-hand turn and came upon a car in front of us in the lane. But the 200-yard view was clear, and before Lucas could even gasp, I'd swung into the oncoming lane and passed the slower vehicle. Only after we were around the next bend did it register the car had *not* been a police officer.

And once I almost kissed a guardrail around a blind left-hand turn whose radius began wide and sweeping, but tightened dramatically halfway through. Traction control kept the rear tires from losing grip, but we used all of the road. Next to a black void.

We passed oncoming cars about four times, quickly. I didn't look at how fast we were going, but it felt insane. Gloriously fun in the moment, but insane on a dark road I didn't know.

After what felt like half an hour, but was probably only four or five minutes, I let up. I didn't see headlights behind us—hadn't for a dozen turns. "I think we lost them."

My heartrate was elevated to a typical race level, and I felt a light sweat all over my body. I glanced at Lucas and laughed at his big eyes and wide smile.

"Holy shit," he croaked, then cleared his throat. "That was fucking amazing! *You* are unbelievable," he shouted.

That's when I remembered I'd heard him whooping and egging me on throughout our wild ride. "You weren't scared?"

"Hell, no. That was fucking amazing!"

You said that already. "How do we get off this road so they can't catch up?"

"Coming up, Coldwater. Take it to the right. Drops right down by your hotel."

"Perfect."

"That—when you—guardrail to the side…better than any roller coaster."

I saw Coldwater Canyon Drive, and turned right, immediately heading downhill. Now that the adrenaline rush was over, doubts and second-thoughts crowded in. I wasn't sure I was happy he hadn't been scared. The drive had been dangerous, and looking back on it scared me some. He'd pushed me into it, and he'd loved it. Like an amusement park ride.

As I drove sedately down Coldwater Canyon, Lucas leaned over. "You are amazing, Kate. I can't believe you. So damn sexy and so powerful." He nibbled at my neck.

Despite the tingling I felt, I shoved him back. "Not while I'm driving."

"But when you stop?" I glanced at him to find he'd turned on the smoldering look to accompany his teasing.

"I...uh." My brain went blank. *Lucas Tolani! Gorgeous man hot for me. What the hell do I do?*

Lucas started to stroke my forearm, and I felt myself weakening. Then I thought about what I'd just done. *You already halfway regret one decision tonight, don't go two for two.*

I snapped my eyes back to the road and pulled my arm away. "Not when we stop."

"Are you sure?" Same smooth voice. I didn't dare look at his face.

"I'm tempted. But I don't do this." *There's always a first time.* I frowned. "It wouldn't be about the real you, it'd be about your fame. That's not fair to either of us."

"I'm not sure I need you to be fair, Kate."

"Now you sound like a bad movie."

He sat back. "Ouch." He laughed. "Can't blame me for trying, right?"

I shrugged. "So long as you don't blame me for saying no."

"Trust me, Kate. It only makes you more intriguing."

Chapter Thirty-eight

The next morning, as I drove through the pre-dawn streets from Beverly Hills to Universal City, I gave Holly a minute-by-minute account of my evening.

She "hmmmed" for a long time. "Interesting that he let you take charge, literally take the wheel, and didn't have to prove his masculinity. Didn't have to play Mr. Macho."

"More than that, it obviously turned him on."

"Not many women could turn down a romp with Lucas Tolani, big, sexy heartthrob."

I shifted in my seat. "Maybe that's why I said no."

"It takes a rare man to convince you to break one of your personal commandments."

"Do I have them?"

"A couple. 'Thou shalt not drive recklessly on city streets' is a big one for you, though I've never known if you don't want to endanger other people or get a ticket."

"Both." If anything, my regrets about racing down Mulholland had grown. There could have been too many awful outcomes, including scaring other drivers into accidents. Including a ticket and a hefty fine. Including the press knowing I was behind the wheel. I didn't want to add the possibility of injury to me or Lucas to the list—I knew my own skill—but I hadn't known the road, and anything could have happened. "Dammit, I hate peer pressure."

"Is that why you did it?"

"Partly. Mostly." I tried to dredge thoughts out of my groggy brain. "I was caught up in the moment, the excitement, Lucas' urgency and concern, the thrill of the car."

"The thrill of the chase."

I sighed. "When I'm in a racecar, I'm prepared to make good, snap decisions. In the rest of my life, maybe not so much."

"Like a ballerina who's graceful on stage, but a klutz walking down the street?"

"You have the weirdest analogies. Yes, like that. I hate that I put us and maybe others in danger. For no good reason."

"You're disappointed in yourself." Holly's voice conveyed support, no judgment.

I didn't like what that behavior said about me. It made me feel irresponsible. Stupid. Even childish, like my behavior with my father. "I'll learn from it."

Half an hour later, I cupped a mug of coffee in my hands while a makeup artist added powder to my face. Holly leaned against the counter next to me, scrolling through her phone in one hand, and downing caffeine with the other.

"Oh, boy." She straightened.

My stomach fell. "I *really* hate it when you do that. Can it wait until after the interviews?" The brief video chat with the network morning show back in New York was first, then a live sit-down with the local anchors.

As I got out of the chair and we walked to the green room, Holly spoke quietly in my ear. "It's about Mulholland last night. They don't have your name, but one of the tabloids speculated. You need an answer prepared if anyone asks you about it this morning."

Thinking hard, I refilled my coffee cup. I'd only gotten four hours of restless, remorseful sleep, and I needed my brain working at full power. Deflection would be the name of the game, though I hoped the topic wouldn't come up.

Of course it did. First thing.

After introducing me as a female driver gaining a toehold in the national consciousness, the requisite perky female anchor asked if I'd heard about Lucas leading the press on a reckless chase through the Hollywood Hills the night before.

"I've seen reports."

"Do you know anything about that, Kate?"

I chuckled. "My guess is Lucas got some tips from Maddie Theabo, who I've been coaching before her run in the Celebrity Race at next weekend's Grand Prix of Long Beach. Maddie's getting quite good, and I know she's talking about racing with everyone."

The male anchor leaned in. "That wasn't you in the car with Lucas? Behind the wheel?"

I tried to look surprised. "A car like the Porsche Spyder? Would you let anyone else drive it? I sure wouldn't!"

To my great relief, they moved on. To something worse… though it started out more sympathetic.

The woman took over the questioning. "We wanted to talk with you about being a woman in racing. You've been in the news this week, with colleagues questioning your talent and dedication. Calling you high-maintenance. Do you have any comment on that, to start with?"

"I've worked hard for the opportunities I've had with teams and sponsors. Nothing's been given to me. I've had to earn every single advancement." I was tense, but I managed what I hoped was an engaging grin. "I know I have an ego about my driving—I'm pretty sure it's a job requirement. But I've always worked hard to leave that ego in the car, to not take it into the team shop or the pits or the rest of the world. My priority, after on-track performance, is being a member of the team. I may be the only one behind the wheel, but the team got me there." I paused. "People will think what they think. I can't do much to change it."

The news anchors were both nodding, and the man spoke this time. "Well said. What I wanted to ask you, Kate, is how you deal with being feminine in racing? We've seen other women in motorsports do provocative shoots for men's magazines or pose nude for fitness magazines. In contrast, you've maybe deemphasized your femininity. Do you feel you have to set it aside to race? To succeed?"

I've taken an unfeminine route? "For me, and certainly for most of the other women I know in racing—drivers, engineers, or whatever—being feminine in racing isn't any different than being feminine in line at the supermarket. We're simply ourselves." I smiled to take the sting out of what I was going to say next. "And frankly, I'd like to take issue with the idea that 'feminine' only means naked or sexy."

The man scrambled to apologize or backtrack, but I interrupted. "I'm not pointing at you. It's a common perception that if we're not sexual, we're not essentially female." I shrugged. "Today, being female or feminine or girly comes down to whatever a female wants to be. Whoever she is. For me, that's wearing makeup and heels sometimes, it's wearing shapeless sweats sometimes, and it's being strong and determined behind the wheel on the racetrack whenever I can. To answer your question, I don't really think about my gender when it comes to racing. Except when I'm looking for the bathroom."

Both anchors laughed, and the woman, who'd frowned at the man as he'd asked the questions, thanked me for my words. Then it was mercifully over…until twenty minutes later, when I joined the local crew on their set.

They were interested in talking about the coming weekend's race activities, especially since their sports reporter was one of my passengers in the pace car during Media Day. When we returned from a commercial break, the female co-anchor looked at me apologetically.

"Kate, we want to touch on an issue you discussed with our national program this morning. If we can play that clip?" She looked to the producer, and we were all quiet as my response about femininity played in the studio. It took every bit of willpower I had not to cringe.

When the crew indicated we were back live on-air, the woman turned to me again. "I applaud your response, and so do many of our viewers on social media. But some of them have a different perspective I wanted to ask you about."

I nodded, wary. "All right."

"No ambush intended," she assured me. "But something I think is interesting for a woman who's a role model. Some of our viewers have commented they think you're not enough of a feminist. That you're not speaking up enough about inequities in the treatment of men and women. You're not doing enough as a role model for young girls. Would you like to comment on those opinions?"

"Who decides what's enough?" I shook my head. "I make a case for women every day I'm behind the wheel or otherwise representing racing. Why is it okay to claim I'm both not feminine enough and not feminist enough? I can't win." I gathered my thoughts. "I'm female, feminine, and a feminist. All I can do is what's right for me."

She smiled. "It's a tough situation, being something of a female pioneer in a man's industry. I think you're doing well, and I'll be rooting for you this coming weekend." She detailed for the television audience the weekend schedule of events and encouraged everyone to attend the race.

The broadcast switched to a different part of the studio, and as I slipped off stage, the female co-anchor leaned over and squeezed my hand. "Great responses, Kate. Don't let the haters get to you. Thanks for being with us."

I thanked her for the support and got the hell out of the building. It wasn't even eight o'clock in the morning, and I felt like I'd done a three-hour stint in the Corvette.

As Holly and I rode the elevator down to the parking garage, I reviewed the headlines from my escapades the night before. "Star's Reckless Nighttime Race" and "Heartthrob's New Role: Dangerous Driver" were the most succinct. There was no end to the superlatives about the danger we'd been in. I felt every word like a pinprick, but I was determined to face public reaction, even if it wasn't reaction to me. I was reading the Ringer's take—he assumed I was the driver, though he had no proof—when I saw a text from Lucas.

Holly saw my reaction. "You just delivered a perfect performance to the media...what could possibly be wrong?"

"Lucas texted me, 'Great job last night. Reporters don't have a clue! Thanks for an amazing and wonderful evening. Do it again soon?'" I stuck the phone in my handbag, tired of it. "I can't believe he's unaffected by what happened."

"From his perspective, nothing happened except getting away from the paparazzi."

"It wasn't only him. The press didn't care what laws they broke. Is that what happens around celebrities? Normal rules don't apply?"

"Hard to tell what's the person and what's the situation." The elevator doors opened, and Holly hurried me to our car. "But I can tell you one thing, sugar, you need to find us a diner for a big, greasy breakfast, so *this* person is happier about *our* situation."

"Good plan."

Chapter Thirty-nine

Holly and I spent most of the rest of Tuesday quietly back at the Beverly Hills Hotel. Holly decided she had to lounge by the pool in her big, floppy hat and oversized sunglasses long enough for someone to either ask for her autograph or tell her she ought to be in pictures. It only took half an hour.

I spent two hours watching raw footage from Nikki's reality show cameras, mostly on fast-forward. I didn't see anything I thought was relevant to Billy's death. Assuming I knew what I was looking for.

Billy was there, of course, as were Don Kessberg, Elizabeth Rogers, Erica Aarons, and a host of others. The most interesting moments were the tense exchanges between Nikki and Billy—validating her frustration with him—and the hard looks Don gave Billy behind Nikki's back. I did glean one useful item from the video. By slowing down occasionally and checking the timestamps, I could be certain Nikki couldn't have killed Billy. I'd never seriously suspected her, but her camera crew's filmed evidence definitely ruled her out.

After hard work eliminating the most unlikely of suspects, I gave up sleuthing for the day and opted for a swim and a nap. By four that afternoon, Holly and I were on the road again, moving slowly through the city streets, back to the Frame Savings headquarters.

I was nervous. We were meeting with Beauté and Frame Savings executives, and it was crucial I find a compromise between them to fund my career. They started with different goals: Frame wanted me in the Indy 500, and Beauté wanted me in NASCAR. As we all talked about how and why, how much and how many marketing "eyeballs," we gradually reached tentative agreement, with both sides giving a little and Frame coming to see the value of NASCAR, with its touted seventy-five million fans, as the ultimate goal.

At the end, we had a plan sketched out, subject to fine-tuning and official board approvals. I would run three preparation races on ovals in the lower-level Indy Lights car this year, as well as a road course IndyCar race. Next year I'd do a partial season of IndyCar, including the Indy 500, and test the waters of stock car racing in a feeder series to NASCAR. The following two years, I'd continue to run the 500, while I moved into NASCAR's Xfinity Series, the second tier below NASCAR's Cup cars. If all went well, I'd move to the Cup cars by the fifth year out, subject to reevaluation and contract renewal along the way.

I'd talked extensively to the people around the table about realistic expectations of performance, emphasizing the dramatically different nature of the cars and series, the importance of a good team and equipment, and the idea of a learning curve. They made the right noises and only condensed my proposed timeline a little bit. As everyone left the room, I slipped back into my seat and worked on calming my nerves.

Holly sat down next to me. "How does it feel to get everything you want, sugar?"

I held my hands out in front of me, parallel to the table, and watched them shake. "It's Christmas, my birthday, and my biggest win all rolled up into one moment. Unbelievable." I turned to look at her. "Is it okay I'm also terrified? Bone-deep, to-my-toes petrified?"

"You're a normal human being, of course you're scared." She hugged me, hard.

"What if…"

"Don't start. Those never end." She sat back.

"There's only one." I paused, held my breath. "What if I can't do it?"

Holly smiled at me in a way that would have been pitying and condescending from anyone else. But I knew she understood. Even though I'd spent the last two hours saying "I can do whatever you want me to" over and over, even though I'd talked two corporations out of millions of dollars of future spending on my racing dreams, sometimes I wasn't convinced.

She tilted her head to the side. "This agreement isn't a contract to perform. They know you probably won't win, and they don't care. They want publicity, and you can sure as hell give them that, even if you're running in last place. This agreement today, Kate? This gives you the support to *try*. That's all you've got to do. Try."

I closed my eyes, feeling the truth of her words.

"And hell, if you can't cut it? We'll talk them into something else."

With a laugh, I popped my eyes open. "Thanks, I think."

"Kate?" My father entered the room. "You're going to join us for a drink out here, aren't you? Before we head to dinner?" A subset of the executives from Beauté and Frame Savings was adjourning to a local restaurant to celebrate the deal.

I nodded. "We're finished."

He frowned. "I should let you know my brother will also be at dinner. I believe Holden and his girlfriend, as well."

I braced myself for the familiar tension that always accompanied those kinds of statements. But I found only echoes of past anger and a feeling of relief. I owed my father some explanations, but this wasn't the right time.

Instead, I held my tongue as our party of ten made our way to a nearby steakhouse. I ended up at one end of the long table, with Edward and Holden at the other. I took the seating as a sign I'd be able to keep the bank as a sponsor, but not have to deal with the people I didn't care for. Except Coleman. At least he didn't seem to hate me the way Edward did.

I shoved those thoughts away and concentrated on my delicious food and on the conversation near me between my father and some of the Beauté team. I had the opportunity that evening to get to know the Beauté executives better, and I liked what I learned. My general discomfort with makeup aside, I knew I'd be happy working with the company for years to come. If they'd continue to have me.

The Beauté team members were still in high spirits as they left, declining the after-dinner coffee that most of the Frame Savings team ordered. We exchanged hugs all around, and my father and I walked them out to the valet parking area. We turned to reenter the restaurant, and I remembered who remained inside.

I stopped my father with a hand on his arm and gestured to the currently empty smoking area on the other side of the restaurant's large entry patio. It wasn't a great time or place for the conversation, but I wanted it done. I hoped Holly would forgive me leaving her at the table with the rest of the sharks.

"What's going on?"

I faced him. "I made another decision recently." I paused. "It's been quite a couple days for life changes."

"Now you have me worried." He clasped his hands in front of him.

"I made a decision, and I owe you an apology." He tried to protest, but I wouldn't let him speak. I took a deep breath. "I've been acting childish, like a bratty kid. Lashing out at you because of how other people treated me. Lashing out because of the past, even when you've apologized and done what you can to make things better for me. I'm sorry."

"Kate, it's all right."

"About the past." I had to stop and take a deep breath. "I don't know what happened. I may never know. Maybe don't want to. But I'm sure whatever you did or didn't do then, you never intended to hurt me. I believe that, and I forgive you. Between us, it's over."

He didn't speak, but stepped forward and enfolded me in his arms. It felt good.

He stepped to the side, keeping an arm around my shoulder and starting to walk me back into the restaurant. I resisted. "I'm not done."

"I see." He dropped his arm and faced me again.

"I want to be part of your family, but only yours. That's you, your wife, and your kids. Not the others with their unreasonable attitudes or anger. Their resentment. I don't like them, and I don't like how I react to them. Who I become around them. I won't do it."

He looked from the restaurant back to me, obviously confused.

"I'll interact on a business level," I explained. "I'll be professional. But I won't see them on a personal level. I won't open myself up to them. I hope you can live with that."

He sighed. "I wish I could change the situation, but I understand. And I'll support you. I'm simply grateful you'll be part of our family. I know Amelia and the kids will be, too."

Whatever nice thing I might have said about looking forward to getting to know them was wiped out of my head by the loathing on Edward's face as he exited the restaurant, Coleman, Holden, and Elizabeth on his heels.

"Finished your money grubbing for the night, dear niece?"

"Edward," my father warned. Even Coleman put a restraining hand on Edward's arm.

But Edward shook Coleman off. "James, you can't claim this meal wasn't about funneling money to our sweet Kate. Though, honestly, it was all I could do to swallow my food the way everyone fawns over her."

Coleman put his hand on Edward's shoulder this time, saying with a laugh, "You had no trouble swallowing those five whiskey sours. Let this go."

Red faced, Edward turned and shoved Coleman back a few inches. "I'll never let this go. Not while my son's dead and this worthless excuse for a human being stands in front of me."

Holden looked shell-shocked, as did Elizabeth, who slipped back into the restaurant, hopefully to get Holly. Or the management. Coleman frowned, straightened his tie, and stepped forward again, but didn't touch Edward this time.

My father was as still as stone, except for the clenching and unclenching of his fists. "Edward. You need to leave now. Right. Now."

But Edward curled over onto himself, one hand rubbing his eyes. He sobbed once. "I'll never let it go. My wonderful son is gone, and she's not. There's no justice."

I watched the angry, grieving, and hateful man in front of me, and I felt nothing. Absolutely nothing. No compassion, guilt, or obligation. Only the tiniest taste of freedom. I knew what came next.

I looked from Edward to Coleman. I was calm. "I'm done. Do you hear me? I will be an outstanding representative of your corporate brand, anytime and anywhere you need me. But," I glanced over my shoulder to make sure my father understood this was for him also, "I won't do this with you. I won't talk about my relationship to you. As far as I'm concerned, James is the only one I'm related to. Between us, it's only business." I looked to Coleman. "That includes looking into Billy's murder. I'm out. No more. Done."

Edward straightened up with a look so vile on his face, I was sure he would vomit next to us on the patio. But no, it was aimed at me. "No one wants you looking into anything! Stay away from my boy, you bitch! NO ONE WANTS YOU!"

Though he roared the last, I didn't flinch. Didn't react. I looked at my father, who was stunned into immobility, then Coleman, even Holden, who hadn't yet contributed anything. I settled back on Coleman. "Consider this my report. Please tell the board of directors I've done what I could, but it's over."

I stepped around Edward and walked back inside the restaurant.

Chapter Forty

I woke up Wednesday morning feeling lighter than I'd felt in a week. Since I'd seen Billy's body. Holly and I had agreed to take a lazy morning, and I lounged around in my yoga clothes after finishing an hour's practice. The only hitch in my mellow mood came when I realized I also needed to inform Nikki and Don of my decision.

I picked up my phone and dialed Don. Voicemail. I left him a message and dialed Nikki, hoping for the same. No such luck.

"Noooooo!" Nikki wailed. "You can't, Kate!"

"I'm sorry, but I'm no longer willing to look into things for you. His father made it clear he doesn't want me asking questions."

"You have to ignore Edward, like Billy did." She tried pouting. "Please, for me?"

I held firm, and she deflated. "Tell me what you've learned up to now."

"To be honest, I haven't gotten very far."

"You must have learned something." She paused. "What are you doing today? Are you going to the premiere tonight?"

As the race organizer, she knew every activity on the schedule, including the animated movie premiering that night featuring the sounds of IndyCars and the voices of a handful of drivers.

"Holly and I are going. Before that I promised her shopping."

"Perfect! Here's what we'll do. Meet me at Dino's on Rodeo. The salon? Both of you should be there at, let's see, red carpet starts at six-thirty for the seven-thirty show, but you don't want to be there at the start…" She kept talking.

I remained silent. She didn't need my input. Or agreement. "Be at Dino's at four this afternoon. Both of you."

"For what?"

"The works, silly! We'll do makeup and hair for you both, my treat, and while that's happening, you and I can talk about what you've learned. Okay, great! Ciao!"

The call went dead in my ear before I could ask about the availability of appointments. Before I could protest Nikki paying for our services. Before I could tell her I didn't want any of it. The last would have been a lie. I wanted every bit of help to look good for the red carpet and the paparazzi. But I'd have refused on principle.

Holly was predictably excited and pragmatic as we made slow progress along Rodeo Drive that afternoon. "Why argue with the woman? Think of it as payment for the work you've done for her, and enjoy it. Besides, it will be my chance to meet her. Ooooh—shiny!" She dragged me into another store.

Whatever reservations I had about dealing with Nikki face-to-face or being pampered in a salon for a couple hours—not usually my favorite activity—were swept away by the VIP treatment we received the moment we gave our names to the receptionist at Dino's. Within moments, a gorgeous man with skin the color of café au lait swept around a corner. He wore bright purple, skintight trousers, a bright blue gingham button-down shirt rolled up to display muscled arms, and a hot pink sweater vest. Plus a purple paisley bow tie. He also wore more makeup than I'd ever seen on most women, let alone a man.

He ushered us through a pair of elegant, frosted-glass doors to the salon itself, a marvel of clean, sleek glass and chrome broken up by at least a dozen styling stations. We followed his mincing lead to a private area at the back where he installed us in side-by-side chairs.

"I am Dino, my lovelies. I hope you are prepared to become even more beautiful than you already are." He noticed my amazement over his outfit and struck a pose. "I know, honey, it's so much to take. Drink in the fabulous."

His response delighted Holly to no end. "Sugar," she drawled, "that would take a month of Sundays."

He preened. "We do what we can." He turned a sharp eye on her. "And may I compliment you, Miss Holly, on your efforts, though I think I can bump you up a couple points on the gorgeous scale." He walked around behind me to lift my hair and look at us both in the mirror. "Miss Kate, you are a diamond in the rough, and I do surely love a challenge."

Holly snorted. "I keep telling her to do more with what the good Lord gave her."

They'd turned into the Southern twins, though I suspected Dino was more a chameleon than a native.

"Not everyone is equipped to field our level of spectacular on an everyday basis, honey. But we'll show Miss Kate what she's capable of." He winked at me, then grew serious, meeting my eyes in the mirror. "Do I have a free hand?"

I felt a pang of fear, and I forced myself to trust the expert. Within limits. "No bleach, no super-short cut, no shaving." I swallowed. "Otherwise, do your thing."

He put his hands on my shoulders. "I'll do what's good for you. Trust me."

I nodded, still nervous. He turned to Holly, his eyebrows raised.

"Anything you want. You're the man."

Dino giggled and clapped his hands together. "One moment while I gather my assistants and my tools." He swished out of the private room.

An hour later, Holly's hair was being dried by an assistant, and Dino was wrist-deep in mine. Brandishing scissors. I tried not to look. That's when Nikki pranced in, with her Yorkie, Teenie, under her arm.

She squealed and waved Dino away so she could give me air kisses, and I introduced her to Holly. Dino snapped his fingers at one of the assistants who ran off, reappearing in an instant with a small, padded bench. Once he set that between our two stations, Nikki sat down facing us.

"Dino, sweetie, I can tell you're creating your typical masterpieces," she said. Teenie barked in agreement, making Nikki reprimand the dog. Nikki looked back to me. "Now, Kate, tell me what you think happened to Billy."

I glanced from Nikki to Dino's reflection in the mirror, and Nikki waved a hand. "Dino won't say anything."

Dino winked. "She's the boss."

"It's great you know each other well, but—"

I stopped when Dino started to giggle. He tilted his head one direction and cocked a hip the other. "This is like that 'Who's on First?' routine. When I say she's the boss, it's not an expression. Nikki owns the salon. What she says goes."

I'd forgotten who I was dealing with. Of course she owned the salon. *No wonder her hair and makeup were always perfect.* "You can't share this with anyone else. Even Don Kessberg." I told Nikki the little I knew, starting with the long list of people who hadn't liked Billy and ending with the short list of suspects: Don, Tara, and Coleman. "But none of them make any sense," I concluded. "I can't see any of them going that far."

Nikki scrunched up her nose. "I think anyone could be capable of killing someone else."

"Even *moi?*" Dino pretended outrage and tossed imaginary hair over his shoulder.

"Even you, sweetums." Nikki blew him kisses. "But I agree motives are thin for Don and Coleman. Tara has the best motive of all."

I agreed. "But I don't think Tara did it. I have no good evidence. Only a feeling."

Nikki held Teenie up to eye level with me, waving one of her paws as she spoke. "Teenie wants to know who Kate thinks was the big, bad killer?" Nikki giggled, Dino smirked, and Holly smothered a laugh. Teenie looked nonplussed.

Nikki lowered the dog and grew serious. "Seriously, who

would you pick if you had to bet on a killer now? What's your gut feeling?"

"Coleman." The name slipped out before I could consider if I should say it.

"He'd be my guess, too," she replied. "Even though he was Billy's uncle. He's a bully. Billy was learning it from him."

"You called Billy a bully before. What did he do?"

Nikki frowned. "He wasn't nice to people he thought were below him…waiters, valets, even Dino's staff."

Dino gave an enormous sniff. "Had to ban his ass from this place." He waved his scissors in the air—snip, snip, snip—for emphasis.

Nikki sighed. "I never understood why he was good to animals and generous to homeless people begging, but rude to workers providing service. I didn't like it." She paused. "Did I remember to tell you about the breakfast club?"

"Not yet."

"I confirmed Coleman and Edward were members, and Billy was a junior member for the moment. Don says Billy was always in Coleman's shadow, and really seemed to be picking up on Coleman's habits and attitudes."

"Don?"

"Sure, Don Kessberg is also a member. Didn't I tell you?"

Chapter Forty-one

Don Kessberg was one of the gang of shady businessmen helping each other get around the law. Including helping men like Richard Arena get rid of people. How connected is Don? How far would he tap his resources to take care of the boy toy screwing his boss and screwing up his business?

"Kate." Holly was trying to get my attention. "You're done investigating, right?"

I glanced at Nikki and caught a sly expression on her face. I looked back at Holly. "Right. Done. Don't care."

Nikki tried a few more approaches to get me to change my mind, including payment, peer pressure, guilt, and promises of handsome men as my slaves. The latter got Holly giggling, though that could have been due to the Latin-lover makeup artist staring raptly into her eyes. I resisted all entreaties.

Nikki finally heaved an over-dramatic sigh and stood up. "I'm not giving up."

"Why is it so important to you she's involved?" Holly asked.

"I want someone on my side to figure out what happened. I want a woman involved. Call it instinct or intuition, but I want Kate looking out for my interests." She paused. "Besides, all three of my spiritual advisors told me she must be part of it if Billy's murder is going to be solved." As an exit line, it was outstanding.

I was still shaking my head over Nikki's proclamation a couple hours later, as a chauffeured Town Car delivered us to the famous Chinese Theater on Hollywood Boulevard for the movie premiere. I had to admit, Dino and his staff knew their jobs. We looked amazing. Our hair had reversed roles for the night: Holly's was blown out straight and sleek and mine was pinned up in a complicated arrangement of curls. Add a cocktail dress and high heels, and I had my social armor on.

Thankfully, I was able to duck through the press line with minimal notice on the part of the photographers. Inside the theater, I was surprised to discover how many drivers, team members, and racing series staff was there. We chatted with Alexa Wittmeier, caught sight of Don Kessberg and Nikki across the room, and waved at SCC Series staff.

The movie delighted everyone in the audience, and we all laughed and applauded when we heard recognizable driver voices. On the way out, Holly and I looked around for signs to the post-premiere reception, on a higher level of the Hollywood and Highland complex adjacent to the theater. I finally spied IndyCar drivers leaving the theater courtyard to walk along the sidewalk.

Holly tugged me forward. "I want to walk through the entrance where the stars make grand entrances for the Oscars." She dove into the flow of humanity. I stayed close behind.

We worked our way across the courtyard and joined the crowd. Hollywood Boulevard, with the stars in its Walk of Fame, attracted tourists at any hour. The stretch of it in front of Hollywood and Highland, a multi-level, open-air mall perfectly aligned for views of the famed Hollywood sign, was always one of the busiest spots on the street. On a balmy spring evening, right after a major studio premiere, it was a mob scene.

I saw three street musicians performing, six costumed characters posing for photos—for a fee—a man preaching the gospel, and a woman reading tarot cards. Plus a group of ten-year-olds doing precision dance steps. All in only a two-hundred-foot stretch of extra-wide sidewalk.

I was next to the curb, nearing the main entryway when my attention was caught by the sight of three Spidermen walking down the block together sporting matching middle-aged paunches. I looked down to pull my phone out of my clutch purse for a photo, when suddenly I was off-balance. Tripping. Dropping my purse. Falling toward the street into traffic.

Time slowed down almost as it did when something went wrong in the car. But I had fewer options on foot on Hollywood Boulevard. Step. Step again! I felt my ankle jam as I stumbled in my ridiculously high heels. Catch yourself! No amount of willing it to happen could put my feet in the right place to keep me vertical. My upper body kept heading out to the street.

Falling. Instinctively, I put my hands out to break my fall. *Can't drive with a broken wrist!* Tucked them into my body. Tucked my head. Prayed there weren't any cars coming soon. That they could stop in time.

Closed my eyes. Twisted, turned. Thumped down onto asphalt on my shoulder and side. Braced for other impact.

The noise I'd blocked came back in a roar. The squeal of brakes, mercifully short. The blare of horns. The screams and shouts of people. In a moment, I was swarmed. I heard one voice above the rest: "Get back. Give her room."

I kept my eyes closed and did a survey. Toes and fingers wiggled. Ankles, knees, and back felt battered but not seriously injured, though one knee stung like crazy. I must have scraped it.

The hip, shoulder, and ribs I'd landed on hurt, but my neck and head seemed fine. I opened my eyes and started to move. A chorus of instructions greeted me.

"Are you okay?"

"Take my hand."

"Don't move."

I ignored them all, focusing on the messages I got from my body. By the time I sat up, unassisted, ignoring everyone gathered around me, I could tell I'd be fine. Bruised and sore, but not really hurt. I'd been lucky.

Finally, Holly's voice. "What the hell?"

"Here, little lady." Another voice, with a Texas drawl, accompanied a big, beefy hand holding out my clutch purse, which sagged open.

Holly took it from him and glanced inside, thanking him.

I looked up to see a big, white handlebar mustache under an even bigger white straw Stetson. "I certainly hope y'all are all right. Your little purse was on the sidewalk, and I'm purely sorry to say there was no cash inside it, but I did look to see if any identification and credit cards were there, and they do seem to be. Plus your phone and a note. I apologize for not catching the miscreant who took your money."

I blinked up at him. He spoke so slowly and deliberately his explanation took a long time. While I sat in the middle of a lane on Hollywood Boulevard, impeding traffic.

I shook my head to regain my senses. "Thank you. Would you help me up?"

The moment I was upright, I knew the shoes were no longer an option. I thanked my Texas savior, leaned on Holly to slip the heels off, and hobbled over to the sidewalk. By this time, the crowd had dispersed, and a police officer had walked over from his traffic duty at the corner. I managed to wave everyone off with apologies, references to high heels, and assurances I'd watch where I was going next time. I didn't have to pretend to be embarrassed.

I limped over to the grand staircase the stars ascended in ballgowns for the awards show and sat down.

Holly settled next to me. "Did you have much cash in your purse?"

"Twenty bucks."

"Do you need remedial lessons on how to walk in those heels?"

I turned to look at her, finally letting down my guard and allowing myself to react to what happened. I was short of breath. Cold. "Holly, I was pushed."

"Seriously?"

I started to shiver. "The Texan said there was a note in my purse. Let me see."

She flipped open the catch. I pulled out the rumpled piece of paper, unfolded it, and read the message aloud: "Stop investigating Billy's death. Leave it alone, or you'll be next."

"But you told everyone you were quitting!"

"Someone didn't get the memo."

Chapter Forty-two

I heard people calling my name, and I quickly stuffed the note back in my purse, as I pulled my emotions together. Holly threw her wrap around my shoulders to warm me as Elizabeth and her boss, Tug Brehan, VP of operations for the SCC, rushed toward us from behind the staircase.

"Are you all right?" Tug asked me.

"What happened?" Elizabeth chimed in.

Alexa appeared, repeating both questions, buying me more time to consider how to respond. My insides still trembled in shock.

I went with the easy question. "A couple bumps and bruises, nothing serious."

"You're sure?" Elizabeth asked, and I nodded.

"We started to hear the wildest stories," Tug put in. "You tripped. You were pushed. You were avoiding a mugger. You bet someone you could jump over a small car parked at the curb." He grinned. "I'd have figured on the latter, but I know you like to keep your superpowers under wraps."

I made myself chuckle. "Nothing so newsworthy, I'm afraid. I stumbled over someone, tried to save a fall, and launched instead. Dumb and very embarrassing."

Holly looked at me, then at the others. "Given the circumstances, we'll skip the party."

Tug narrowed his eyes, studying my face. "Entirely your choice."

"You're sure you're all right?" Alexa stepped forward and took my hand.

I smiled at her. "I'll be fine, thank you."

"Good, stay in shape for the weekend." She paused. "We may have a situation you could help us with. I'll be in touch when I know."

That did a lot to calm my nerves. What worked even better to help me relax was the bubble bath I soaked in back at the hotel.

Holly perched on the wide ledge next to the tub. "That enough bubbles for you, sugar?"

I nodded, happy to feel tensed muscles starting to relax.

"It's time to ask who did this. The obvious answer is Billy's killer."

"Which means Billy's killer isn't anyone at last night's dinner. Or Don or Nikki."

"Unless someone didn't believe you."

"Or wanted to keep me on the job."

Holly tapped a finger to her lips. "The rational person would stay away, like the note says. You know, when the haunted house tells you not to go in, you don't go in?"

"I tried to stay away. I told people I was going to!" I smacked the water, spraying bubbles. "I can't sit here waiting to be attacked again." I sobered, reliving the shove and my fall in slow motion. Feeling the panic again. The loss of control and the certainty I'd be hurt. The fear. I shuddered. "I was lucky."

"True. So if the result of being attacked is you keep investigating, who benefits?"

"Nikki. But only if she thought threatening me would make me keep going."

"It only takes knowing you a little bit."

I flicked a bubble at her. "I might really have been hurt."

"Or killed," Holly put in.

I swallowed hard. "But if whoever shoved me expected it to make me stop…"

"We're back to people who didn't know, didn't believe you, or wanted to be sure your decision stayed made because you were scared or out of commission. Which doesn't narrow down the field much."

"Try not at all." I sighed. "It's not that I want to keep at this. Or that I feel I've made any progress. Anyone I suspect has an alibi I can't break, like Nikki or Don. Or they have no motive at all and they're people I can't possibly investigate, like Coleman or Holden."

"Or it's someone you don't want it to be. Meaning Tara or her sister."

"Maybe I should stop." I stared at the bubbles. "I'm not doing anything but sticking my nose into everyone else's business. I've got no results, and I'm taking time away from the job I'm paid for. I might even be jeopardizing my future with my sponsors."

"Your mood has more swings than a park. Turn your brain off. The circus comes to town tomorrow, so you'll have a change of scenery and a whole new set of people to talk to." She meant the racing community, set to arrive at the Long Beach track the next day.

I sank down further in the water. "Thank goodness we can go to a racetrack. This Beverly-Hills-and-Hollywood lifestyle is too much for me."

"You'll feel better tomorrow."

She was right. Even after a night of brooding and the occasional nightmare about falling, I woke up Thursday morning equal parts upbeat, pissed off, and determined. Determined to be a good little soldier looking into Billy's death for my sponsor and the racing organization. Pissed off at the coward who'd pushed me. Or had me pushed. Adamant I wouldn't let him win. I'd keep doggedly asking questions—even if I didn't know what I was doing—until the cops caught Billy's murderer.

I also woke needing answers from Don Kessberg. He'd be busy that day, with the race weekend starting. But at least I knew where to find him.

As I drove the rental car south to Long Beach, Holly asked if Coleman Sherain was still my number one suspect.

"That's what you told Nikki yesterday. I wondered what his motive could have been." She tipped her new, oversized Gucci sunglasses down her nose at me. "Mind you, I agree. Coleman is the sleaziest of a pretty sleazy bunch, except for maybe Uncle Edward. But you can't figure Edward killed his only son."

"Fathers have killed their sons before. But no, I don't think Edward had anything to do with it." I watched traffic in the lanes ahead as I considered. "If Coleman did it, I think it was to preserve his lifestyle. His West Coast wife and kids, connections to sketchy businessmen, access to power. Probably some kind of illegal business practices. He's that type. While that doesn't mean he's a killer, it's a motive if Billy was messing things up for him."

"Or drawing too much attention to their practices." She looked out the window at the rows of palm trees visible over the high wall of the 405 freeway. "If it was him, how did he get to you last night? We didn't see him. And why?"

"With his connections, he could hire someone. Maybe he didn't believe I was serious, so he thought he'd make sure of it."

She might have said more, but my phone rang. She batted my hand away from it. "Hands free, remember? It's Alexa." She put the call on speakerphone.

"Kate, how are you feeling today?" Alexa began.

"A little stiff, but nothing that won't work itself out. How's everything at the track?"

"Setup's going fine, but we've got a problem. I'm sure you know Sasha Ivanov is our Indy Lights driver. He's had a visa problem, and he's stuck at home in the Ukraine. Can't get out for the race. We're short a driver."

I grinned at Holly. "Is that something I can help you with?"

"I'm hoping," she replied. "Would you like to drive that car for us this weekend? I know it's not an oval, but it'll still be good practice for you. And good exposure."

I clamped down on my emotions and nerves. "I need to check the schedule. In addition to the SCC times, I need to be available for the celebrity race sessions, to fulfill my obligations there."

"I heard you're coaching Maddie Theabo. How's she doing?"

"She's got skills. She should do well."

"Great. I'm looking at the schedule now, and of course, nothing's on track at the same time. Indy Lights qualifies right after the Pro/Celebrity race ends, but as I remember, there's time in between. I think we can get you where you need to be for all three."

Holly mouthed the word "sponsors" at me, and I nodded. "Alexa, do you need to check this with your sponsors?"

"Already cleared. After the tabloid photos from the test day that included sponsor logos on the car, they're thrilled. If Frame Savings or Beauté want to kick in funding to get their logos in, we can find them a prominent location. But it's not a requirement. Funding is covered. We need a hot shoe. You in?"

"I'll need to clear it with Jack at Sandham Swift Racing, as a courtesy. But assuming he's fine with it, heck yeah, I'm in. Thank you."

"Great. Find me in the IndyCar paddock this afternoon. I'll get a seat dug up, and we'll get you settled in the car."

It took me two miles of highway to find my voice again. "It's starting."

"Sugar, you're gonna be busier than a one-legged man in an ass-kicking contest." She laughed at herself. "But it sure is starting."

Chapter Forty-three

After turning in my rental car at the small, charming Long Beach Airport, Holly and I piled into a taxi for the seven-mile drive across town to the Renaissance Hotel, our home for the next few days. We checked in early, tossed our bags into our rooms, and crossed the bustling Ocean Boulevard to the main entrance of what was quickly becoming the Grand Prix track.

Thursday was setup day for everyone. The larger track structures and miles of fencing had been installed over the last couple months, and with cars scheduled to take to the track for official practice at seven forty-five the next morning, kicking off three days of nonstop activity, it was time for the final touches. Those included the large concert stage on the plaza in front of the Performing Arts Center, vendor setup in the convention center's exhibition hall, and the arrival of the racing competitors.

The evening before, semi-trucks containing cars and equipment had rolled in to four different areas of the track compound: IndyCar teams in the center of the infield, Indy Lights teams inside the sports arena building, World Challenge cars at one end of the exhibition hall, and SCC teams in a parking lot outside the track next to Turn 11.

Today was a day of business, before the fans arrived and the show began, as teams set up their equipment and cars. My first stop, first priority, was Sandham Swift Racing in the SportsCar Championship paddock. Holly and I waved to friends as we cruised down the row of teams, finding Sandham Swift's assigned spot near the end of the main aisle, directly across from the technical inspection tent.

Aunt Tee, our team mom, unfolded chairs and spread table-cloths in the small hospitality area at the rear of our space, while the crew was hard at work prepping the 28 car, which Mike Munroe and I shared. Since this race was for only two of the four SCC classes, our sister car, the 29, wasn't racing with us this weekend. The paddock felt extra small with only one Corvette.

"About time you got here, Reilly." Mike leaned against a toolbox, watching the crew.

I gave him a quick hug. "Good to see you, too."

He turned to Holly to tease her about her NASCAR debut, and I enjoyed the sight of my big, burly co-driver towering over my petite friend. I went into the hauler we used for our gear and team meetings and greeted our team owner, Jack Sandham.

"I hear the test went well last week," Jack offered.

I wondered who he'd heard from, but didn't ask. "Well enough they're asking me to drive their Lights car this weekend because their driver's stuck in the Ukraine."

"That Sasha kid?"

"Right. I told them you needed to be on board if I was going to do it."

Jack crossed his arms over his chest and glowered down at me. He wore nothing but black on his tall, lanky body, and he was as intimidating as a man twice his bulk, all due to attitude. Except I knew better. He had a hard outer shell and a soft center.

I faced him, crossing my own arms. "The Corvette stays top priority."

"I should let you do this? What's in it for me?"

I knew he wouldn't stand in the way, but I kept playing the game. "A mention in every interview, though it'll be awkward if they're asking me for beauty secrets."

He barked out a laugh. "You do that. Tell them I say women should only wear black eyeliner."

"It's the classic for a reason." I eyed him. "Are we good?"

He finally smiled and dropped his arms. "Go do your thing, kid. You'll be busy."

"Thanks, you're right. Saturday'll be tight because of the celebrity race also."

Jack rubbed his hands together. "Right. Madelyn Theabo. How's she doing? Should I put my money on her?"

"I'm taking her in the pool to win." Sandham Swift Racing put together a betting pool every year for the celebrity race, each of us picking a winner and the first to crash. There were always crashes in the celebrity race, usually multiple wrecks. In fact, it wasn't unusual for half of the ten-lap race to be run under caution to clean up accidents.

"Then I for sure won't pick her to wreck," Jack replied.

We talked through Friday and Saturday's schedules for a few moments, working out where I needed to be, and when, for Sandham Swift. Then I hollered at Mike to join me toting our firesuits, helmets, and other gear to technical inspection for approval. While we stood watching the Series technical team sort through our clothing, I explained to Mike the triple-duty I'd be pulling that weekend. "I figure that means you'll do the qualifying."

He nodded, his shaggy brown hair flopping around. "It was my turn, anyway. That's great for you. So your Indy plans are moving ahead? For next year?"

"Looks like. For a couple years, along with other things I'm not ready to talk about."

"I'm going to hate when you're not my regular co-driver." He hooked an arm around my neck and rubbed his knuckles on the top of my head.

I batted at his hands to extricate myself. "I'm not leaving soon, Mike." But his words made me sad at the thought I would someday.

He smiled. "We'll kick ass together until you do. And I'll come see you at the 500."

"I'll hold you to that."

Once inspection was done, I promised to meet Mike again in an hour for a track walk and headed off to check in with Alexa. She took me over to the Beermeier Racing Indy Lights team inside the round sports arena and introduced me to the crew of the car I'd be driving: the number 47, sponsored by Kremer Building Supply. They were different men than I'd worked with at the Beermeier test the week before, since that had been the IndyCar Series team. Tristan Rhys, the race engineer, was especially welcoming.

I sat in the car, using a seat for a recent test-driver they said was a similar size to me. They weren't wrong, but that other driver wasn't female, so the fit was pretty tight in the hip area. I squeezed into it, though it wasn't what I'd call comfortable, especially with my right hip sore from my fall the night before. I'd make it work.

One of the mechanics leaned over me to buckle the seatbelts and ratcheted them down with ridiculous, unnecessary force. I gasped in surprise and pain as he yanked straps across my bruised side.

I heard him muttering under his breath. "Don't belong here. Think you're better than everyone else. Don't deserve this." And more in the same vein.

It was so unexpected, I didn't know how to respond. Tristan saw the stunned look on my face and the angry one on the mechanic's and hustled over to pull the guy away, talking to him sharply and sending him out of the building. I wondered if the mechanic knew my father's family or if he hated me for me.

Tristan knelt down next to the car. "I'm sorry, Kate. What did he say?"

"That I didn't belong here."

"I hope you know that's not true. We're happy to have you, and I'm sorry he didn't make you feel welcome. He has a nephew who tested with us, so he may think his nephew should be here. But that's no excuse. I'll speak to Alexa about him."

I didn't ask if I'd displaced the mechanic's nephew. I didn't want to know and didn't care. That was racing. We scrambled for every opportunity we could get, on the track or off, and sometimes it came down to luck and timing. I'd been on the opposite side of it myself. If he was good and persistent, the nephew would get his chance. But not this weekend.

"We'll keep him out of your way for the weekend." Tristan looked down at my lap. "The seat okay?"

"It's a tight fit, but it'll work."

"Great, let's get the pedals fitted." He turned to the rest of the crew. "Pickle, help us?"

A young, slender man with a buzz cut trotted over and cheerfully adjusted the pedals forward and back to suit me, and we got the car set up. I spent a few minutes with Tristan discussing my past experience with Lights cars, my car setup preferences versus those of their regular driver, and what radio communication I liked to receive while in the car. We also went over the timing of meetings and on-track sessions, and I added them to my master list. Everything was doable except for the Indy Lights driver autograph session, which was scheduled at the same time as the mandatory SCC Series driver meeting. Tristan assured me he'd get approval for me to miss it, and we parted, satisfied on all sides.

Holly waited for me in the sun outside the big rollup door of the arena, where the Lights cars went in and out. The angry mechanic stood to the side, smoking. I ignored the glare he shot me.

"What's his problem?" Holly asked.

"Nothing I can fix. There's the weekend's head honcho, Don Kessberg." I waved as Don walked by, and he returned the gesture.

Holly turned to watch him as we started back through the IndyCar paddock to reach the SCC area. "That's interesting."

"Don is?"

"If he's asking you to look into Billy's death. Also ironic. Don didn't like Billy."

"You didn't know who Don was, how do you know that?"

"It's my assumption, based on the screaming match I heard at Petit last year."

"Billy was at Petit Le Mans?"

"I didn't tell you I saw him. You didn't need the added stress."

I wasn't sure how I felt about that. "Go on."

"I saw Billy and a man—who I now know is Don Kessberg—in an argument behind the Series hospitality tent one day. At least, Don was arguing. Billy stood there with that insufferable, smug rich-kid look he has. Had." She shook her head. "I never figured out what they were talking about, but Don wasn't happy about it. He was using colorful language. Telling Billy he'd beat the tar out of him if he tried anything. Said he didn't care who Billy was sleeping with, he'd stop Billy from throwing her money away. Said Billy would ruin everything only over Don's dead body."

I looked at Holly. "Or Billy's?"

Chapter Forty-four

Holly cocked her head to the side. "Maybe it's strange Don asked you to find out who killed Billy. Or maybe it's clever, if he did it. We've certainly learned motive doesn't mean opportunity or action."

"True. I need to have a conversation with Don."

That would have to wait. It was time for the annual track walk: the two hours reserved for drivers and teams to examine the track on foot, bicycle, or golf cart. It wasn't that we'd never seen the track before, after all, the team had raced here for half a dozen years, and I'd been there twice. But it was never a bad idea to get out and look at the turns, surface, and curbing before getting in the car and going like hell.

And in a way, we hadn't seen the track before, in this specific incarnation. Long Beach was a temporary track, meaning for 360 days a year it was city streets and parking lots. Each year, the city rebuilt the racing curbs, smoothed out the surface, and put up walls. Every year, therefore, the track was a bit different. I'd been on it a few days prior for Media Day, but Mike and I needed to see everything up close. We also needed to discuss how the Corvette C7.R was last year, how any changes might make the car better or worse where it was good and bad, and how we might want to adjust the setup.

While Holly wandered off elsewhere, I collected Mike and we hopped into a golf cart piloted by our crew chief, Bruce.

The information-gathering trip paid off for us in Turns 5 and 8. Turn 5, a right-hander around the Long Beach Aquarium's parking structure, had been reconfigured to offer more room to track out. Extra space was especially useful since the turn itself was off-camber or slanted and cars tended to slide to the outside. The inside had a sharp, aggressive curb we'd use to cut the radius of the corner…but with caution, so it didn't upset the car too much.

We also needed to study the unchanged Turn 8, because it was one of the most difficult corners on the track, due to its wide-open entry and an exit that didn't match. That meant less space to run out of the turn if you got into it too deep, which was pretty easy to do, given the downhill, sweeping approach. It was a sure thing someone in every on-track session—practice, qualifying, or the race—would spank the wall on the way out. If they were lucky, they'd get away with a little body damage. Unlucky ones ended nose-deep in the stacks of tires.

"I hate this turn," I muttered.

Mike laughed. "You haven't found your rhythm yet."

"Not sure I ever will." But of course, I was determined to do so, this year.

After Turn 8, we cruised down the back straight as it curved in near the braking zone, narrowing the track slightly. Then Turn 9, Mike's least favorite due to a bumpy and dirty braking zone. The bumps came from manhole covers and the transition from street to parking lot. The dirt came from rubber and other debris that accumulated from four different series of cars running over the same surface.

"They've even repainted the traffic markings on the street to make it more slippery," Mike groused.

Back at the Sandham Swift paddock, we conferred with Bruce about changes to the Corvette's setup from the prior year, Mike arguing for tweaks he thought might give us better grip coming out of Turn 8 and the hairpin. Bruce wasn't sure he agreed, but we decided to give it a try.

I slapped Mike on the back. "With that, you voted yourself first in the car tomorrow for practice, in case the adjustments make the car suck. They can fix it before I get in."

"Works for me."

I spotted Don Kessberg walking past our setup, and excused myself to run after him. I didn't bother with any preliminaries or with asking if he had time. "Why did you argue with Billy back at Petit?"

He stopped and put his hands on his hips. "How'd you find out about that? I thought you were done investigating."

I shrugged. "Maybe I'm not. You were in the paddock. People know."

"Fan-fucking-tastic." He rubbed the back of his neck. "That's when Billy shared his idea to form a new team with Nikki's money. I didn't think it was appropriate."

"You objected by saying you'd beat the tar out of him?"

"I was upset. Protective of Nikki. But I calmed down and talked with her. She assured me she wouldn't be taken in by him, so I let it go."

Had he? "Then what were you arguing with him about at Media Day?"

"The SCC paddock logistics. I'd just had the head of Porsche Motorsports North America on the phone raising hell over Billy's screw-up. I was explaining that to Billy mid-morning. I left him alive."

"Are you sure you want to find out who killed him?"

"I might not be sorry he's dead, but the killer should be punished." His eyes were steady on mine. "And I'm not the killer."

"Since you brought it up, where were you after one o'clock that day?"

"Mostly with Nikki."

I wondered about *mostly*. "That's not what her evidence says." I meant the videotaped testimony, but I hoped being vague might rattle him.

Which it did. "What? I can't...I don't know—I was there!" He took a breath. "There may have been a couple minutes I wasn't with her, but never long. Not enough to kill that idiot, at least. If anyone says different, they're lying. If Nikki won't tell you the truth, ask Elizabeth. Or Erica from my staff. They were all around."

"Hmm."

"Come on, Kate. This is why we wanted your help, to get past me and Nikki being suspects. We're the easy targets, but we didn't do it."

"You hated him. More than a lot of others."

He shrugged, a jerky, irritated movement. "He was a useless twit who thought he should get a cookie for showing up. A gold star for meeting expectations. Thought he was entitled to everything. Didn't understand we all have to work for money and success. We don't get them because daddy hands them to us." He turned away to look at the rows of trucks in the paddock. "You know what really burns me? Jackasses like him. They aren't capable but have money, luck, and position handed to them. Others, the talented, capable ones, work their tails off and go bankrupt trying to achieve a fraction of what he squandered. Yes, I hated him, particularly when he rubbed that entitlement in my face." He stopped abruptly.

"What happened?"

"Damn my mouth." He sighed. "Early on in his relationship with Nikki, I thought I'd give him a little friendly advice. Instead, he turned on me, called me an old man, out of touch…all the typical shit. Then he took it a step further. Taunted me. Saying *he'd* be telling Nikki what to do with the race. *He'd* be running the race next year, and I'd be out of a job."

"How'd you respond?"

Don wasn't as red-faced and angry as I might have expected for rehashing the argument. He seemed embarrassed. "I yelled at him. Almost shoved him, but held myself back."

"I understand that wouldn't have been the first fight you were in."

"That was a long time ago, Kate. A different life." He eyed me sideways. "And you claim you're no investigator."

"Why was that a different life? It was about racing, right?"

"I was young. I was a heavy drinker. I'm neither now. Sober twenty years, and it's changed me."

"Good for you."

"I admit I still have a temper. But I let it out in words, not violence." He looked down the paddock again. "I might think Billy represented everything that was wrong with the younger generation, and I might have thought he'd be terrible for Nikki and racing. But I didn't kill him. In spite of it all, I still hope you'll find out who did."

I stared after him as he walked away. I wondered if he was telling me the truth.

Chapter Forty-five

After wrapping up with the Sandham Swift team and meeting Holly at the media center to do a quick interview with a motorsports journalist, I made it back to the Renaissance with enough time to change clothes and freshen up before the evening's activities.

First on the agenda was our fledgling support group for women in racing. I knew at least half of the ten women there: Holly, Elizabeth, Erica from the race organization, and a junior race engineer for an SCC team. The others I'd seen but never met included two women doing media for different IndyCar teams, a female mechanic on a World Challenge team, a fill-in pace car driver for World Challenge, and the only full-time female driver in Indy Lights. We settled around tables in the open lobby of the Westin hotel, two blocks down Ocean Boulevard from the Renaissance, with an assortment of water, soft drinks, and beer.

Elizabeth got our attention. "We're all here for extra support from our female colleagues as we go about our jobs. I thought we could set up a meeting like this at each race weekend, and I encourage everyone to exchange contact information. I think we're all happy to stay in touch in between races."

"Can we bring others to future gatherings?" one woman asked, and everyone around the tables agreed.

Holly and I sat together at one end of the group. Erica was on my other side, with the other driver beyond her. Next to Holly were the mechanic and the race engineer. That small group of us started getting to know each other, talking about what each of our jobs entailed, where we were from, what road we took to racing, and so forth. With one exception: Sofia Montalvo, the twenty-year-old Indy Lights driver from Spain, turned her back on us and spoke with the women at the other end of the tables.

I didn't take it personally until later, when I specifically tried to engage her in conversation. "Sofia, I'll be racing with you on Sunday," I said, after reaching over Erica and tapping Sofia's leg.

I got the barest hint of a polite smile and a stiff nod. "That is what I have heard. Congratulations, I wish you luck."

"Thanks. Any tips about the cars or competitors?"

She pursed her lips. "I do not think so. I think with your great experience—for this is why you get the ride, yes?—you will have little troubles understanding where to press ahead and when to stay out of the way."

She excused herself to the bathroom and when she returned, she sat at the far end of the gathering, next to Elizabeth.

After she left, Erica shivered next to me. "It got cold in here. Did you hit her in a race years ago?"

"Never interacted with her before, on- or off-track. I wonder what the problem is."

"Competition, I'd say."

"I really hate that." I sighed. "It's not as if there's only one seat for a female driver."

"When there's only one, she gets more attention. You'll draw some away from her." She paused. "Do you run into that a lot?"

"I don't run into other female drivers very often, but the ones I've met are usually pretty supportive. Glad to have someone around in the same boat." I thought about my friend Colby. "Even one I beat out for a sponsorship wasn't like that. We've driven together since then, and we're friends."

"That's impressive."

"What's your experience? Are women supportive or competitive?"

"A pretty normal mix, I think." She shrugged. "But there are more women in management, hospitality, and media, and we're not fighting over limited spaces as you are."

"Have you worked for a team or series before?"

"Did before, working on doing so again. I like this organizing committee, but I prefer being the traveling circus, not the empty field."

I studied Erica and liked what I saw. She was about my age, open, friendly, and articulate. "Where are you looking?"

She cut her eyes down to Elizabeth and back to me. "Maybe a series."

Interesting. "They're a good group. Tug seems to do a good job as the VP of operations and seems to be a decent boss." Though I'd questioned Tug Brehan's ethics and moral fiber in the past—when I met him, he'd been allied with Billy and Holden—he'd cleaned up his act in the intervening year.

"Do you know Elizabeth well?" Erica asked.

"We've gotten closer recently, but she's hard to read. I'm never sure where I stand with her." In contrast, I felt an easy connection with Erica.

"That's my feeling exactly." She lowered her voice, though only Holly could have heard us, and she was involved in her own conversation. "I think things aren't all rainbows and unicorns in that team."

"The Tug and Elizabeth team?"

"From her I've heard frustration she's not advancing fast enough or being given more responsibility. He thinks she's pushing too hard but not delivering enough. I can substantiate the pushing. She's been a demanding contact from the GPLB standpoint. About unimportant details."

"She doesn't have Tug's charm to soften the demands."

"So she ends up being pointlessly bossy." She shook her head. "I think Tug wants me to come on and get trained in case she leaves. He's concerned she'll make it official with her boyfriend and leave with no warning."

"I had no idea it was that serious. I can't imagine Holden would have her leave her job...but I don't know him."

"That's his name?"

I made sure Elizabeth couldn't see what we were saying. "Holden Sherain. He's sort of related. He was Billy Reilly-Stinson's cousin, too. They were best friends."

"Interesting." I watched her absorb the information and make the connections. "All I'd heard was he had money."

"The family does. Like I said, I don't know him. Maybe that means a good opportunity for you."

I repeated the bit of gossip to Holly as we walked to dinner later.

"Erica is sharp," Holly noted. "She'd suit Tug better than Elizabeth, and maybe she'd have less baggage."

"Baggage?"

"Needs. People who have to be handled carefully, like cousin Holden. *Causes. Intensity.* Elizabeth is serious all the time." Holly grinned. "And serious all the time is tough for our naughty friend Tug."

"What does she need?"

"Advancement, recognition, reward. Tug's annoyed because she's always trying to connect the Series with the non-profits she wants, instead of the SCC-standard charities. But even there, I understand. I have my pet cause, too."

"Autism organizations, because of your cousin." I thought a minute. "What were hers?"

"Foster care organizations." She paused. "Tug told me in confidence. Apparently Elizabeth's abusive mother was murdered, and then she went into foster care and had a horrific experience. Kudos to her for rising above."

"It gives me new respect for her, and it explains why she's reserved and serious all the time. Did Tug have any other good gossip?"

She smacked my shoulder. "Call it information."

"Sorry."

"He'd also heard rumors about Billy wanting to field a new team with Nikki's money—he didn't know whose money, but he could guess—as well as how furious Don was about it. Do you think Don is secretly in love with Nikki?"

I missed a step. "What? No. Why?"

"He's so angry, so protective." She shrugged. "Which keeps him on the suspect hook."

"I suppose it's possible. I should look at the footage again tonight, make sure I didn't miss him with Nikki, since he swore she was his alibi." I spied the restaurant a block ahead.

"Why don't you let me look? Fresh eyes and all that. Plus, I have a lot less to do this weekend than you."

"That would help."

"Tug also says Stuart Telarday might come to the Lime Rock race in July." I could tell she was worried about how I'd take the news.

Why should I be upset? My ex-boyfriend who was almost killed is doing well enough to come to a race, and I heard about it from someone else? I cleared my throat. "That's great. It would be nice to see him."

"You haven't spoken with him in a while?"

"He doesn't call me, and he told me to go the hell away, so I don't call him." She opened her mouth, but I stopped her. "Not a good time, and I don't want to talk about him anyway."

She smirked. "I guess you have enough boys to juggle here in L.A. Think about them instead."

"I'll think about the race."

Chapter Forty-six

I got to the track at six-thirty Friday morning to prepare for our first practice session: two hours starting at seven forty-five. Before that, Mike, Bruce, Jack, and I gathered around a table in the hospitality area of our paddock setup, huddled into fleece jackets against the morning fog.

We talked through the changes we'd seen in the track the day before, what basic setup had been applied to the car, and what we'd particularly watch for and try to improve on during the morning runs. If the car was handling well, Mike and I would split the two-hour session evenly. If the car needed more work, Mike would stay in longer. As the meeting ended, I ordered Mike to make the car perfect for me and went to change into my firesuit.

One of the crew sat in the Corvette for the tow over to the pits. Mike and I caught a ride on the back of a small flatbed cart carrying bottles of fuel and a car's worth of crew.

I picked up a radio headset and settled myself on the pit box next to Bruce, ready to watch Mike go to work. Activity and anticipation slowly picked up as we neared the magic minute, and when the clock turned over to forty-five minutes past the hour, the word came down from race control: "The track is green. Track is green."

Engines fired, and we were off. Twenty minutes in, I found myself grinning listening to Mike complain about the car's

handling down into the "the bitching Turn 9," as he referred
to it. I hadn't had this much fun in days. I was so glad to be
back racing—doing what I knew I was good at—I could hardly
contain myself.

As he got out of the car after his stint, Mike stuck his helmeted
head next to mine and yelled. "I'll get on the radio. Track's slippery, but the car's pretty good."

I gave him a thumbs-up, tucked my seat insert into the Corvette, and climbed in. I felt giddy. For at least the next forty-five
minutes, no one would have expectations of me I couldn't meet.
I wiggled my butt in the seat the fraction of an inch allowed
by my belts.

"Radio check," came Bruce's voice.

Time to focus. I pressed the radio button. "Copy."

"You settled?"

"Ready to go."

"Crew's done, she's all yours."

"Copy that." I pressed the ignition button. A lone crew
member checked pit lane and waved me on. I dropped the car
into gear and pulled away without drama.

Yessss! The car felt great. Like a big, warm, rumbling cocoon
around me. Like home. I took three deep breaths as I puttered
down pit lane at the required 37.5 mph and relaxed my shoulders. I focused ahead. Smiled.

Past the end of pit lane. Push the button to turn the limiter
off. Throttle, shift to second.

"Clear on track." Bruce meant no one was coming my way
down the straight.

I moved left, turning directly into Turn 1. Throttle, shift to
third. Then braking, downshift to second for the minor left-
hander of Turn 2. Arcing around Turn 3, the dolphin fountain
in front of the Long Beach Aquarium. Seeing the purple and
white petunias planted in a checkerboard pattern around the
fountain's base. Third gear out of that turn. Braking, back to
second for the ninety-degree Turn 4. Using the curb at the apex,
moving carefully, feeling the lack of grip Mike warned me about.

Throttle. Shift to third. Pointed to Turn 5. *Remember the off-camber exit, more room, careful on the curb.*

"Bunch of cars coming up on you, then another gap after," Mike told me.

I went through Turn 5, came out of the exit wide left, and stayed off the throttle, letting six cars sweep by. I picked up the pace again through Turn 6. Third gear, slight rise, throttle, watching flag stands for the blue flag that would indicate more faster traffic approaching.

Out of Turn 6, moving from the right edge of the track to the left, over the crest in the track. Now downhill, looking at Turn 8. Fourth gear, wait for it. Looking at the apex. Brake. Downshift to third. Turning right, on the brake, feeling the car rotate. Track out, wall approaching. Wall approaching. Feeding throttle on. Not seeing how close the wall is because I'm focused down the track. Full throttle now. Up to fourth. Engine spooling up. Fifth gear. Sixth gear right before the braking zone. Back down to third, grinning under my helmet at Mike's "bitching turn."

Through 9, directly into 10, the now-empty SCC paddock on my left. Staying tight to the curbs of 10, second gear. Out of 10, as far left on the track as I can go without scraping the wall. Down to first gear. Steering full right, wondering again if the car will fit through the famous hairpin, Turn 11, a tight, 180-degree corner marking the start of the long front straight.

Unwinding as quickly as possible, power down cautiously to ensure grip. Flying down the front straight, flat through the middle banking, climbing up through the gears. Freedom.

Then around again, my warmup lap over. Push myself for speed, grip, and time.

The session was over before I knew it, and following Bruce's instructions, I went past the checkered flag on the front straight. I continued around the track at reduced speed and, between Turns 9 and 10, turned directly into the paddock. I pulled carefully into the 28 car's assigned space and quieted the engine. A couple of the crew had hotfooted it over from pits to paddock to help me get out. The rest of the team trickled back slowly, towing tire racks and fuel bottles.

Jack strolled in as Mike, Bruce, and I chatted next to the car while I tried to cool down. As usual after a stint, I'd sweated through every layer I wore. Even though we had in-helmet and in-cabin air conditioning, we could still feel the difference between a hot, sunny day and an overcast, cool one. Left alone, the interior of a closed-cockpit racecar ran thirty degrees warmer than ambient. The AC could only do so much when we worked so hard every minute. We still got plenty warm.

Jack faced us with his usual wide stance and crossed his arms over his chest. "How'd it feel? Going to be good for qualifying?"

Mike and I glanced at each other, and Mike spoke. "Pretty good." I nodded and resettled a cold towel around my neck.

"I sure hope so," Jack replied. "Given that's all you get before qualifying. Stupid, short schedule."

There was a lot of on-track activity to fit into three days here in Long Beach, and only the marquee event, IndyCar, got what anyone would consider a normal amount of practice time. However, every sponsor and manufacturer wanted us here in the great consumer mecca of Southern California, so we griped about it, but we played the game.

"Who's qualifying?" Jack asked.

Mike raised his hand. "She's got enough to do."

I checked the time on my phone. "Speaking of which. We good here? Anything I owe you for the next couple hours?"

They assured me they'd call if they needed me, and I headed into the trailer to dry myself off and climb back into street clothes. Holly was waiting for me when I emerged, helmet and second firesuit in my hands.

"Morning, Sleepyhead," I greeted her.

She gave me a warning look. "I've been awake and dealing with a media deluge."

I flopped down in a chair with a groan. "Don't tell me, I'm having an alien's illegitimate love child. I'm really a man, and

Lucas is having a secret homosexual affair. I'm having a psychic channel the late Dale Earnhardt to help me drive better."

"You want to know or you want to make stories up? I can sit here all day."

I took a deep breath. "Tell me."

"You're driving SCC and Indy Lights, and you're coaching Maddie. That's it."

"What a relief."

"I've got it sorted out. We'll stop by the media center on our way to or from Maddie, and you can talk to the important people."

"Thanks." My phone buzzed in my pocket, and I smiled at the message. "Maddie is here and either freaking out or excited out of her mind, she's not sure which."

"That your next stop?"

"After dropping my gear off at the Lights team."

Holly stood up and settled her sunglasses on her face. "Let's saddle up and head out. I'm ready for my Hollywood close-up."

Chapter Forty-seven

Maddie was fretting by the time we made it into the Celebrity Race paddock. "Thank *God* you're here." She threw her arms around me.

As I hugged her, I felt her shaking, and I glanced at Penny, a question in my eyes.

Penny mouthed, "She's fine."

Maddie pulled back and looked straight into my eyes. "Get me out of this. I can't do it."

I bit back a laugh. "Maddie, this is my best friend and manager, Holly Wilson."

Holly knew exactly what to do. "Maddie, I'm so glad to meet you. I'm a big fan of your work on screen, and I'm excited to see you on track. Kate's told me you're a natural. Are you excited about getting out there today?"

Maddie detached herself from me to shake Holly's hand and froze, staring at Holly wide-eyed. "Really?" She turned to me. "No lie?"

I took Maddie's hands in mine. "Close your eyes." I made her take three deep breaths. "Listen to me and believe me. You've got this. You picked up the basics fast, and you have good instincts. Don't get so over-excited or worried you can't think. Focus on what you were taught. Think about the next turn, going full throttle, hitting your braking point. You'll hold the wheel straight while braking, then turn, hitting your apex. Track the wheel out of the turn, and throttle back on. One thing at a time, one turn at a time. Channel your energy into that concentration on what's in front of you." I paused. "Open your eyes now."

She did so with another deep breath. I could still see nerves shimmering around her, but she seemed less frantic. "Okay." Another breath. "Now I can do this."

"No backing out?" I tested.

"If you tell me I got this, I believe I've got this."

"Go out and focus on you and your car. Don't worry about how anyone else is doing. Do your best." I glanced across the enclosure and lowered my voice. "And maybe kick a little soap opera behind."

Maddie chuckled. One of the other competitors was a rising, but still minor, soap opera star, as well as the biggest ego in the celebrity group. He'd talked endlessly about attending driving school and doing his own stunt work, though we never figured out what driving stunts he'd need to do for a soap. He strained even Maddie's patience, as nice as she was, and her goal throughout training had been to be faster than him. She squared her shoulders. "Take that to the bank, sister."

Celebrity drivers were called to their cars, and Maggie panicked for a second. Then she relaxed, smiled, and moved off.

Holly and I followed the forty-five minute practice session from the top of pit lane where we could see cars exit the hairpin and start down the front straight. More important, we could also see one of the track's giant video screens, which followed action all the way around the track and ran a crawl of average lap speed for each driver. The six drivers considered professional—past racing champions, current drivers in other forms of racing, and the prior year's celebrity winner—occupied the top spots, as expected, followed by the twelve celebrities. Maddie ran about tenth overall, fourth in the celebrity category, which I could tell surprised a lot of people. It satisfied me to no end, especially when she kept herself out of trouble, even as a driver right in front of her speared into a tire wall.

I checked the time. Getting in the Indy Lights car was next. "Holly, I don't think I…can you tell Maddie she did great? Tell her I swear I'll get to her before she pulls out to qualify, even if I have to cut my practice session short. I wish—I just—"

"Slow down. Take a breath. Take your own medicine, Kate." When she saw me calm down, she answered me. "I'll take care of Maddie. You need to do two things."

She fished in her small backpack and pulled out a protein bar. "First, eat this. You aren't going to get lunch. Second, do the same thing you told Maddie. Focus on the next thing only. Don't freak out, don't second-guess yourself. Focus on what's in front of you. Don't let the doubting voices in."

"I didn't say that to her."

"That's my addition for you." She slapped the protein bar in my hand. "Go, eat, focus."

I walked and chewed, thinking over Holly's words. *Don't think about this as the start of everything. Don't think about other people watching, evaluating, or criticizing. Don't worry about what anyone else is doing. Get in and focus on yourself and the car. Do your best.* I hoped I'd listen as well as Maddie had. I paused outside the sports arena, taking one last deep breath before going inside to find the Beermeier Indy Lights team.

Half an hour later I stood in pit lane, fastening my helmet strap. I'd talked through setup and approach to the session with Tristan Rhys, the race engineer who'd be on the radio with me. Alexa had also shown up to make sure I felt settled in the car and with the team.

She cautioned me about feeling I had something to prove. "You don't. The point today is for you to get more comfortable in an open-wheel car to help your future. It's not about winning this race." She'd flashed a smile. "Not that we don't want you to do everything you can. But we'd rather you take the checkered flag in last place than run first but crash out on lap ten."

I wasn't thinking yet about finishing the race, starting the race, or even qualifying. I was thinking about the initial lap of the practice session ahead of me. I knew from the seat of the Indy Lights car, the Corvette I was used to would seem slow and lumbering, and I tried to prepare myself for the initial shock of the first couple laps.

I was accustomed to piloting a heavy, front-engine, normal-height, almost-production car with a roof. In it, I sat up straight and made use of plenty of technology, including a rear-facing camera that highlighted the speed and direction of approaching cars. Since we drove in multi-class competition, part of racing meant playing a chess game with the other cars on track, using them as picks for passing or as blocks to keep from being passed. With multiple manufacturers in every class, strategy was key, and we focused on how our Corvette used tires and fuel that was better or worse than how the BMWs, Porsches, or Ferraris used them.

They were both racecars, but the Corvette and the Indy Lights car could hardly have been more different. Like its bigger brother, the IndyCar, the Lights machine was open-wheel and open-cockpit, meaning no roof. I'd drive a spec package: the same chassis, engine, and tire package as every other competitor, with all cars built to the same formula and a known, proven window of peak performance. Differences between cars were entirely due to teams' setup and tuning tweaks and driver skill.

I put on my gloves and climbed over the wall from the Beermeier Racing pit box to pit lane, eyeing the car. I climbed in, squeezing my hips into the almost-too-narrow seat, and helped Pickle, the crew member, get my belts fastened. Compared to the sitting-in-a-chair position of the Corvette, the Lights car was like sitting on the floor. The foot box was narrow, and the pedals were close together, but at least I didn't have to move my legs or feet around much. Brake with my left foot, throttle with a flex of my right ankle. Once again, I was lucky to be short with small feet.

Pickle patted the top of my helmet and gave me a thumbs-up, which I returned. He grinned and climbed back into the pit box.

Tristan in my ear. "Radio check, Kate."

My heart jumped into my throat, and a roaring filled my ears. *Knock that shit off! Do not screw this up.*

I pushed the button. "Copy, Boss."

I heard engines firing up and down pit lane as he replied. "Session is now green. Let's get you started, nice and easy."

I shut down the scared, nervous part of my brain. No more time for that. I was ready. I pushed the starter button, and a crew member waved me out. I took a breath, shifted into gear, and pressed the throttle.

I stalled it.

The most rookie of rookie moves, and I'd done it. On a big stage. I felt my face flame, even under my helmet and balaclava. I was mortified, but had no time to dwell on it. I started the car again.

I stalled again.

Chapter Forty-eight

This time, I wanted to crawl in a hole. I wanted to unbuckle my belts, climb out of the car, and disappear. A millisecond later, I was mad and ready to stop screwing around.

I clapped both hands to the side of my helmet, then nodded at the crew.

Tristan spoke to me again. "Tell me if there's an issue with the car. Otherwise, be sure you're giving it more throttle."

"My fault."

I started it up again, and I focused intently on pressing my foot more firmly down on the throttle. This time, I launched out of the pit box and down pit lane with decorum and control.

First hurdle down. Keep moving forward.

The first four laps I swallowed my embarrassment—telling myself I didn't care how terrible I looked to the rest of the paddock—and went slowly, staying well out of everyone else's way. I wasn't as slow as pace car speed, but I did move at "what's wrong with that car?" speed. It couldn't be helped. I needed to get comfortable, and I gave myself four laps for the basics.

The next six laps I spent increasing my speed as I got more familiar with the nimble, balanced handling of the car, which was worlds different from the Corvette. As in the Corvette, in the Lights car I braked well into the turn to transfer weight forward and help turn the car, pushing that traction circle I'd cautioned Maddie about. But in the open-wheel car, I also carried much more speed into a corner, through it, and out again. Its engine felt like a rocket behind me.

Logically, I knew the Lights car's turbocharged, four-cylinder power plant didn't produce as much horsepower as my Corvette's V8, but the chassis weighed so much less, I felt like I was flying. Less weight also meant I had more aerodynamic grip, so I felt more stuck to the ground. But I was tossed around more by the track's bumps and slippery surface.

I started working on refining my approach to corners, braking later and lighter to carry more speed. Pushing to find the edge in the trickier corners: how much of the curb could I use in Turn 5, how bumpy it was when I did it right, and how fast I could take Turn 8 and stay off the wall. How stable did I need the rear of the car coming out of Turn 10 to be set up correctly for the hairpin, and how slow was Turn 11.

The biggest surprise didn't even come in a turn. It came on Shoreline Boulevard, the three-quarter-mile front straight. I'd forgotten my first time down the "straight" in the Corvette, how the arc and banking of the turn messed with my mind and made me want to lift. How the first time I was flat out through there, I'd done it because Mike assured me I could, not because I was convinced. After doing it once, doing it again was easy.

Then I got into the Lights car that had more grip and a greater sensation of speed. It took three laps to find the courage to hold the throttle flat to the floor in top gear down the front straight. I'd never relax through there, in any car.

Tristan finally broke into my thoughts. "How're you feeling, Kate?"

I unspooled the wheel and put the throttle down out of Turn 8. Shifted up through the gears on the back straight. Called back to the pits. "Getting better."

"Let's take a couple more laps, no more than four. Then come in."

"Copy that."

For three more laps, I worked on being smoother, faster. Then

I pitted. While one of the crew checked the car over, Tristan spoke to me from the pit box.

"You're looking more comfortable."

I pushed the radio button. "Feeling better. I'm still not sure I'm getting enough speed down Shoreline, or through the one-two-three complex."

"There's a gusty wind on the front straight, which may be affecting you."

"Not used to feeling wind here. Track's also bumpier in this car."

"We started with maximum downforce, so you'd feel secure while you got comfortable. I think we'll dial that back a little bit. Maybe a little more later, see how you do. See if that helps your speed on the front straight."

"Copy that, thanks." A mechanic made the quick turns of a wrench, and I pressed the starter again. Leaving was the next test.

"Pit lane clear, Kate. Go ahead." The crew member in front of me waved me out.

I let out a breath, focused, and pulled smoothly away this time. *Good. Enough with the rookie crap. Let's go put a decent time on the board.*

By the end of the hour-long practice session, I'd redeemed myself for my shaky start. My best lap speed and time put me in last place of the fourteen cars, but I wasn't far off the field, and there was another practice session the next morning before qualifying. My goal was to be in the top half of the field, and while I wasn't yet where I wanted to be, I knew I'd keep improving with every lap. I'd done enough in this hour.

Alexa and Tristan agreed, if their smiles as I climbed out of the car were any indication.

Alexa patted me on the back, sweaty firesuit and all. "You had me worried at first."

I stripped off my wet balaclava and peeled my earplugs out of my ears. "Sorry."

"Don't apologize, just don't do it again."

Tristan laughed and handed me a towel. "Get used to that phrase. It's her trademark."

"I can live with it." I wiped off my face and bent forward at the waist, running my fingers through my hair to loosen it where it was matted to my head. I stood up again, and thanked Alexa for the cold bottle of water she handed me.

"Shall we go debrief in the air conditioning?" Tristan gestured back toward the sports arena and the paddock.

I looked up pit lane where I could see the celebrity cars staging. I turned back to Tristan and Alexa, unsure how they'd take my request. "Can you give me about twenty minutes? I need to reassure someone before qualifying. Unless it's a problem, in which case, I'll text instead."

Tristan frowned. "Who's qualifying now?"

"Celebrities," Alexa told him. "She's been coaching Maddie Theabo."

"She's nervous," I added. "I wanted to give her a pep talk before she qualifies. But if that's an issue, I'll skip it and come back with you now." These kinds of talks got delayed all the time, but I didn't know them well enough to know if they'd mind.

Tristan retained his frown for a moment, then looked sheepish. "How about I take you up there on the scooter, and you can introduce me?"

Alexa laughed, and I turned a concerned face to her. She waved a hand. "Take your time. Find me in the IndyCar paddock when you're ready to talk."

Maddie was relieved at my arrival, and she was pleased to meet Tristan. After introductions, I pulled Maddie aside.

"How did you feel about practice this morning?"

She wiggled a hand in the air. "Better by the end."

"You looked great. You even handled yourself when others freaked out around you."

"I kept hearing you. 'One thing at a time.' I stayed out of my own head and focused."

I grinned. "Now you know what I do every time I'm on track. Go do exactly the same thing now. Don't think about it as qualifying, focus on driving the track as smoothly and cleanly as you can. The speed will take care of itself."

"I'm beginning to think I can do that." She saw my expression and nodded. "Scratch that. I *know* I can do it."

"That's better." I gave her a hug. "I may not see you after, but I'll be watching how you do, and I'll check in with you or Penny." I put my face right in front of hers. "You got this."

"Yeah, I do."

Thirty minutes later, she proved it, qualifying third in her category. I sent a text message congratulating her and telling her to get a good night's rest.

By then I'd debriefed with Tristan, Alexa, and the rest of the team, and I'd changed out of my damp racing suit into dry street clothes. Pickle offered to take charge of my firesuit, promising to hang it to dry overnight. Since the first on-track activity I'd have the next day was Lights practice, I left my helmet with him also. Then I hurried over to the SCC paddock, to find the team rolling our Corvette into the huge line of cars and carts waiting at the break in the wall. The minute IndyCar teams cleared the track from practice, the barrier would swing open, allowing our vehicles access to the track and pit lane.

Mike was suited up for qualifying and sitting shotgun in the team golf cart. I grabbed a bottle of juice, a banana, and a bag of cookies and hopped onto the rear seat next to Tom Albright, our media guy.

"Busy, busy Kate."

"No kidding. Sorry I've only run past you so far this weekend."

"Such is the life of the famous driver-slash-detective. How's that going?"

"Which?"

"The detecting. How's the family doing after Billy's death?"

I shrugged. "You know I'm not close to them. I haven't a clue who killed Billy. I've found people who weren't happy with him, but I can't tell if they did it. Or maybe I can't believe they could."

"Maybe you need to ask Lucy Rose, Lily, or Violet."

"Who?"

Chapter Forty-nine

"I'm not sure who Lucy Rose, Lily, and Violet are," Tom replied. "A month ago, at Sebring, I heard Billy threatening someone. It was nighttime, and there was one of those momentary breaks when all the cars are on the other end of the track and it's suddenly, weirdly, quiet. I heard Billy's voice, sort of low and hissing. Angry. Saying, 'I'll make sure everyone knows about Lucy Rose, Lily, and Violet'…I remember the names since they're all flowers. Anyway, he'd make sure everyone knew about the three women, he said, 'and you'll never see anything but a cell.'"

"Who was he talking to?"

"I never saw the person. Didn't even hear the voice."

"At Sebring." *Who'd been at Sebring that Billy could have been threatening? And who were the three women?* "Was Don Kessberg at Sebring?"

Tom's eyebrows shot up. "You think Don killed Billy?"

"How about not saying that out loud?" I glared at him. "I'm trying to figure out who it *could* be, given what I know about motives."

"Sorry," Tom muttered, almost inaudibly. "He was there. Race organizers attend other races on the schedule."

It could have been Don…who else? Tara wouldn't have traveled across the country with her sister in crisis, no matter how much she blamed Billy and Coleman for it. But Coleman had been there, and he had a mistress named Lucille. That had to be Lucy Rose. I'd bet he had two daughters also.

I was delighted to have a solid clue. In the next instant, I felt sad for my father. Things could hardly get worse for his family.

Our cart started forward with a jerk as the mass of cars and equipment poured out onto the track. I pushed thoughts of crime from my head and leaned forward next to Mike's ear.

"I expect you to be spectacular out there," I told him.

"If that's what you want." He sighed. "It simply takes so much out of me."

"You'll have almost twenty-four hours to recover." The next day, race day, we weren't on track until pre-race ceremonies. No morning warmup, no additional practice. A long day of waiting until our four p.m. green flag.

I patted Mike on the head and turned around to keep an eye on the crew towing our gorgeous, black Corvette C7.R. I hoped the car had what it took to fend off the BMWs, which had been fastest in practice.

In the end, though Mike did all he could—and he was excellent, delivering a time half a second faster than either of us had managed in practice—we qualified fourth behind both BMWs and one of the factory Corvettes, which had also found speed. The top six cars were only separated by two tenths of a second, which told us the racing would be close and tight the next day.

By the time we were done, the crowd had thinned considerably. Drifting cars would practice and qualify after an hour and a half break for dinner, but most of the day's race attendees had gone home. The IndyCar paddock was buttoned up for the night, and the SCC teams moved at a measured pace, putting cars away and closing up shop. Only one or two teams dug into repairs or fixes—we heard mention of a gearbox rebuild as we passed one team. The rest of us hung up our tools and headed off for dinner. The next day would be long, since everyone would arrive first thing in the morning to tweak and polish, if not disassemble and reassemble, their racecars.

I was free for the night. Unusually free, in that we had no team obligation for dinner. I looked forward to a hot bath and room service. Holly added another item to that list: re-watching the footage of Media Day from Nikki's cameras.

We settled into my room, burgers and salads on trays in front of us, eyes on my computer screen.

Half an hour in, I did a double-take and jumped the footage back a few seconds. "That voice. That's Don talking, right?"

"Sounds like it."

We kept watching and kept hearing Don's voice, talking to Nikki, off screen. We also caught glimpses of Coleman in the background, even one time interacting with Elizabeth, looking annoyed, and brushing her off. Billy was in and out of the cameras' view, though surprisingly he didn't stick by Nikki's side for long, and he left sometime in the hour before he was killed. Elizabeth and Erica also appeared and disappeared throughout the day.

When I saw myself walking toward the parking structure in the background of a shot, I stopped the video player. "Don stayed with Nikki the whole time. I didn't see that before."

Holly wagged a finger. "That's why you can't watch on fast-forward."

"I'm relieved he couldn't have killed Billy, and I'm not sure I believed in my gut it was him. He was convenient, and he had assault in his background. Plus he could have been the mystery person at Sebring." I filled Holly in on the threats Tom had overheard and who I thought the female flower names belonged to. I snapped my fingers. "I'll get Ryan to verify it."

I pulled out my phone and sent him a text message asking if Coleman and Lucille had two daughters named Lily and Violet.

He replied that he'd see what he could find out, but I'd have to tell him why I wanted to know when he saw me at the race. He wished me luck.

"I take it you like the FBI boy?" Holly asked.

"He's helping with information."

"You think I don't know that look on your face?" She snorted.

I gave up. "I do like him. He's nice and interesting. Smart."

"Sexy."

"That, too."

"But sexy in a different way than Lucas."

"Lucas hits you over the head. Ryan is a sleeper. He sneaks up on you."

"Is Ryan also interested?"

"He says he's coming this weekend."

"You might have to make a choice, sugar."

"You don't have to sound so satisfied about it." I stood up and gathered our meal debris to set out in the hallway. "And I'm not doing, thinking, or choosing anything until after tomorrow's over. I've got enough to deal with."

By seven-thirty the next morning, we were headed over to the track for one of the biggest days of my racing career. First on my packed agenda that Saturday was a second Indy Lights practice, where I again made improvements, lapping twelfth quickest of the fourteen in the field. After that, I hustled to the Sandham Swift tent, arriving as Jack, Bruce, and Mike sat down in the office of the main hauler. We had twenty minutes before the SCC Series drivers meeting with the race director, and Jack used them to remind us of our strategy and our responsibilities.

Since this race was only an hour and forty minutes long, compared to our typical two hour and forty-five minute "sprint" races, there wasn't much to say beyond the plan to stop once for the driver change, fuel, and tires. And to stay out of trouble. Plus the ever popular, "Run your own race" and "Don't hit shit" dictums.

The SCC race director echoed Jack's sentiments, at least in terms of contact, reminding us the track was narrow and the concrete walls unforgiving. We all knew how too many cautions could doom a race: one of the first times sportscars had run here in recent years, the race featured more minutes under caution than under green, which made no one happy. As the race director made that point again and transitioned into procedures for the race start and all restarts, I checked my phone for the time.

Not only was I missing the Indy Lights autograph session, for which I'd had to get special dispensation from that race director, but the celebrity race was about to start. I had twenty minutes to see Maddie before she took the green. Holly was there in my place, and I texted her, asking her to tell Maddie I'd be there soon and to remember what I taught her.

Holly sent back an acknowledgement, but no details, and I tried not to fidget. Finally, we were released, and I dashed out of the room. Two steps later, I slammed into Lucas Tolani. He barely caught me before I fell flat on my face.

"Falling for me, Kate?" He murmured, kissing my cheek.

Great, another public spectacle. I pushed my embarrassment aside and focused on his all-access credential. "Let's go."

"But where—?"

"No time. Move." I grabbed his hand and headed for the door.

Chapter Fifty

As we ran from the media center to pit lane, Lucas alternately huffed, puffed, and exclaimed over the pace I set.

"You're in shape, use it," I tossed back over my shoulder. If nothing else, rushing through the crowds of people kept fans from recognizing Lucas.

We shot past the security guard, waving our credentials, and arrived at the end of pit lane to see the celebrity field pass us on the front straight behind the pace car.

"Son of a bitch." I'd missed her. I spotted Holly in a patch of shade created by one of the media booths above the grandstands and moved toward her. I saw flickers of surprise, awe, and amusement on Holly's face as she recognized the man with me.

"Lucas, Holly Wilson, my best friend and manager. Holly, Lucas. How's Maddie doing? Is she okay? Did you tell her what I said?"

Holly rolled her eyes for effect and held her hand out to Lucas. "A pleasure, Lucas. Kate's told me so much about you."

"She hasn't told me nearly enough about you. Hopefully you'll fix that." He deployed his magic, movie-star grin on her.

She basked in it, which irritated me. "Hello? Race time here?"

The cars came around again, still with the pace car in the lead.

Holly patted my arm. "Don't worry, we've got one more lap before green. Maddie is great. I gave her your messages, and she repeated them with me. She understood you couldn't be there, and it's fine. I think she's in good shape."

"Okay. Thanks. Okay." I shook loose the tension that had collected in my shoulders and arms and turned to watch the giant screen above us showing the celebrity cars on track. The pros were in their own pack behind the celebs; their handicap was starting thirty seconds behind the celebrity field and having to work their way through it to take an overall win.

I watched the screen as the celebrities rolled down the back-stretch and wound their way toward the front straight, talking to Maddie as if she could hear me. "Stay focused. Watch for the flag. Watch what the cars ahead of you do. Think about your braking, turning, shifting." I felt as nervous as if I were the one behind the wheel. More nervous. If I were behind the wheel, I could control the situation. Watching Maddie, I was helpless. "This is it!"

The pace car peeled off. The field of celebrities surged forward, Maddie tucked up behind the pole-sitter. Right on the leader's bumper. Green flag in the air. The cars sweeping down to Turn 1 slower than any of the racing series did, but still fast for non-professionals. Braking. Cars wiggling around. Starting to turn.

The pole-sitter went in too hot, couldn't brake hard enough, and couldn't turn. He went straight instead and impacted the second-place car to his right, nosing them both into the tires on the outside of the left-handed Turn 1.

Which left Maddie to brake perfectly, hit her line, apex the turn, and move into first place. I couldn't believe my eyes.

"No yellow. No yellow. No yellow." I chanted the words, willing the two off-track drivers to collect themselves and keep moving. The rest of the celebrities made it past them, as the original second place car backed up and steered around the pole-sitter.

"Oh!" I reacted along with the crowd and the track announcers as the second-place car purposefully nudged the pole-sitter in retaliation. Then the pros took the green flag, with a buzzing of engines roaring past me. I watched the situation at Turn 1, holding my breath until the pros made it through and the pole-sitter extricated himself and moved forward again.

That's when the cameras went back to Maddie, still in the lead and now with a gap on the car behind her. Holly and Lucas stepped forward next to me, mouths similarly agape.

"That's?" Lucas pointed.

I wasn't sure I could speak for the lump of pride in my throat.

"Holy shit," Holly said.

I reached out to grip her hand. Lucas took my other hand, and we stood that way for the eternity that the next nine caution-free laps took.

When Maddie made the hairpin turn for the last time and surged forward to take the checkered flag, I jumped up and down and yelled. Threw my arms around Lucas, Holly, and the startled paramedic near us. I shouted myself almost hoarse in the five minutes it took Maddie to do her cooldown lap, pull her car into pit lane, and climb out.

She zeroed in on me on the other side of the car and ran. We both whooped as we hugged and jumped up and down. I helped her pull her gear off, and Penny arrived instantly with a towel, baseball hat, and sunglasses.

Once Maddie was settled, I took her hands. "You kicked everyone's ass. You're freaking amazing." I glanced over her shoulder. "And now you need to do an interview and a victory lap."

She gave me another quick hug. "Couldn't have done it without you. I'll find you later."

I turned around and walked right into Lucas again, but this time he was waiting to grab my face with both hands and plant a big kiss on me. I reeled and stepped back. Lucas smoldered and followed, but I held up a hand. "It's not the time for that. I have to go qualify."

"But—"

"Not now. I have to *work*." I was almost angry as I stepped around him.

Holly fell in beside me and didn't speak until we were halfway to the Indy Lights paddock. "He looked stunned."

"That I didn't melt in his arms? At a race, of all places?"

I could hear the grin in her voice. "Something like that."

"The second most stressful moment of the whole weekend for me is right now, when I've got to go qualify this brand-new car."

"Sugar, believe me, I get it. But Mr. Movie Star doesn't understand."

I started up the ramp into the sports arena. "He'll have to figure it out." I dismissed Lucas and everything else from my mind, ready to focus solely on making the Lights car go fast.

Every team had a different strategy for the forty-five minute qualifying session. Some cars went out for only three or four laps. Some went out early, waited to see how their speeds held up, and then went out near the end of the session to try to better their position. And others, like Beermeier, used every minute of the time to work on their cars. Or drivers, in my case.

But it helped. During the session I made another leap in pace, and when the checkered flag fell, I'd qualified in eleventh place. Tristan assured me he and the team were thrilled with that result, and I promised I'd find more speed and rhythm in the race itself.

"I have no doubt you will, Kate." He patted me on the back. "Even Sasha, with his year of experience in the car, would be looking for a top-ten result here. From you, for your first race in the car, we want to finish. That's the only pressure we're putting on you. Okay?"

"Sounds good." I didn't tell him the pressure I was putting on myself. To prove myself to the team as capable—of more than only Lights races—I needed to match their regular driver, if not exceed him. Finishing was a given. A top ten finish would be acceptable; a top seven would be my goal.

I thanked Tristan again and made the rounds of the crew, thanking them for their effort and telling them I'd be there bright and early in the morning, ready to race. I left Pickle my suit and spare balaclava again to air out overnight, and I slung my helmet bag over my shoulder for the trek back to the SCC area.

Holly was outside the arena, a container of street tacos in her hand. The smell of roasted, spicy meat reached me, and my stomach growled audibly. "I hope those are for me."

"You bet, but we have to walk like civilized people back over to Sandham Swift, not like we're in a footrace."

I laughed. "I've been a little bit nuts."

"Focused and busy. But you have forty minutes now to relax. And eat. You only have the Lights series driver meeting before the SCC race, right?"

I steered us down the row of IndyCar setups toward the Beermeier paddock. "Lights meeting at three, pre-race for SCC three-thirty. I missed that autograph session, which feels wrong." I saw Alexa under her awning, talking with a mechanic. "Let me check in."

"Do your thing." Holly moved to a patch of shade.

I passed the fans lined up against a barrier, and I ducked under the belt stretched between two stanchions. Three minutes later, I emerged, feeling reassured, since Alexa had seconded everything Tristan had told me. With that validation, I could relax. Briefly.

Chapter Fifty-one

My calm lasted until we reached the Sandham Swift paddock, where we discovered a crowd of twenty fans, all waiting for me. I was starving and dying to sit down, but I was touched they'd stuck around after the autograph session ended, wanting a photo or a signature. No way I'd let them down.

I had about twenty minutes to recover before my next meeting. Four tacos, a banana, and two bottles of Gatorade later, I was refueled and on my way again across the track's infield. This time, I was back in a firesuit, but I'd left my helmet and other equipment with Holly, who would ride to the pits with the team. I hoped like crazy I wasn't forgetting some essential item or someplace I needed to be. I'd never been this busy at a race weekend, and I was starting to feel the strain.

This is what success looks like, Kate. Suck it up! I walked a little faster.

Out of the crowd, I heard my name. I turned and saw Erica, from the Long Beach race committee, waving at me and jogging to catch up. "Do you have a sec?"

I checked the time. "I have seven minutes to get to the Indy Lights drivers' meeting."

"I'll head that way with you. Walk and talk."

I started moving again. "What's up?"

"Something odd I remembered from Media Day. I don't know if it means anything."

I took my head out of cars, speeds, and angles. Remembered Billy. "Why tell me?"

"Don explained he and Nikki pressured you into investigating."

"I really prefer 'looking into things.' What happened?"

"An argument. Or a conversation. I don't know. It was one voice, but it was a threat." She sighed. "I don't know who was involved, except I think Elizabeth must have been one of the people. I heard a male voice yelling something about 'Holden will never marry you. I won't let him.' I wouldn't have remembered hearing it if you hadn't told me Elizabeth's boyfriend was named Holden."

"When was this?" *Was it Billy? He didn't have a problem with Elizabeth. Was it Coleman, who didn't approve of his son's girlfriend?*

"Right after lunch."

Coleman. "You need to tell the police about this."

"You think it's important?"

"It could be." *It proves Coleman was here and meddling in others' lives that afternoon.* "Promise to call them?"

"As soon as I have a free minute." She surveyed the race activity around us and laughed, then saw my expression. "Tonight. Also, I've got a couple journalists wanting quotes from you about Lights versus the Corvette. After the meeting?"

"If they can come to me on the grid, that'd be fine. Or in the pits before race start. Thanks for telling me." We'd reached the sports arena, and I headed up the ramp toward the drivers standing around the Series truck in the center of the paddock.

The Indy Lights driver meeting was only unusual for the race director singling me out. At the start of the meeting, he welcomed me to the Series, and near the end, he reminded everyone there'd be a new driver in their midst this race, and he suggested they all play nicely.

Sofia Montalvo, stationed at the far edge of the group from me, rolled her eyes at that comment, which provoked chuckles from the drivers next to her. I ignored them. After the meeting ended, I introduced myself to the drivers standing near me, stopped by the Beermeier Racing team to say hello, and took myself off to the SCC pits.

I was ten minutes early for the pre-race ceremonies, though the car was already in place and the team was setting up. I had a word with Mike as he put his earplugs in and pulled his balaclava on. Then I climbed up on the empty pit box, closed my eyes, and got my head back in the Corvette. I hadn't been in the car since the day before, and I'd driven a very different racecar in the meantime. But I had a well-developed habit of visualization, and it proved useful once again.

By the time Mike fired up the Corvette, to drive it on a single recon lap of the track and line it up on the front straight, I'd banished thoughts and sensations of more downforce and less cockpit. I was ready.

Once all the cars cleared pit lane, I hopped the pit wall and crossed the stile at the start/finish stand to join Mike and the Corvette on the front straight. Unlike other SCC races, fans weren't invited onto the pre-race grid here at Long Beach, since the logistics of clearing the grid in the short amount of time we had available were too difficult. But we had officials, dignitaries, cameras, and journalists. Most importantly, we had my grid girls. They attracted a lot of attention.

The four women ranged in age from late twenties to early sixties. They represented all shapes, sizes, and heights, but they all wore jeans with identical pink tee-shirts and pink baseball hats, logoed with Beauté and the Breast Cancer Research Foundation. Each held a flag of some sort, from the American flag to a solid pink one, and they all were breast cancer warriors. I loved them.

Tara was there, and I went immediately to hug her. "I'm sorry I haven't seen you before now. How are you doing? How's Jenny?"

She braced the flag she held, a pink ribbon on a white background, and grinned at me. "Jenny's holding her own. I'm fantastic. This is amazing." She looked at the other women. "Thank you so much for including me."

"You bet. I need to introduce you to Maddie. Maybe right after this race starts?" I thought about how to make that happen, since I expected to see Maddie in our pits for the race.

"We've already been in touch. Don't worry about it. You think about your race."

"Great. We'll talk later also. If not today, soon."

I moved on to greeting the other grid girls and the Beauté executive on hand as the roving cameraman from the broadcast network appeared. My friend and sometime-mentor Zeke Andrews trailed the camera and made a beeline for me and the women I was talking to.

Zeke gave me a quick side squeeze, to avoid head-butting me with the giant radio headset he wore. "Let's do a live bit with you and the girls—sorry, your cancer warriors. You set?"

I waved to the women to stand around us with their flags. We waited two minutes, posed and ready, for the live shot to be tossed to Zeke.

He turned to me. "Thanks guys. One of the best stories on the grid today comes from Sandham Swift Racing, and this bevy of strong, courageous women here with Kate Reilly, one of the drivers in the number 28. Kate, why don't you tell us what your new twist on the classic 'grid girl' is all about?"

I smiled. "Glad to, Zeke. In the last couple months, my primary sponsor, Beauté, has worked closely in partnership with the Breast Cancer Research Foundation to run a contest in each race city from Long Beach forward, asking fans why they're breast cancer warriors. We're picking a couple winners, bringing them out to the race, outfitting them, and sharing their inspiring stories."

Zeke turned to the women behind me. "Let's have you all introduce yourselves very quickly and tell us why you're here." He went down the line, holding the mic for each woman.

"Erin Charlton," said the woman I'd met earlier in the week. "I'm a survivor and supporting my sister-in-law Janel Jernigan through her fight."

The short, round, sixtyish woman: "Riley Warren. My daughter died a year ago, leaving two gorgeous children. I'm here in her memory."

"Good name," I noted, and she winked at me.

A tall, slender woman with a blond pixie cut that formed a halo around her head was next. "Debbie Mariol. I've had breast cancer twice, and I'm still here. Still strong."

"Tara Raffield. I'm here for my sister, Jenny Shelton, currently fighting her battle."

Zeke's eyes were as damp as mine. "Ladies, you are an inspiration to all of us. We all wish you and yours continued health." He turned to me. "Kate, if anyone's interested in joining you at a future race, they can get information on your website?"

I nodded. "Plus social media or Beauté's site."

"Excellent. Keep up the good work, all of you!" Then he was gone.

Free of the camera's eye, I turned around and thanked the women for being there and promised to visit with them after the race, as well as to answer any questions they had during their visits to the pit. They were all thrilled to be a part of the race weekend and honored to represent the cause.

Before we knew it, it was time for Mike to pull his helmet and gloves back on and slide back in the car. The invocation was given, the anthem sung, and a local business leader gave the command to start engines. Our grid girls, along with the other flag-holders from other teams, filed off the grid, walking to the end of pit lane and around the dividing wall.

I reached in the car and fist-bumped Mike. "See you halfway."

Back in the pits, I waved at Maddie on our pit box, put on a radio headset, and took up station in front of the display screens on the backside of the pit box. The field did three warmup laps behind the pace car, the tension slowly rising. The pace car dove into pit lane, and the faster prototype class led the field of twenty-two cars down the front straight.

"Green, green, green!"

We held our breaths as the field thundered down to Turn 1.

Chapter Fifty-two

Careful, careful, I cautioned every driver on track, and Mike most of all. There was one near miss at the rear of the prototype pack, right in front of our class leaders. Including Mike. But the driver who'd bobbled under braking dove into the runoff area and didn't cause a ripple effect through the field. Everyone got through cleanly, straggling into a single-file line by the fountain turn. With all the jostling for position, Mike snuck forward one spot into third, and we exchanged high fives in the Sandham Swift pits. Early days, but a good step.

In our Grand Touring or GT class—those being the sports-cars—the lead BMW had gone out like a rabbit at the start and maintained a five or six second gap on the rest of the field. The other BMW, the two factory Corvettes, a Porsche, and Mike in our Corvette remained bunched up in second through seventh place for the whole of Mike's stint. As the commentators liked to say, you could throw a blanket over those five cars, they were so close together.

The tight racing and lack of yellows piled on the pressure for the single pit stop we'd make. Our strategy was to pit as soon as a full fuel load would get us to the end of the race, around sixty minutes in, regardless of where and when cautions fell. Most other teams would do the same, leading to a ten or fifteen minute window of time when pit lane would be a very busy place. Because the action on the track was so close, the pit stop was the best opportunity to pass your competitors. But only if you and your crew were flawless. One stop, one chance to get it right. Or to blow it.

I felt the pressure mounting as I climbed up on the pit wall a couple laps before Mike was due to hand the car over. I'd been calm and collected a few minutes prior, answering questions for our visiting grid girls. But nerves hit, as always, in the fifteen-minute period between pulling on my helmet and jumping down from the wall to get in the car.

I fidgeted. Talked myself through the pit stop procedure. Thought about pulling out onto the track, into Turn 1. Talked myself through the driver change again. And again.

Then Mike was puttering down the long pit lane toward us. He stopped. The crew sprang into action. I opened the driver's door for Mike. He already had his belts and cables undone and was unfastening the window net inside the car. He pulled himself out and hurried out of my way.

Seat insert in place. Right foot into opening. Grab the railings above the door, pull. Left leg in. Pull, slide, twist my head so my helmet cleared. Find the center seatbelt buckle, find the right lap belt, fasten. Our driver helper Bubs leans in the window, doing the same for my left lap belt. Find the right shoulder belt, buckle. Bubs fastens the left shoulder belt. Reach up, check both shoulder straps sit correctly. Tilt the steering wheel down. Bubs plugs in my helmet air hose and the radio/transponder cable. He fastens the window net while I tighten my shoulder straps.

Thump—Bubs closes the door.

"Radio check," from Bruce in my ears.

Car shakes, still up in the air. *Problem on a tire?* Waiting on fuel. Car shakes again. My eyes on the crew member with the outstretched hand telling me to wait. Wait.

Push the radio button. "Copy."

Wait. One of the factory Corvettes goes by. Wait. A Porsche goes by. Car jostled, fuel line out. Still waiting. *Let's go!*

Finally tires done, air jack removed. A BMW goes by. Car bounces down on the tires, crew member waving me forward.

Press the start button, the engine roars. Throttle to the floor, check pit lane limiter is on. I snugged up behind the BMW. Found my drink hose and stuffed it in the front of my helmet. Tightened my belts more.

On the display screen showing my rear camera feed, I saw another Porsche behind me. My right thumb hovered over the limiter button on the wheel as I approached the pit exit line. Closer. Now. Press the button. Foot on the floor as the Corvette leaps forward.

Bruce: "Single prototype coming on track, Kate. You're coming out in sixth. When you can, change the engine map to three." I twisted the dial on the steering wheel to the correct number, changing the mixture of air and fuel, as well as the ignition timing, to give me optimum power and efficiency for my stint. I turned into the first corner, letting the faster prototype nip through ahead of me.

Through Turns 2 and 3, I got a feel for the car. Tweaked the brake bias. Stayed in line with the prototype ahead and the Porsche behind. Catching up to the BMW in Turn 8 when he wiggled on his cold tires. Staying in a train with the same cars lap after lap.

Once I found my rhythm, I called back to the pits. "I'm P6? What happened?"

"Sorry, Kate. Problem with the wheel nut on the left rear, took some extra time."

"Wheels okay now?"

"Wheels, tires, everything fine now. Crew feels terrible. Do what you can. The BMW in front of you is P5."

"Copy." *Nothing like starting in a hole.* I shoved that thought and sympathy for the crew out of my head and focused on the car in front of me.

As my tires warmed up, I adjusted the traction control with the dial on the wheel, tuning in a little more grip, a little less slipping of the tires than Mike liked to run. Lap after lap, I studied the car ahead, alert for weaknesses in the car's handling or the driver's skill in different parts of the circuit. I didn't find any.

But I kept on the car ahead. Anything could happen, which became clear only twenty minutes into my stint.

I was in Turn 5 when Bruce radioed. "Yellow, Kate. Double yellow. Full course. Prototype on the front straight. Lots of debris. Leader is in Turn 8." A pause. "Safety car will pick up the leader in Turn 10 and lead the field down pit lane."

"Copy, must be a mess." I slowed.

Two turns later, Bruce called again. "Red flag, Kate. Now red. They're going to stop the field at the end of pit lane."

Dammit. With every minute under red or yellow, my window of opportunity to gain positions closed further. "Going to be long?"

"Don't think so. No repairs, just a huge debris field, and they don't want you running through it."

Bruce was right. We sat only five minutes in pit lane, then circulated under yellow to allow for pit stops.

But by the time we went back to green, only twenty minutes remained in the race. I was frustrated, mired back in sixth, wanting more. I had one idea, a pass I'd seen done by experts but never attempted myself. I'd have only one chance to surprise the driver ahead, and if I screwed up, I might give up a position. It was a longshot, but I didn't have much to lose.

I stalked the BMW in front of me, planning my attack, and suddenly it wiggled under braking for Turn 8. Instead of turning right, it went straight into the runoff area. Now I was fifth. I wanted fourth, to finish where Mike had started the race. I set out after the Porsche ahead.

Two laps later, I started my move, staying well left on the back straight and pulling in tightly to the apex of the right-handed Turn 9, signaling I wanted to pass on the inside there. Two laps, three laps, the same maneuver. Close up behind the orange and yellow Porsche, almost bumping him. Smooth transition, driving straight from the exit of 9 into Turn 10, taking a tight line on the double left-handed apex.

Keep the car as far left on the track as possible out of 10. Braking. Downshift. Looking to Turn 11. Knowing better than to sneak inside the Porsche here. Single-file corner. First gear, full steering wheel lock. Turning right. Car barely fits to make the turn.

Too slow! Too slow! I ignore the recurring thought. Focus on unwinding the wheel, feeding the throttle on. Careful over the bumps, careful on the throttle so I don't tap the wall.

Wheels finally straight. Upshift to second. Throttle on the floor. Take a breath, relax my shoulders. Upshift to third. Porsche pulls away a tiny bit. Fourth. Fifth. Road bends right, the camber adding to the feeling of speed. Focus. Staying flat through the bend. Shift to sixth. Touching 157 mph before getting on the brakes. Catching up with the Porsche there, right on his bumper to funnel through Turn 1.

Swing left for Turn 2, line up for 3, the fountain. Up on the curb next to the flowers. Careful line on exit. Right-hand turn through 4. Right into 5, onto the high, rough curbing, over the crest of the turn. Move left out of the turn, use every inch of track, careful the camber doesn't toss me into the wall. Wheels straight, throttle down. Upshift to fourth. Fifth.

The prototype behind me takes a tighter line, passing me through Turn 6. Coming out of the turn, I move all the way to the right wall, against the tires. Up the rise, move all the way left, prepping for Turn 8. Downslope, braking into 8. *Get the apex right, Kate. Square off the corner.* Wide entry, braking into the turn to help the car rotate through it. Apex. Throttle.

The Porsche ahead of me was better out of the turns, but the prototype had gotten in front of it and balked it slightly. This time, I didn't lose ground in the drag race off the corner down the back straight. *This is it!*

Move right down the back straight, again signaling a pass on the inside. The Porsche ahead moves over to take the line, which isn't blocking if he doesn't move again in front of me. Drafting down the back straight, holding to the right. Upshifting through the gears to sixth. Holding. *Now!*

At the last moment before braking, I pulled left, creating a second lane around the outside of the Porsche making the right-hand turn. *Don't flinch, there's room.* Brake as late as possible. Turning, willing there to be grip on the outside of the turn. Turning. Pulling even. Next to the Porsche at the apex. Turning. Track wider on exit. Focus only on the apex for the next turn, seeing my car there with no Porsche in front of me.

I held the line on the left side of the track out of Turn 9, straight into the left-hand carousel of Turn 10. The Porsche tried to stay with me as I inched ahead through 9 and into 10. But he couldn't keep up around the outside of 10 and had to fall in behind me to navigate the single-lane hairpin.

Slow, slow, slow through the hairpin. Our cars concertina into each other as we downshift to first gear and go single-file through the turn. The Porsche buzzes in my rear-view. *Don't try to pass me, buddy, it'll never work.* The turn required discipline to accept the slow-speed turn with patience, without trying to pass, and to launch out of it carefully, not getting on the throttle too quickly and unsettling the back of the car.

Porsche in my mirror. *Don't panic, don't jump on the throttle. Don't give away the hard-earned position.* Accelerating down the straight. Take a breath. Focus through the kink in the straight. Start/finish line. No flags.

Ten minutes later, I took the checkered flag in fourth with mixed emotions. No podium, but no broken car parts. On the plus side, I'd be the toast of the paddock, earning kudos from my team and others, impressed I'd pulled off the pass. I was, too. But we'd missed the podium. While everyone behind me in the order would have gladly traded places, I wanted podiums.

And wins. I hated to lose.

I drove the car directly into the paddock from the track and pressed the button to quiet the engine. I smelled hot car and fuel and felt my heartbeat slow from its galloping race pace. I sighed. All the effort and money to be an also-ran. That was racing.

A crew member opened my door, and I unbuckled. I pulled myself out, done with my sulking and ready to tell the world I was happy to collect points for the season championship.

Chapter Fifty-three

I could easily have collapsed into bed when I got back to my hotel room that evening, but the day wasn't over for me yet. One of the SCC sponsors was hosting a cocktail party that evening, and nearly everyone associated with the Series was invited. My team owner and my new, big sponsor required my attendance, so instead of curling up in pajamas, I put on team gear, khakis, and lip gloss.

Holly and I walked down Ocean Boulevard to the Sky Room, a restaurant on top of a fifteen-story building from the 1920s. The art deco décor was stunning, but the focal point was the three-hundred-sixty-degree views of the City of Long Beach and the racetrack.

I'd heard about the restaurant during past visits, especially the life-size statue of Humphrey Bogart in the women's restroom, but I'd never been inside. I went immediately to the windows, while Holly went to the bar. She joined me a couple minutes later and handed me a glass of juice.

"You can't hide on the edges of the party all night." She sipped her pink, blended drink.

I turned around to face the crowd. "I could try."

"What's going on? You don't usually mind these things."

"Tired from today. A race still to run tomorrow. Don't want to deal with people."

She nodded toward the entrance. "Like them."

Coleman and Holden Sherain walked in, looking like they owned the place, and my father joined them a moment later. In a flash, Elizabeth wove her way through the crowd to reach Holden's side. She tucked her arm in his and led him away. Annoyance flashed across Coleman's face, before he smoothed his features and touched a hand to his tie. He and my father moved toward the bar.

"At least Edward isn't with them." I pointed Holly to the farthest end of the room, where we joined Jack and Tom Albright chatting with a mix of media, Series staff, and sponsors.

I managed to stay away from the Sherains, father and son, for nearly two hours. But a third trip to the buffet table proved my undoing. That's when I fumbled a meatball onto my shirt and decided to sneak around the bar the long way to reach the bathroom. I had my head down, dabbing at the brown stain—on my white shirt, of course—when I heard familiar voices among the hubbub of the bar area. I stopped in my tracks, halfway down the narrow aisle.

"You're calling me an idiot?" Holden, sullen and resentful.

"If anyone has the right, I do," Coleman shot back. "Your stupid cousin, he'd have ruined everything. And you listened to him. Be grateful I got everything back on track for both of us. I cleaned this up for us. For *you*. You hear me? Don't screw this up again."

They saw me. I involuntarily fell back a step.

Holden surged forward, his fists clenched. "I am so *sick* of you."

I glanced around, hoping he was speaking to someone else. Hoping for backup. The party was a few yards behind me, but no one looked our way. I figured I could outrun any physical violence, so I stood my ground.

"I've done nothing to you, Holden." I put my hands on my hips, wishing the stain on my shirt didn't undercut my authority so much.

He took another step, menacing. "You're always *there*. Go away. Get out of our lives."

Coleman moved forward, all traces of pleasant sponsor executive gone. "How would it all be different if you weren't here, Kate? Interesting thought, Son."

What the hell? Are they talking about bumping me off? I wanted to retreat so badly I could taste it, but I stayed put. "I'm not leaving. You can't get rid of me."

Coleman only raised his eyebrows and smiled. My breath caught in my throat.

Holden's face went red. "You are a leech. A worthless, blood-sucking freeloader. What do you do for anyone? You're a pair of tits in a firesuit, and you think that makes you special. You're a novelty item."

Coleman made no move to stop Holden's rant. Instead, he crossed his arms over his chest and watched the show.

I was stunned at the bile spilling from Holden's mouth, still surprised anyone could be that cruel.

"You're a public relations trick, not a real driver, which means you're as useless on the track as you are in the rest of your life." He leaned forward and down, to get in my face. "Useless. Worthless. Unwanted. Same as when you were a baby and your own father didn't want you. Get it? If you had any integrity at all, you'd stop wasting everyone's time and go away. Permanently."

My resolve to ignore the other members of my father's family went out the window with the feel of Holden's hot, alcohol-soaked breath on my face. I felt sick. And mad. Really mad.

I spoke in the same low, angry tone Holden had used. "Enough! You have no right to talk to me like that. No right to comment on my driving or my career. None!" I wrinkled my nose at him, heaping on the scorn. "And look who's calling who worthless. You couldn't even cheat effectively, let alone drive."

Coleman clamped a hand on Holden's shoulder, stopping his son from lunging at me.

I was loud now, angry and reckless. "That's right. Have Daddy hold you back, take care of you. How about being your own man? Oh that's right, you can't be. Like Billy couldn't. Your daddy had to fix things for you both." I turned to Coleman.

"Isn't that what you said? You 'cleaned things up'? Things Billy was ruining? How'd you do it, Coleman? Did you kill him?"

Holden looked stunned, but Coleman remained impassive. I sensed movement behind me, but I was beyond caring. My suspicions had coalesced into certainty when I'd heard Coleman's words. I knew he was the killer.

"Kate, is everything all right?" my father asked.

I glanced around to see him, Elizabeth, Tug Brehan, Don Kessberg, and others crammed into the narrow aisle behind me.

I turned back to Coleman and Holden. "Fine. Now that I've figured out Coleman killed Billy."

Someone behind me gasped, and my father exclaimed "What?"

Coleman hadn't moved a muscle.

"That's right," I went on. "Billy was causing problems for Coleman at the bank—with his poor management and sexual harassment—and in the business community. What's wrong, Coleman? Was he going to expose your shady business connections? Or your multiple affairs with subordinates in the workplace? Or maybe he was going to introduce everyone to Lucy Rose, Lily, and Violet." For everyone else, I added, "His second wife and children."

Coleman reacted with a flicker of confusion. Holden looked from his father to someone over my shoulder, a question in his eyes.

My father stepped forward, between me and his brother-in-law. "I'm not sure I understand. Is there an explanation for this, Coleman?"

I crossed my arms over my chest. "The explanation is he pressured me to look into who killed Billy when the answer was him all along."

My father turned incredulous eyes from me to Coleman. "Coleman? I don't—what she said?"

Coleman relaxed and smiled, which immediately made me nervous. He shot his cuffs and tightened the knot of his tie. "You're wrong. I should sue you for slander."

"Not all of it. Not the second family." I couldn't be.

"I don't know those names." He shrugged. "I'll gloss over the rest for the moment, but James, we will talk later about the appropriate venue for this kind of discussion."

I started to sweat.

"I'll tell you this, Kate." Coleman's expression was icy. "I hope you're a better driver than investigator, because you're wrong. Totally, completely wrong."

To my horror, my father nodded.

I tried again. "You were there at the track that day. You were mad at Billy. Weren't you?" Reports of overheard arguments whirled in my head. "You were mad at Elizabeth. But you were also mad at Billy."

I could feel Coleman growing stronger as I crumbled.

My father moved to me and put his hand on my arm. "I can almost guarantee it wasn't Coleman. I was on a conference call with him most of the time he was at the track that afternoon."

Don Kessberg spoke up from behind me. "I saw him leave, and Billy was still alive."

I gasped for air. I was embarrassed, horrified. *How did I get it wrong? Was I wrong about everything? No, he's still an asshole. Still unethical. But maybe not a murderer.* I looked at the faces around me and saw shock, confusion, and pity.

I bolted.

I was unable to comprehend the magnitude of the mistake I'd made as I stumbled out of the elevator into the brightly lit night. I stopped on the street, bewildered at the crowd of people spilling out of restaurants and bars, shouting at each other across the street. The noise of the rock band performing on the plaza stage next door hurt my ears. The smell of beer and cigarette smoke turned my stomach.

I slumped down on a low wall between buildings and leaned over, holding my head with my hands. I was still in shock. My brain refused to settle on anything coherent.

I latched onto one thought: I might have ruined my career. At the very least, I'd finally ruined my sponsorship deal with

Frame Savings, which probably meant kissing the Indy 500 goodbye. And the move to IndyCar. Beauté's funding would get me partway there, but I'd have to hustle to make it work. I wasn't confident I could make up the difference.

A different future stretched ahead of me, and I knew I'd have to adjust my expectations. Give up on the dreams I'd started reaching for. I was furious with Don and Nikki for forcing me into the investigation and with Coleman for being an asshole. With Billy for dying. Mostly, I accepted, I was angry at myself for messing everything up.

Part of me was also relieved to no longer have to interact with the rest of my father's family. *Silver linings.*

I sat up straighter and the scene replayed itself in my head. I tried not to cringe. Coleman hadn't reacted with guilt, unless he was a great actor. And apparently the three flower names—Lucy Rose, Lily, and Violet—had nothing to do with him. I pulled out my cell phone and sent a text to Ryan asking what he or the FBI knew about them.

People will find out I falsely accused Coleman. I can't face telling Ryan…a real investigator? I'll look like an idiot. A failure.

I pushed those thoughts away to deal with later, when I didn't feel so raw. I typed the names into Google on my phone, more to keep my mind off my embarrassment than because I thought I'd find results. I scrolled through page one. There, at the bottom: "The Tragic Childhood of Lucy Rose." I clicked on the link and the article loaded, detailing the story of a foster child suspected in the deaths of her mother and a foster sister.

I expanded the photo that accompanied the article in disbelief. I was looking at a young Elizabeth Rogers.

I raised my head from my phone in shock and looked up into Elizabeth's eyes.

Chapter Fifty-four

"Get up." Elizabeth moved her hand in the pocket of her over-sized, loose jacket. Something in the pocket was pointed at me.

"Elizabeth. What? What's going on? I just—" *Figured out you're a killer from way back. Coleman didn't kill Billy,* you *did.* I tried to work moisture into my parched throat.

"Get. Up." She snarled. "Meddling bitch."

I was tired of insults, but I stood, slowly, warily, glancing around to see how I might get help.

She plucked my cell phone out of my hand and slipped it in her left pocket. Then she stepped forward and linked her left arm through my right, pulling her right hand in her jacket pocket around her. I went numb with fear as she jabbed me in the side.

"We're going to take a walk." She tightened her arm to bring me closer. "Two girlfriends. And my weapon. Don't try anything stupid."

I needed two attempts before the words came out. "Why are you doing this? Why did you kill Billy?"

She turned to face me. I marveled at her calm. Only a flicker of excitement in her eyes hinted at any emotion. She smiled. "Billy was going to ruin my life. He was going to keep me from what I want, and he was so happy about it. You understand, Kate. I did you a favor also, getting rid of him. He wanted only people he deemed worthy to succeed. The rest of us, you and me, he wanted to destroy." She shrugged. "Unlike you, I wasn't going to stand for it. I remove obstacles to my success and happiness."

I'm not like you. I'm no killer! I took a breath and tried to understand. "Is that what happened with your mother and sister?"

"Foster sister," she snapped. "Come on, let's move." She tugged me forward.

"You had to learn to stand up for yourself early on. I wish you hadn't gone through that."

Elizabeth pulled me along the sidewalk, moving toward the plaza and the racetrack. "Gee, thanks. It's a shame I grew up with a mother who beat me and whored me out. A shame I went into the foster care system and was subjected to another bully who abused me and wanted to keep me down." Her tone dripped with sarcasm. "But it made me. I know how to get what I want."

I felt no sympathy. "You want Holden?" I walked as slowly as possible, trying to prolong the time we were out in public. I looked around, trying to figure out how to get away.

"I'm going to have Holden. All that lovely money and power. Not to mention his stamina in bed. Mmmmm."

That was an image I didn't need. Focus! "Billy would have stopped you?"

"Slow tonight, aren't you? The mighty investigator." She laughed and jerked me forward. "Billy threatened to expose me, disclose my former identity. He said I'd marry his cousin over his dead body." She giggled. "Now, I will."

"Where are you taking me?" I couldn't make my mouth form the question I really wanted to know: what she would do with me once there.

"I thought returning to the parking structure would be nice symmetry."

"You won't get away with it."

She snugged me up against her and put her mouth to my ear, as if we were best friends sharing a confidence. "I'll find your body after you tragically take your own life, distraught over the mess you made. Unable to cope with your own failure."

"No one will believe it." I lied. Most people wouldn't believe it. Some would.

She lifted a shoulder. "We'll see."

Time slowed down, as if I were behind the wheel. *If I let her lead me to the parking structure, she'll kill me. If I try to get away, I might still die. But I'd have a chance.*

I needed to get lucky. We reached the main entrance to the racetrack, the sidewalk right outside the plaza where the concert was taking place. Where the band played their last notes. Within moments, the crowd started streaming out of the outdoor venue.

Right in front of us.

All of a sudden, we were surrounded by sunburned, drunk, half-deaf concertgoers jostling us, pushing each other, and swearing. I'd never seen a more beautiful group of people.

Buffeted by the crowd, Elizabeth jerked my arm and jabbed with her gun. "Stay close."

Not gonna happen. My heart pounded in my throat as I watched the movement of the crowd and saw my opportunity. A young family navigated the steps down from the exit to the sidewalk, three paces away. Dad held a toddler by the hand, mom pushed a stroller. *A metal concert with kids?* Two paces away. They stopped in the middle of the sidewalk to adjust something, right in front of us. We pulled up short. Elizabeth was startled and off-balance. I was prepared.

I shoved her, leaning my right shoulder in and heaving. I ripped myself away, and I ran. To my left was a crowd waiting for the walk light to cross Ocean. *Sidewalk crowded, go wide.* I dodged into the street as cries went up from every direction.

People near Elizabeth thought she was my victim. They helped her up, yelling after me. People near me shouted at me to stop, angry I was cutting in front of them or warning me to stay out of the street. I didn't care. Movement was vital.

I glanced left. Traffic, but moving slowly. I darted into lanes, meaning to put a six-lane street between myself and Elizabeth's gun. Tires squealed and horns honked. *Déjà vu, but at least this time I'm on my feet.*

Police whistles. More shouting.

"Stop her, get her back here."

"Thief!"

I made it through two lanes of traffic, but had a close call in the third, when a driver took issue with me in his space and didn't slow down. I lunged for the median, and as I landed, I felt my ankle wobble under me. Hands reached to help me up, and I looked up to see the walk sign.

Relief trickled through me until the hands that lifted me up refused to let me go. I was marched, limping, back across the street, where I saw Elizabeth pointing at me and explaining something to a group of people.

We got close, and I heard what she was saying. "My cousin, just let out. She's confused and off her meds."

I shook my head. "She's lying. She's the criminal. We need the police." I saw officers fifty yards away, in the direction we'd come from. I shook off the people holding me and jog-hopped toward them as quickly as I could.

Cries went up behind me. "Stop her! Police! Don't let her get away!"

The four cops closed the distance between us and one of them grabbed me. "Hold on."

I nodded. Babbled. "Help me. She's trying to kill me like she killed Billy." I turned to identify Elizabeth and saw her weaving through the crowd, trying to escape.

Oh, hell no! "Stop her!" I pointed and ran after her, my ankle improving with every step.

Two of the police officers grabbed me, and two went after Elizabeth. A minute later, both of us sat on the steps leading to the plaza, cuffed with enormous zip ties. My heart still pounded, but I finally felt safe. Even while cuffed.

One of the officers loomed over us, his thumbs hooked in his equipment belt. "Now, what's this all about?"

"She's trying to kill me. She killed Billy Reilly-Stinson here last week—" I found myself on the verge of tears. I labored to breathe, realizing how hysterical I sounded.

Elizabeth spoke. Calmly. "Officer, I'm so sorry. My cousin has been off her meds for a week, and I'm trying to get her back home." She sighed. "She's delusional, poor thing. Thinks we're all trying to kill her."

I was almost impressed with her for trying to brazen the situation out. I cleared my throat. "Officer?" I said, proud of my even tone of voice. I took another deep breath as the cop turned to me, looking skeptical. "Check her right jacket pocket for a gun."

He took me seriously, even if he still thought I might be crazy. I breathed deeply again, ready to be vindicated. He straightened and held up a six-inch, metal tube. "No gun."

Elizabeth gloated, while I thought unprintable words.

I regrouped. "She told me it was a gun. What is it?"

The cop flicked his wrist and the tube snapped out to its full length. "Expandable baton. Illegal in this state. Can be lethal. But not a gun."

Key word: lethal. I met Elizabeth's eyes and slowly smiled. "Officer, call Detective Barnes about the murder here last week. You might be holding the murder weapon."

Elizabeth seemed to collapse in on herself. I focused on the cop. "Please, call Detective Barnes. You've caught a murderer for him. He'll remember me. I'm Kate Reilly, a driver here for the Grand Prix. I identified the victim's body. I'm not crazy."

He frowned but nodded at a second officer standing next to us, who pulled out a phone.

"Also," I spoke again, "if you check her other jacket pocket, you'll find my cell phone."

As the second officer turned away, speaking quietly into his phone, the cavalry appeared, in the form of my father. Between him vouching for my identity and sanity, and Detective Barnes on the phone, everyone finally believed my story. They still kept a close eye on me and put me in a car to take me to the police station, but they cut me free of the zip ties and treated me like a witness instead of a suspect.

My father wanted to come with me in the patrol car, but I insisted he go back to the party to find Holly and meet me at the station instead.

As we watched the officers exchange the plastic cuffs on Elizabeth's wrists for metal ones, my father still wore a stunned expression. "I'd never have guessed she killed Billy."

"Me either." I let out a long breath. "I'm glad you got here when you did. She was pretty convincing that I was the crazy one."

"I'm sorry I wasn't here sooner. I would have been, but Coleman stopped me, trying to explain himself, condemning you. Holden was complaining, making excuses." He ran a hand through his hair, an uncharacteristic, nervous gesture. "I stood there, listening to him and ignoring the voice inside telling me to go find my daughter."

"I guess you managed both."

"I walked out on him mid-sentence. Realized I don't care what he has to say. Tonight needed to be about you."

"Thank you." I hugged him, initiating the gesture for the first time.

"We'll be there right away." He choked up. "Sure you don't want a lawyer?"

I stepped back and looked at Elizabeth, restrained and scowling in the back of a squad car. "I don't think I'll need one."

When I walked out of an interview room three hours later, well after midnight, my father was still there. Holly, I'd expected to see. But I hadn't thought to find her curled up in a chair next to my father, showing him something on her phone and making him laugh. They saw me at the same time and both stood up to hug me.

"I'm fine," I replied to their anxious questions. "They don't need anything more from me, at least tonight. Let's get out of here."

Holly eyed me. "After all, Detective Kate still has a race tomorrow."

Chapter Fifty-five

Twelve hours and a lot of coffee later, I sat on the Beermeier Racing pit box, watching their star driver, Mick Poirier, suit up for Sunday's main event, the IndyCar race. I enjoyed the minutes of quiet, figurative and literal, after the activity of the day so far.

Despite little sleep the night before, I'd turned in a respectable performance in the Indy Lights race that morning, grateful it wasn't a twenty-four-hour endurance competition. A one-hour sprint had been exhausting enough. Still, I'd pulled myself together, banished thoughts of cops and killers, and hit my goal of a seventh-place finish. That was three positions lower than Sofia Montalvo, but I couldn't have everything. The team was ecstatic, and the press, attentive.

After cleaning up at my hotel, I'd made my way back through the crowds to the pits. I looked forward to watching the IndyCar race, glad there was one event on the weekend schedule I had no responsibilities for. I was worn out from it all, though my reputation and standing as a professional driver had improved significantly over the course of the weekend. I'd caught the attention of the IndyCar paddock, which meant I wouldn't be laughed off the track when I lined up for a race. And meant a number of teams might discuss fielding a car for me at the Indy 500.

If I had the funding.

I still had no idea what the repercussions would be from falsely accusing Coleman of murdering his own nephew. I winced at the memory. Even though the rest of the charges I'd hurled at him were true, I was afraid he'd brush them off. Maybe I underestimated my father, who'd promised me a long, serious talk about Coleman and the rest of my father's family. I hoped my father would listen and take some action. I didn't want to be ashamed of my sponsor.

If Frame Savings is still my sponsor.

I stopped thinking about my future and instead tried to figure out how I'd missed the signs pointing to Elizabeth as a killer. How I'd missed the fact she didn't even *like* me. When I'd wrapped up with Detective Barnes at the end of the night, he'd told me Elizabeth admitted planting my hero card and phone number on Billy's body to draw me into the murder investigation and implicate me as a suspect. "To mess with me," she'd reportedly said.

I heard my name above the noise of IndyCar's pre-race ceremonies, and I turned to see Tug Brehan, Elizabeth's boss at the SCC, standing in the narrow walkway behind the Beermeier pit space. I climbed down from the pit box and walked with him to a quieter spot nearby.

Tug was wide-eyed. "I've been trying to catch you all day. No one could believe when the news hit the party last night that Elizabeth had killed Billy—and that you figured it out and caught her for the cops."

I suppressed a wince. "That's not exactly how it went."

"What I don't understand is why she did it. Someone said you knew."

Detective Barnes had told me not to discuss details of evidence—like the baton that later proved to be the murder weapon—but he hadn't told me not to talk about *why*. "She said Billy was in her way. She killed him to preserve her new life, her job, and her path to future riches and power. That being Holden."

"Murder seems extreme."

I laughed, which felt good. "You think?"

"Katie!" I was enveloped in scents, chiffon, and diamonds as Nikki gave me air kisses and a real hug. "You solved it! Who'd have thought, Elizabeth?"

"Not me."

"But you did it! I have to run, but I owe you. Talk soon! Kiss, kiss!" She tripped off in her skintight white pants and standard five-inch heels. Strangely, she looked almost naked without a dog.

Wide-eyed, Tug watched Nikki's departure, then turned back to me. "If Elizabeth killed Billy to hang onto Holden, that explains why Holden looked so shell-shocked last night."

"What happened?"

"Your father came in, looking distraught, and went straight to Holly. Then he pulled Holden and Coleman to the side of the room and talked with them briefly. Coleman kept trying to speak, and your father kept cutting him off. Coleman looked upset. But Holden," Tug paused, shaking his head. "You could tell he was stunned. Shaken to the core."

"I would think so."

"I understand how he feels, I mean, I was sure I knew Elizabeth. She isn't who I thought she was."

"Literally. Her real name was Lucy Rose something. She changed it after she killed her mother, was put in foster care, and probably killed a foster sister."

Tug's mouth dropped open in shock.

I shrugged. "To be fair, her mother's death was probably self-defense. But I think she killed her foster sister because she stood in Elizabeth's way. Like Billy did."

"Never would have guessed by looking at her."

I patted his shoulder. "Tug, if there's one thing I've learned in L.A., it's that people are rarely what they seem." I remembered Lucas' description of the movie he and Maddie were filming. "You never know how people will react or what they're capable of. Even what we're capable of ourselves."

Tug went on his way, and I pondered my own words. My behavior the night before was inconsistent with my resolution about how to handle and react to my father's family. I knew I'd have to consciously work on a calm, non-emotional response to them in the future.

I felt my cell phone buzz in my pocket, and I frowned. No doubt a responsible adult wouldn't ignore her messages, as I'd been doing all morning. I thought it might be Holly chastising me for not responding to her texts. Instead, it was a message from Ryan Johnston, standing a hundred yards away on the other side of the pit-lane gatekeepers.

I walked over to him, thinking he could have been a "Hottest in Hollywood" candidate himself with his clean-cut good looks, simple tee-shirt-and-jeans attire, and aviator sunglasses.

He didn't return my smile. "I was glad to hear you weren't hurt last night."

"You heard about it? How?" Detective Barnes had assured me the Long Beach police wouldn't talk to the press or the racing community for a while. I'd assumed that meant no one would know the details yet.

"I have a friend in the department." He paused and stuffed his hands into the front pockets of his jeans. "Good race this morning. And yesterday. Great pass."

"You're not going to yell at me for putting myself in danger?"

"You're an adult, and I'm not your keeper." He finally grinned at me. "Though I'd like to discuss ways you could stay out of trouble the next time. Over dinner tonight?"

The next time? Dinner tonight? I studied him. "You saw the race yesterday? Were you here?"

"I was. You were too busy to interrupt." He took one of my hands. "Come on, Kate. Have dinner with me again? Please?"

I felt a fluttering in my chest and the slow spread of pleasure that a nice, sweet—and okay, slightly dangerous—man liked me.

I thought about a text message I'd been avoiding. Lucas Tolani, wanting to hear about my races, to talk about the murder suspect the police had in custody, and to see me. Tonight. Trying to tempt me by suggesting I try Mulholland again with the Lamborghini he had in his garage. Not understanding my thrills came from the racetrack.

This time, I'd heed the warning signs. The problem wasn't the different worlds of racecar driver and movie star. I wasn't interested in his brand of reckless. I didn't want flash and flame-out, I wanted a man who looked good in his tight tee-shirt *and* who understood I had a job to do.

I squeezed Ryan's hand. "I'll find you after the race."

As I reentered the pits, I saw my father shading his eyes and looking down the row of teams. The IndyCar drivers were pulling out of their grid positions for pre-race pace laps, and in the roar as they launched, I knew he couldn't hear me. I tapped his shoulder.

He waited until the noise level dropped to speak. "I was looking for you."

"How are you today?"

He smiled and tugged me out of the way of a crew member laden with tools. "Forget me. How are you? You drove well in the race this morning. That should bode well for the future."

For the future?! "Thanks. Were you here?"

"Of course. I never miss an opportunity to see you drive." He saw my face. "I'm sorry that surprises you."

"I didn't know before, but now I do. Thank you." I hugged him and discovered reaching out got easier the more I did it.

His eyes were moist when I pulled away, but I pretended not to notice. "You mentioned the future. Am I—last night..."

"Last night changes nothing about your contract with the bank."

I nearly wilted from relief. "Thank you. I've been worried."

"I'm grateful you opened my eyes to what's been going on. I needed to know, and I'm angry with myself for not noticing." He clenched his fists. "Though I'm much angrier with Coleman. And Edward. Trust me when I tell you there will be plenty of changes at Frame Savings."

"Really?" I tried to keep my tone neutral.

He started to speak, then stopped himself. "I deserve you questioning me. I know I have something to prove to you—to quite a few people, including myself."

"What are you going to do?"

He squared his shoulders and took a deep breath. "I'm going to clean up the bank's management. Coleman and Edward will have to go."

"Can you actually fire them?"

The IndyCar field went by, and my father paused until the last of the cars disappeared down the front straight. "I can sideline them, if not remove them from the organization entirely." My father grimaced. "Though my sister might want Coleman's head, let alone a divorce and his resignation."

"I know you're the president of the bank, but I wasn't sure how much power you had to make changes like that."

"I haven't often exercised it, because it was easier to let more ambitious people take the lead." He paused. "Of course, that attitude resulted in my brother and my best friend—former best friend—dragging the bank into questionable business circles, betraying their wives and wedding vows, and repeatedly abusing their power. Unforgivably." He looked sad. "I trusted them because I thought I knew them."

"People can surprise you."

"We've found that out, haven't we?" He laughed, a terse, rueful sound.

"Tug Brehan said Holden especially looked shocked about Elizabeth last night. I suppose Holden didn't know anything about her actions?" I'd woken up that morning remembering his quick glance over my shoulder the night before—at Elizabeth, I assumed—when I mentioned Lucy Rose, Lily, and Violet. If Holden had recognized the names, I wondered what else he knew.

My father shook his head. "I saw him again this morning, and he's almost catatonic with shock. Truly shattered. He had no idea what Elizabeth was up to, and he feels responsible now for Billy's death."

That didn't surprise me. "Will you get rid of him along with Coleman and Edward?"

"I'm not sure." He hesitated. "I know you're no fan of Holden's, but I think this situation has the potential to change

3/16

him. Coleman and Edward are unrepentant—both trying to feed me excuses and stories, which I'm no longer listening to. But Holden might be redeemable…if I can get him away from their bad influence. I may give him a chance, but keep him under a strict watch."

I kept my doubts about Holden to myself as the cars came around again and drowned out conversation. Instead, I thought about my future, which still included sponsorship from Frame Savings. And which no longer included Edward or Coleman. *I have a future in racing, I drove well this weekend, and I never have to think about Billy's murder again. I never have to think about Billy again. Or any of the family I don't want to deal with.*

As the car noise died down, I saw my father beaming at me, with an unfamiliar expression I thought was fatherly pride. I took a deep breath. "Thank you for choosing to come after me last night instead of staying with the others. It meant a lot."

This time he definitely blinked back tears. "You're welcome. Thank you for letting me help. Letting me in. I hope this is a new chapter for us."

"I'd like that."

We moved forward together into the pits, and stood there, his arm around my shoulders, watching as the cars thundered down the track to take the green flag.

Next year that could be me.

To receive a free catalog of Poisoned Pen Press titles, please provide your name, address, and email address in one of the following ways:

Phone: 1-800-421-3976
Facsimile: 1-480-949-1707
Email: info@poisonedpenpress.com
Website: www.poisonedpenpress.com

Poisoned Pen Press
6962 E. First Ave. Ste 103
Scottsdale, AZ 85251